ALLEGIANCE *to* ALSACE

MARTA ANNE TICE

North Carolina

Disclaimer

The characters in this novel are fictious, but the events and dates are accurate regarding battles, historical figures, and events during the Napoleonic era (1799–1815). The towns and provinces are real; however, the estates of Friedensthal, Adlershof, and Blumenthal are fictitious. Some of the distances between cities could perhaps be longer when traveling on horseback or carriage. The incident regarding the Duke of Enghien occurred on March 21, 1804, not in 1806 as it is written in the story.

Published in the United States by BQB Publishing
(an imprint of Boutique of Quality Books Publishing Company, Inc.)
www.bqbpublishing.com

978-1-952782-55-8 (p)
978-1-952782-56-5 (e)

Library of Congress Control Number: 2022932357

Book design by Robin Krauss, www.bookformatters.com
Cover design by Rebecca Lown, www.rebeccalowndesign.com
First editor: Allison Itterly
Second editor: Andrea Vande Vorde

Praise for
ALLEGIANCE TO ALSACE
and Marta Anne Tice

"I was part of Marta's journey in discovering Annaelise and bringing her to life on the pages of this most extraordinary book. Marta's attention to detail, especially with her historical accuracy, makes this story all the more real. Readers will easily become attached to Annaelise and feel her joy and her sorrow as she lived through one of the most fascinating periods in history. If you are an avid reader of historical romance novels, you will love *Allegiance to Alsace*."

—Joanne DiMaggio, MA, CHt, author of
Soul Writing: Conversing with Your Higher Self

"On a visit to the Pfalz in Germany and the Alsace-Lorraine region of France as a young girl, Marta Anne Tice had a vivid déjà vu experience of living in the eighteenth and nineteenth century. So it comes as no surprise that her novel brilliantly recreates the sparkling pageantry and powerful history of the Napoleonic era of that bygone time. A wonderful read!"

—Stefan Bechtel, author of
Through a Glass, Darkly and *Mr. Hornaday's War*

To my daughter, Lauren Peterson Michalka, for her talent in journalism and production. Keep creating the many books and films within you!

To my father, Captain William Preston Tice, MD, who served in World War II as a physician. Thanks for your inspiration: "Teach your daughter about her ancestors; we hold their memories in our DNA."

To my mother, Dorothy Adams Tice, a poet of life and creator of "My Song."

To my brother, Captain William Preston Tice, Jr. Your passion for Mozart and listening to this great composer while I was writing was the inspiration that spurred me on!

ACKNOWLEDGMENTS

David Albert Juergens for his love, patience, and encouragement.

Richard Rust, author of The Renegade Champion, for his inspiration to write our story.

Richard Leahy, author of Beyond Jefferson's Vines, for his friendship and knowledge of viticulture and the German language.

Joanne DiMaggio who believed in the story.

Millicent Reynolds for her support, and for her mother who was passionate for this period of history.

Allison Itterly, my editor who went further beyond to create a finished product that has made my story become a reality.

BQB Publishing made it possible for me to create my dream.

All my friends over the years who were patient with me while I created this novel.

HOW THE STORY CAME TO BE

This novel has been a part of me throughout my life, and I kept coming back to it through many seemingly unrelated but interwoven discoveries and coincidences. Eventually, I chose to retell these experiences as fiction even though they are, in a certain sense, as true as my ongoing everyday life. Let's say this fiction is based on my *soul story*.

My *soul story* came alive at the impressionable age of fourteen in the summer of 1965. My family and I were in Germany visiting my father's cousin who was serving with the US Army in Nuremburg. While taking a tour of the medieval town of Rothenburg, I experienced a sense of having been there before, the sensation often referred to as *déjà vu*.

When we left Nuremberg and were traveling on a back road, the area looked all too familiar to me, and I "recalled" a quaint church that was farther down the road. As we approached the small church, I told my father to stop.

The Herrgottskirche Church, also recognized as the Church at Creglingen, is known for an elaborately hand-carved wooden masterpiece of Mother Mary and scenes of her life, including the Annunciation. When I entered the church, a sudden chill rose up my back. Before me stood the elaborate work of art, a beautiful altar in all of its splendor. I somehow knew in my spirit that this was not the first time I had seen this magnificent masterpiece. This affected me in the years to come, enabling me to weave this glorious altar into my story.

As an avid equestrian since the age of eight, horseback

riding came naturally to me. When galloping across open fields, flashbacks of battle scenes of German calvary soldiers sometimes appeared in my mind. I maintained my connection with riding for many years and have owned horses of my own. This has been an essential part of my life. The boar hunt in this story is reminiscent of my thirty-five years of foxhunting.

When I was in college, my interest in art history came alive when I studied the Napoleonic era between 1799 and 1814. I was particularly interested in the furnishings, fine art, fashion styles, and the architecture of that period. I was fascinated by this era, and I soon became obsessed with researching the French Revolution, as well as the American Revolution and the ideals and philosophy of our Founding Fathers, which are expressed in this novel.

When I became a member of the Daughters of the American Revolution (DAR), I learned that men from both my mother's side of the family (Adams) and my father's side (Theiss; in English pronounced *Tice*) fought in the American Revolutionary War. In my research, I discovered that my ancestor, Phillip Anglin, came from France and fought in the Revolutionary War. Even more curious, Phillip Anglin II was born in Albemarle County, Virginia, where I resided for many years, and his descendants married into the Tice family. It is no wonder I was drawn to live in Albemarle County where not only do I have lineage, but it is also the place where Thomas Jefferson resided.

My mother relayed to me that my father, a neurosurgeon from Roanoke, Virginia, expressed an interest in the theory that we could possibly carry memories from our ancestors in our DNA. On the morning of my father's death, he came to me in a dream and said, "Make sure you tell your daughter about her ancestors."

At that point I started researching "Theiss," my German name. The only information I obtained was from records from the Mormon Church, which indicated that a Jacob Theiss from the Pfalz came over on the ship *Sally* and landed in Philadelphia, Pennsylvania, in 1772. This information from the Mormon Church came before internet websites such as Genealogy or Ancestry were available.

When I traveled to Europe in 2006, I had phenomenal luck in locating the Theiss ancestral village through the Ancestor Center in Kaiserslautern, Germany. It was there that I verified Jacob Theiss, a bottle maker, came from Leisel, Germany, on the ship *Sally* to Philadelphia in 1772.

Upon discovering this information, I sped north on the Autobahn for an hour and a half to Leisel. Arriving late that hot summer afternoon, to my disappointment, I found the church was closed. However, I succeeded in exploring the Theiss cemetery of my ancestors. A sudden breeze blew out of nowhere on that hot afternoon and seemed to whisper to me, "Welcome home, Marta."

The landscape was breathtaking. The late afternoon sun cast shadows across the newly cut hay bales in the meadow that were silhouetted slightly from wisps of feather clouds that were reminiscent of a Monet oil painting. Totally mesmerized, at that moment I felt a connection with my soul I had never experienced in my life. It was without a doubt the most magical feeling I have ever encountered.

I also visited the wine country in Alsace-Lorraine in France, which brought tears to my eyes, somehow knowing I had been there before as well. It was at that point when I started writing my story.

I hope this book will encourage you to look deeper into

the lives of your ancestors and that it will fill your heart with intrigue, joy, and purpose as much as it has filled mine, and hopefully will for my descendants to come.

"In matters of the heart, nothing is true except the improbable."

—Madame Germaine de Staël

"I hold it that a little rebellion now and then is a good thing, and as necessary in the political world as storms in the physical."

—Thomas Jefferson

"The history of the life of women is an episode in that of men."

—Madame Germaine de Staël

FOREWORD

During 1805 Napoleon Bonaparte personifies the emerging Romantic era and is rampaging across Europe and conquering its old regimes, allegedly to replace them with Enlightenment ideals. But between these ideals and political upheaval, the megalomania of one man, and the struggles of great armies, where is a place for the thoughts, dreams, and actions of individuals, especially those of a young woman caught in the midst of this great upheaval?

Mark Twain once remarked, "There are some books that refuse to be written. They stand their ground year after year and will not be persuaded. It isn't that the book is not there or worth being written—it is only that the right form for the story does not present itself." I'm pleased to say that Marta Tice has found an original, skillful, and artful way of telling the story of a young woman's life and her archetypical struggles in the turbulent upheaval of the Napoleonic Wars.

This was a time often thought of as the Rise of the Great Man theory, and women were not in the forefront.

Annaelise Theiss, a young Alsatian woman, struggles with the same life issues most women struggle with; the transition from youth to adulthood, negotiating new relationship and roles with parents, the search for a true love, and the start of a new independent life with him. What's new and captivating about *Allegiance to Alsace* for me is the added layers of identity and loyalty with which Annaelise struggles. Her mother and uncle played a big part in the Parisian society before the French

Revolution, and her father is a German vintner and brewer. Is her loyalty to Napoleon's France or to Germany? She discovers her father not only is a student of The Enlightenment, but his study of Hegel and Humboldt as well as the American Founding Fathers have led him to be loyal to Prussia instead of Napoleon. She falls in love with a dashing cavalry officer, but he turns out to be more than he seems on the surface, raising more questions of loyalty.

The choices others have made put Annaelise in the position of having to continually make decisions of her own about her multiple levels of loyalty to her family, to her country of France, to the German states, to her political ideals, to her lover, and finally to the future of her child.

This story is a rare work of romantic fiction at its best, and original. It is as if Tice were a contemporary of Goethe's, writing authentically of life and romance before "Romantic" became a tacky genre of literature on which the fortunes of soap opera advertisers were built. Annaelise is doing her best to be loyal and true on all levels, being both honored and challenged as a woman, and the reader will find her sympathetic, authentic, and easy to identify with.

Tice's professional background in interior design and long experience with equestrian arts gives color and detail to the story without clutter. Her patient study of the historical record of the time and place knits the personal and the larger political details together artfully, from the details of Napoleon's campaigns to the interior décor and equestrian details of her characters and their lives. The combination of a gripping personal narrative with a pleasingly accurate and rich background makes this a story that both moves swiftly and has vivid and colorful details.

Annaelis Theiss not only navigates the normal challenges of life, but in struggling with the larger questions of loyalty, she enters an archetypical, mythic realm, taking on questions of fate and destiny and how to make choices to be true to herself but to honor the others in her life, especially her daughter.

While this story will appeal to female readers of all ages, male readers will appreciate details of the horses and the hunts, as well as following the fortunes of Napoleon on the battlefield in the first decade of the nineteenth century, and they will sympathize with the hero and his loyal attendant. Students of The Enlightenment will enjoy seeing many of their philosophers quoted or referenced, and many will be pleased to meet the proto-feminist philosopher of the time and ardent foe of Napoleon, Madame de Staël, whose comments seem just as relevant today as they did 200 years ago.

This novel operates on many levels; most fascinating perhaps is the fact that the story was inspired by feelings of déjà vu. Ms. Tice experienced when visiting both Germany and Alsace to trace her genealogy in 2006. Instead of thinking this story up, it came and found her, which I believe gives a lot of authenticity and power to the narrative.

As a historian, I'm impressed that Ms. Tice took the time and trouble to integrate the details of the characters' lives with the actual historical record on many levels, from food and wine to the philosophy and music of the time, including many historical figures of the period.

For anyone who has read or watched the *Outlander* and *Poldark* series or is a fan of fine historical fiction, especially of this period of history, or for anyone who loves fiction that illustrates the struggles of the individual caught up in much larger forces and rises to be as authentic and loving as they can be, this will be an inspiring and rewarding read.

Richard Leahy, May 2020
Author of *Beyond Jefferson's Vines*

PROLOGUE

Benjamin Franklin, the Ambassador to France, was predictably late in arriving at the lavishly ostentatious celebration at the Palace of Versailles that warm night of July 30, 1778. Respected as a scientist and statesman in all of Europe, Ambassador Franklin was also known to have a taste for the ladies, especially the French ones. It was no doubt that one of them, somewhere in the palace, was entertaining the distinguished older gentleman in her boudoir an hour or so before the soirée began. Franklin had lived in France for several years, and he adored all the extravagant amenities of life in the French court, including the fine wines, the cuisine, the sculpted gardens and fountains, the gilded carriages and fine horses, and the fabulous architecture. During his stay he had developed a reputation as something of a novelty, dressed in his racoon-skin fur hat and leather clothes. One wondered if he might soon take to wearing a powdered wig. He had also become fluent in the French tongue, which the French loved him for.

But it was the women of the French aristocracy that he found most irresistible. With their towering wigs, their powder-dusted bosoms spilling out of extravagant dresses, and their easy morals and taste for the delights of flesh.

Gustave Guerlain, a fussy, eccentric little man who served as Directeur de Soirées for the Royal Court, was the mastermind behind this splendid banquet, and he intended for it to be the most lavish and elegant affair ever given for King Louis XVI and the queen of France, Marie Antoinette. Ice sculptures of dolphins, mermaids, and cherubs graced the enormous high-ceilinged hall. There were glistening mounds of exotic tropical fruit and trays of game, including pheasant, duck, and wild boar. The gold-gilded flatware that bordered the best of Sèvres gilded china set for a table of seventy-five.

For the night's entertainment, there was to be a performance by none other than the twenty-two-year-old Wolfgang Amadeus Mozart, who had performed as a child of seven for the court at Versailles and so astounded the royals that they had repeatedly invited him back. He'd been recently offered a career at the palace as court organist, but after he refused the position he had agreed to perform tonight for this grand, very special event. Wonderment of the young genius's gifts had swept through the court, and there was a sense of hushed anticipation for tonight's performance of Mozart's Sonata No. 8 in A minor, performed by Mozart himself on the harpsichord, and the Paris Symphony.

Meanwhile, as the crowd of magnificently overdressed aristocrats spread throughout the banquet hall, one distinguished guest after another arrived in their carriages to Versailles's massive twenty-foot entrance doors and flourished into the palace as their names were announced to the crowd.

The ostensible point of the great banquet was to celebrate the monarch's first child, who would be born before the end of the year. After eight years of marriage, the king and queen of France were finally going to have an heir, and everyone was hoping for a boy who would one day claim the throne.

There were other reasons to celebrate. The French had played a significant role in waging war on the British for the American

Colonies, which secured victory for the new American Republic in 1776. The Treaty of Alliance was signed on February 6, 1778. This was why Dr. Franklin was the guest of honor.

But Dr. Franklin wasn't there.

Instead, in a different wing of the palace, in a highly ornate Louis XV Rococo boudoir, Ambassador Franklin was tasting the delectable flesh of a beautiful and willing mademoiselle, who happened to be a bit older than most. Her bright red hair had come undone, and in the next minute they were in the elaborate gold Louis XV bed.

Suddenly, there was a knock on the door. The valet had arrived.

"Sir," the valet said demurely, pushing open the boudoir door. "Pardon my disturbance, but you are almost late and the festivities are about to begin. Would you mind if I dress you now?"

Franklin gently pushed the older courtesan aside. "Madame, please put yourself together, my dear."

At that moment, the sound of an ecstatic explosion of an erotic release could be heard through the wall. The courtesan threw her head back and laughed. None of this was any surprise to anyone in the room, since the sport of making love was a way of life in the French court.

With the help of the young valet, Franklin changed his costume for the party. Rather than donning his raccoon hat, which he sometimes wore to amuse his audiences at the expense of the oafs of the American frontier, the valet placed a tricorne hat of navy-blue silk on his head, wrapped him in a gold-threaded jacket and ceremonial American Republic sash where he placed a pin representing the French monarchy, and handed him a gold cane. Franklin glanced at his image in the mirror for one last approving look at himself—a little too thick around the middle, his graying shoulder-length hair a bit disheveled, but overall rather jolly and even a bit noble.

Franklin left the room and walked down an expansive hallway that was adorned with paintings, which were highlighted by the eight-foot-high windows that looked out onto the main courtyard. He gazed at the approaching carriages for the night's gaiety.

Almost immediately, Franklin encountered the young musician he knew to be Wolfgang Amadeus Mozart.

"Monsieur Franklin, I presume?" Mozart asked sweetly but with a wry smile.

"Why yes, Master Mozart, I so look forward to hearing you perform this evening."

At that moment, a servant appeared with a tray of champagne flutes, and the two distinguished guests raised their glasses for a toast.

"To your great success!" Franklin said.

"And to yours," Mozart laughed, draining his glass in a gulp. "Including *amour* with the ladies!"

With that, Mozart quickly made his way down the long corridor to join his orchestra. Within minutes, the music of *Adagios Horn Duos* began to set the stage for Ambassador Benjamin Franklin's entrance into the majestic banquet hall. As he entered, he took the arm of his friend, the lovely Comtesse Camilla Bassett. Her wig was so impossibly high that it made Franklin's own rather unimposing five-foot-nine look a bit comical by comparison. Behind them walked envoys Arthur Lee, a doctor and American spy, and Silas Deane, a Connecticut delegate to the Continental Congress.

The grand ballroom had a black-and-white marble floor.

The walls had gold molding set in the asymmetrical design of acanthus leaves inset with mirrors. Gold crystal chandeliers hung from the tall ceilings illuminated with candles that reflected in the surrounding mirrors. At the end of the room were two gilded thrones each for the king and queen. Women donned towering wigs holding interesting ornaments attached like faux birds in cages. Their breasts were almost completely exposed. Rouge overaccentuated their cheeks and lips in red. The men all wore silk, wigs, and several also wore rouge. It was comical and somewhat amusing.

In a booming, pompous voice, Gustave Guerlain, Directeur de Soirées, announced the dignitaries' names as they entered the hall. Monsieur Guerlain's hair was covered with a wig. He wore silk pink pants, and his jacket was embroidered with roses. His cheeks were blushed with rouge. He was not a tall man but was muscular due to his training with horses.

"The Ambassador to France from America, Ambassador Benjamin Franklin, and the Comtesse Camilla Bassett."

Immediately, a member of the orchestra announced their entry with Mozart's Sonata in A minor as the distinguished guests descended the two rows of notable personages, nodding at the members of the Court, watching them as they bowed and curtsied before the king and queen, who sat on their gold thrones. King Louis the XVI wore a cape of purple velvet trimmed with ermine fur. His face was round with pouty lips, and his expression was frozen with a slight smile. Marie Antoinette wore an elaborate silk dress with a bustle on each side of her hips, and it appeared that she could hold a plate of food from each. Her bouffant towered almost a foot in height and was adorned with feathers and jewels.

Approaching King Louis XVI and Queen Marie Antoinette,

seventy-two-year-old Ambassador Benjamin Franklin leaned into his gold cane and bowed stiffly in honor of the royal monarchs.

The celebrated guests then proceeded back down the lines of introduction while Monsieur Gustave Guerlain nodded to his staff of sous-chefs and waiters, indicating that it was time to pour the wine while the first course was set upon the seventy-five seating places. The tables had been pushed together to become one long table and covered in the finest white linen from Marseilles. Gold candelabras graced the tables. The king was seated at one end of the tables and the queen was seated one hundred feet away.

Over the course of the night, as the crowd of dignitaries grew and the volume of the hall's festive air grew, Gustave had grown ever more frantic and ever drunker. By now, he was fairly well inebriated. *"Faite-vite!"* he shouted at his staff to hurry up as he hustled down a back hallway to the kitchen, grabbing open wine bottles along the way and sipping them as he went. He was excited beyond measure, and also terribly anxious, because this was, after all, his grandest banquet, and perfection was his highest aim. The king and queen of France and their guests required perfection since this was a grand occasion.

Originally, Gustave came to court as a well-established horse trainer from the small French village of Obernai in Alsace-Lorraine near the German border. His task was to make certain that all the mounts for the Court were civil, mild-mannered, and safe. He also had exceptional gifts in the art of décor for setting tables and arranging flowers, including coordinating the coloration of floral arrangements with the colors of the cuisine. It was because of his talents and tastes in these areas that he was appointed Directeur de Soirées of the Royal Court.

But Gustave's flaws were as excessive as his gifts. He drank to excess on frequent occasions, and this night was no exception. Certain ladies of the Court often sought his advice on fashion and decorum, and then lingered with him as the moon rose in the night sky, spreading moonlight over the boudoir.

At age twenty-four, he liked the high-born ladies. He was often seen leaving Parisian apartments in the wee hours of the morning after sleeping off a drunken adventure or escaping from a dangerous midnight liaison with a courtesan.

Gustave lived in a Parisian apartment and had custody of his sister, Louisa Guerlain, who was fourteen years his junior and his pride and joy. Their parents were victims of smallpox, and Gustave and Louisa lost them when Louisa was at the tender age of five. Louisa was spoiled and was raised by nannies and her doting brother. Gustave, however, was less active in her care because of the increasing demands made from the palace or his late-night escapades.

After shouting at the cooks in the kitchen, Gustave left in a huff and stormed down the hall toward the ballroom. It wasn't that they were running out of food, but that the servers weren't being quick enough to replace the platters.

"Ah, Monsieur Guerlain, how are you this evening?" a woman said as Gustave walked past her. She was wearing a soft red silk dress with elaborate jewels of rubies and diamonds and red lips to match. She had enjoyed her wine and was somewhat tipsy.

Gustave put on a fake smile. "I am quite well," he said. "I do hope you are enjoying the festivities. Have you tried the boar? If I am not mistaken, I believe your husband was part of the hunt that caught the beast."

The woman giggled, placing her gloved hand over her mouth. "You are wildly entertaining. My husband is no hunter, but he is a bore."

Gustave laughed to appease the woman, then bowed to her. "Enjoy the rest of your evening."

As much as Gustave enjoyed the high life of French society, there was always a nagging feeling that he didn't belong. That he was a fraud. That one day these people would find out that he was not of noble blood, nor did he have a wife or heirs. Maybe he was a fraud.

Wine flowed like water, and Gustave stumbled from person to person, table to table. Laughter floated through the air. After the elaborate dinner, desserts filled the table with chocolate mousse, crème brûlée, and apricot tarts. People were dancing to Mozart's music, from his minuet to a few livelier country dances. Secret rendezvous were arranged between couples married or not married. Women were fawning over younger men. Ménage à trois were in the making, and men seeking the company of other men was prevalent. Ambassador Franklin had disappeared. The king and queen had left long ago. Despite her reputation to enjoy such a celebration, Marie Antoinette had retired for the evening. Guests continued dancing to Mozart's melodies long into the night, a frenzy of enjoyment and chaotic energy that Gustave thrived on.

The next day, word got out that the celebration was a success. Gustave Guerlain had done it again. He was the man everyone turned to for extravagant parties.

The social and economic inequality further divided France while the aristocrats and royals continued their lavish lifestyles. The debt of the government grew and grew while Gustave and others continued throwing their wild parties.

Gustave, however, relished in his claim to fame. People spoke of him in social circles. He was at the top of his game. Every soirée he threw was bigger and better than the last, all paid for by the French taxpayers. But as the soirées grew more lavish, so did his drinking. He became erratic. He demanded exotic fruits and game meats. He fired half of his staff after a miscommunication over ostrich feathers. He partied late into the night, not even emerging until the afternoon, hungover and dressed in the previous night's clothing.

It was only a matter of time before everything would come crumbling down like a house of cards, when the masses would starve in the streets, and thousands would protest the wealth of the monarchy and storm the Bastille in the name of revolution.

CHAPTER 1

A NEW AWAKENING

July 15, 1805

T he night was restless. My neck was sweating under my white lace nightgown. The north-facing windows were open in my bedroom. The cool breeze lifted the lace window curtains all around me, but I was not cool or calm.

My dreams were haunting me again. I had tossed and turned under my sheets all night as I dreamt of cavalry horses in battle, cannons blasting, soldiers dying on the battlefield and calling out to their mothers.

A rooster crowed in the distance, a faint sound that signaled the start of the day even though it was still dark outside. The sun had yet to peek its head above the horizon. I shook my head and brushed my long brunette curls from my face. My heart was racing, as I was still shaken by my dream. I didn't know why these visions came to me when my mind and body should be resting. But they were becoming more frequent, and it was unsettling.

The breeze picked up, the fresh air calling to me. A ride on my horse would bring me relief and clarity. I always found peace when I rode my horse in the woods.

I got out of bed and splashed some water on my face. I

looked at myself in the small wooden mirror. My curly hair was wild and sticking up in all directions, and my green eyes were swollen and puffy. Perhaps I'd had too much wine the night before in celebration of my eighteenth birthday. It was also the anniversary of Bastille Day.

Tiptoeing over to my wardrobe, I selected my dark green culotte skirt, a cotton shirt, and tucked my hair under my hat. I crept quietly down the old oak staircase, careful not to make any noise. The house was silent at this hour, though I still made sure to be light of foot. The wooden floorboards had a tendency to creak and moan, and I didn't want to get caught. My father, Count Karl Theiss, strictly forbade me to ride alone.

"Annaelise, you must promise me that you will not leave this estate by yourself. It is not safe for you to be out alone when we are at war," he would say.

It had been sixteen years since the French citizens and revolutionaries protested the French monarchy and stormed the Bastille on July 14, 1789, a day that changed France forever. Thousands of people died, many of them executed by guillotine. The bloody Revolution finally came to an end in 1799 when Napoleon Bonaparte staged a coup d'état and overthrew the government, thus establishing a new Consulate with Napoleon as leader. Napoleon had brought hope for France and promised a united government, but things grew even more chaotic. He had been on a war path in trying to make France the most dominate country in all of Europe.

My family's estate, Friedensthal—the Peaceful Valley—was built in 1686 in the wine country of Alsace. The Rhine River ran straight through the valley on the border of Germany and France, dividing the land to the east and west. We lived on the German side of the Rhine just outside the village of Kehl. The nearest city was across the Rhine in Strasbourg, France, where we often visited.

Napoleon's armies were increasing in our region. While we were far enough out, it was becoming dangerous because Alsace served as a station for supplies for Napoleon's army, who were crossing the Rhine and traveling east into the areas of Germany, Austria, and Prussia.

The barn was quiet, and I was relieved that my friend, Sergeant, was happy to see me. He was content to have a small breakfast of oats while I saddled him. When I was twelve years of age, I graduated from riding my pony, Schotzie, and was gifted with Sergeant, Maman's horse. Maman hardly ever rode, and when she did, it was always sidesaddle. Sergeant was half Belgium and half Andalusian. Typically, the Belgium breed was a draft horse and used for pulling wagons and sometimes heavier carriages. They were stronger in bone and calmer in disposition. We had a pair of Belgium horses, Rosie and Robert, that delivered our wine. One fall, my Uncle Gustave's prized Andalusian stallion, General, jumped over the fence and bred with Rosie, the female Belgium. Sergeant was born the following spring. He was smaller in bone like his sire and reddish in color with a flax mane and tail like his dam. I loved that little fellow and played with him often. He had been like a pet until he became my riding horse.

I chose to leave quietly by the back of our property off the main roads. The forest was lush with ancient evergreens, and the smell of fresh plants permeated the forest floor. Autumn would soon arrive. It was as if summer was having the last hurrah by showing the remaining dark green foliage of the season. We slowly crossed the stream, and Sergeant was cautious with every step. A woodpecker drilled into an ancient hemlock tree, searching for insects.

I never felt more free than I did while riding. When I was

younger, Papa and I would wake up early to ride. Maman would insist that I drink goat's milk and have a bite to eat before venturing out, but I was always too excited and would hurry. Then I would get a bellyache while riding. Papa would shake his head at me and smirk, knowing that I would suffer later for it. But I didn't care. I would do anything to ride.

Suddenly, I heard a voice in the distance. Sergeant stopped, his nostrils flaring in fear. He hesitated to move forward, but I felt compelled to see if anyone was in trouble. The homes and farms were spread out. Our nearest neighbors, the Muellers, lived a decent ride away. They were an elderly husband and wife who had struggled with hard times ever since their son, Claude, had died in battle in Napoleon's Egypt campaign. They had no other members of the family to help them work the farm. The harsh winter of 1803 seemed to have permanently damaged their soil, as they were struggling to make ends meet to grow vegetables as well. Papa was always checking on them to make sure they were taken care of.

I quietly dismounted and was glad I was dressed in dark clothing and that Sergeant's reddish coat was adequately camouflaged. We carefully approached the commotion, avoiding twigs and stones, until we came upon our neighbor's small cottage in the woods. The cottage was surrounded by a dozen soldiers, a regiment of Napoleon. We hid behind a huge hemlock.

The soldiers were wearing blue militia uniforms with a white sash. They had sabers by their sides. One mounted solider wore a bicorn hat, and appeared to be a commanding officer. Some were on horses, others were foot soldiers, and there was a wagon pulled by Percheron horses. The soldiers were loading the wagon with supplies.

A lieutenant stood before the Muellers. Next to him, two

foot soldiers held rifles with a bayonet attached to the end. The Muellers looked terrified as the lieutenant barked orders to the soldiers to take whatever livestock that would fit into the wagon, as well as cabbages, potatoes, and carrots. I couldn't believe my eyes as I watched the soldiers take chickens, sheep, and other small livestock for the French regiment.

"But, monsieur, what will we eat?" Mrs. Mueller cried.

"Your husband can hunt and fish in the forest," the lieutenant snapped. Then he ordered three soldiers to force the smaller livestock into the covered wagon.

"No!" Mr. Mueller shouted. "That is our livelihood! We will starve!"

The lieutenant nodded to a soldier, who pushed Mr. Mueller to the ground with the butt of his gun.

"Please don't hurt him," Mrs. Mueller begged.

The lieutenant smirked. "Let it be known that no one has been hurt today. Emperor Napoleon cares about every citizen, even lowly farmers such as yourselves. Your contribution to the French Army has not gone unnoticed. We will continue to expand our nation for France and further our reach in Europe."

As I watched from the shadows, anger coursed through my veins. So this was how Napoleon was winning the hearts of the French and German citizens? By threatening and stealing from good, honest people? I felt sick to my stomach.

I slunk back and grabbed ahold of Sergeant's reins, then swiftly left. Fortunately, I would not encounter any soldiers on the road back to Friedensthal.

The air was cooler, and I tried to keep my head down to avoid the wind. I had to tell Papa what I had seen. With the upcoming winter, we would have to offer whatever we could to the Muellers in this time of need.

The road opened up to a slight hill. It was still dark, though the sun was just starting to rise. The edges of the dark sky were slightly pink. It wouldn't be long before the sky brightened and I would be seen. I pushed Sergeant to go a little faster. I didn't want to get caught being out by myself, especially after what I had witnessed.

As we rounded the bend near a small creek, I could see our stable in the distance. Just a little farther and I could slip in unnoticed before Henri, the barn manager, awoke and tended to the horses. It was quiet—even the birds were silent. A fine mist hung in the air but was slowly dissipating.

Then, in the distance, I saw a figure on horseback riding horizontal to my position.

My body tensed, and I pulled back on the reins to slow Sergeant down. Panic seized hold of my movements for a moment, but then I guided Sergeant toward a grove of trees to hide behind.

The sound of hooves pounded against the earth. The rider was getting closer. Was it a soldier? The figure wore a red cape that billowed in the early morning breeze. They were heading for the stables. I gasped when I saw Henri standing there. What was he doing? He was never up this early.

The rider slowed once they reached the stable. The sky was getting lighter, and I squinted at the figure. They dismounted. I recognized the steed—it was Bravo, my father's Andalusian horse. Bravo's nostrils were flaring, apparently exhausted from a hard gallop.

The figure whipped off his cape and flung it over his arm.

"Papa?" I whispered.

He handed the reins to Henri, then disappeared into the early morning mist.

CHAPTER 2

LIFE AT FRIEDENSTHAL

"Keep your chin up," Uncle Gustave yelled.

I gritted my teeth as I stood up from the carefully laden table. Beautiful dishes, their rims gilded in gold, glittered in the early morning sun.

"So now you decide when to leave the table?" Uncle Gustave said with a wave of his hand. His belly protruded from his tight silk shirt. He was balding with gray hair and had a distinct mustache and beard, which he kept trim. He had a long boney nose that was enhanced when he peered over his glasses. His face was blessed with high cheekbones, and his blue eyes were large and expressive, but there was always something lurking behind his eyes, as if he kept all the secrets in the world.

"I am no longer hungry, Uncle," I said with a sweet smile. "Besides, a young woman must maintain her figure if she is to find a husband. Isn't that correct?"

Uncle Gustave rolled his eyes. "A young woman must watch her tongue."

"Enough, you two," Maman said with a smirk. "Don't you ever tire of bickering? I know I'm exhausted of hearing it." She was sitting at the end of the table working on an embroidery.

Maman was a beauty in her own right. She had luscious eyebrows and eyelashes with a small cherry mouth and bright rosy skin. When she smiled, her hazel eyes sparkled and a small dimple creased her right cheek. I always envied that dimple; it added so much to my mother's smile. Her long dark hair was coiffed with one lock that trailed down her shoulder. My own hair was always wild, with curls sticking out every which way even when I tied it back. Many people said I inherited Maman's beauty, although I was taller like my father.

"You are right, my dear sister Louisa. We should curtail our bickering. I still think Annaelise has a lot to learn," Uncle Gustave said with a smile, revealing crooked teeth. Sometimes I wondered how my mother and uncle were related.

"I believe I have learned everything there is to learn from you, Uncle. After all, I am eighteen now. I am forever grateful, but the time has come to absolve myself of these lessons." I curtsied. "Good day."

Uncle Gustave shouted at Maman, "You're going to let her get away with this? The ungrateful, little—"

I didn't wait to hear the rest. With a pep in my step, I dashed out of the room. It felt good to leave my uncle in a tizzy. He had a tendency to get very fussy and overwhelmed, and he was easy to tease.

I had been receiving etiquette lessons from my uncle since I was a young child. For years we would sit in the dining hall, and he would instruct me on the proper use of silverware, which fork to use for dessert, how to cut meat with a knife, and which spoons were used for soup. I was taught how to curtsy and speak properly when addressing royalty.

When I was younger, Uncle Gustave would play various roles, but he often took on the role of a made-up character, Madame Calais.

"Mademoiselle Annaelise, you have been cordially invited for tea with Madame Calais at four o'clock this afternoon in the grand salon," he would say.

I would put on a pretty dress and we'd set up my dolls and stuffed animals on the French chairs in Maman's salon. I always thought it odd that my uncle would dress up as a woman with a wig and rouge on his cheeks and pretend to be Madame Calais.

"Ah, welcome for tea, my dear Annaelise," he would say.

"I am delighted to be here," I'd respond in French, and then I would curtsy.

Using Maman's Louis XV silver tea service, Madame Calais would show me how to hold a teacup with my little finger pointed up, and how to pour tea without spilling. Maman would show up and remark, "Oh, how kind!"

I was entertained for a little while, and then I would grow bored and couldn't wait to go to the stables and pet my pony.

"Our lives are quite different in Alsace! We are not formal!" I would whine.

"One never knows where you will be someday, Annaelise," Uncle Gustave would say in a definite manner.

Uncle Gustave and Maman were Parisian born and lived at Versailles for a number of years. My uncle was employed as a horse trainer, and through his talents, he had become the Directeur de Soirées, the event coordinator for the palace during the reign of Louis XVI. I never knew that life. They often stressed the importance of my learning so I would one day find a husband. Their hope for me was to enter high society with fabulous balls, parties, jewelry, and a husband who had a title, an estate, and plenty of land.

But their dream wasn't my dream.

Despite the late-August warmth, it would soon be time to harvest the grapes in the fall. I awoke early so I could find Papa and talk to him before the busy workday. He had been fairly absent the last few weeks—disappearing for business and holing himself up in his study—as we readied for the harvest. Even Maman commented that he needed to dine with us once in a while. Papa was always busy, but there was nothing like the bustle of the winemaking season. I had gone over what I would say to him about where he had been so early in the morning. It was a question that hung heavily on my mind.

Today I would drive the carts, my first time this season. I was dressed in my torn work smock and my hair was tucked under my hat. As I walked around the estate, relishing the fresh air, I made my way toward Papa's study.

Friedensthal was a sprawling landscape of lush green valleys and rolling hills. The grapevines were planted in long rows far into the horizon. The manor home reflected the early Alsatian home construction with timber posts, beams, and plaster holding up a thatched roof. My father, Count Karl Theiss, a Prussian and a distant cousin of the Hohenzollern of Prussia, was awarded this land after his service in the Seven Years' War. Thus, he became a land baron and acquired the title of count. Through my father's impressive management skills, he made a remarkable success of his brewery at Friedensthal and was also able to revive old vines on the estate and start a winery.

Maman was not interested in the workings of the winery or brewery. Instead, she threw herself into rather superficial social activities, leaving not only the responsibilities of business and estate to my father, but also all of my schooling to him, Uncle Gustave, and my nanny, Isabelle. Papa, on the contrary, was prudent, scholarly, and sought refuge in his reading and mysterious studies away from the frivolous parties that held the attention of Maman and my uncle. Managing both the vineyard and winery was more challenging than the brewery, and it took quite a lot of Papa's focus to produce a good yield of quality grapes. This suited his temperament, as it required dedication and discipline, something he was innate with in his German heritage.

When Papa acquired the estate, it had been run-down. He immediately replaced the thatched roof to a slate roof with dormer windows. Window boxes adorned with bright red geraniums hung below the leaded glass windowsills. A large fountain stood in the center circle of the driveway—the figure in the middle of the fountain was of Neptune surrounded by dolphins. This was to Maman's request, and Papa complained that it was not only frivolous but atypical to the Alsatian style. But I had loved it and found it enchanting. It was what had compelled me to study Greek mythology.

After Papa married Maman, they made more renovations. A new kitchen was added to the back of the house, the animal trophy heads were removed and relocated to Papa's study in the old Banquet Hall—as per Maman's request—and the home was altered to a more Parisian style so Maman's friends from Paris would be impressed when they visited.

The circular driveway veered off to the east of the house, continuing straight to accommodate the winery and stables, and down to the old Banquet Hall. One of the old barns was reconstructed to accommodate the winery. Every space was utilized, and the complex was compartmentalized for easy access and convenience, so more acreage was acquired for the vines and there would be more pasture for the horses.

"Hallo, Fräulein Annaelise," Jürgen called. He had been the seasonal worker for a number of years. He was a sweet boy with a feisty temperament, but he sure could pick a lot of grapes.

"Good morning to you. Are you going to ride today?" I

shouted. Jürgen had a beautiful horse.

"There's a lot to be done before the harvest—maybe I can go for a ride later. Would you like to join me?" Jürgen asked. At age fourteen, he had just sprouted some hair on his chin. I believed he fancied me, though he was too young and immature. But I enjoyed his company, and I did enjoy our rides together, which didn't happen often.

"Maybe another day," I said.

It was necessary to hire extra staff from the village of Kehl, which was our closest town. Women were not encouraged to participate other than supplying food for the workers in the field. Maman had an aristocratic past at Versailles where servants provided all the service. Over the years, however, she found it rewarding to ride sidesaddle down the rows of grapes in her latest Parisian straw bonnet, absorbing all the workers' bows and admiration for the Countess Theiss while she led the food wagon into the fields.

I wanted to experience it all. When I was ten, Papa led me into the fields and let me pick my first grape off the vine. The workers picked the ripe bunches and put them into baskets. Then they were transported in small wagons driven by donkeys or ponies to the winery.

At first, Maman refused to let me pick grapes. "That is not for a lady of your class," she'd said with her hands on her hips.

"She will be managing this business after I am gone, Louisa, and there is no guarantee that your brother will participate except for the tasting," Papa said to Maman.

Eventually, Maman agreed that I could drive the pony cart for collection. She knew how much I loved horses and riding, as well as driving harness horses and carts. Papa was thrilled with my participation.

Smoke billowed out from the chimney where the cooks busily prepared the food. My stomach growled. I made my way into the kitchen for a bite to eat. Giselle, our head cook, was already baking bread for the workers.

"Fräulein Theiss, why are you up so early?" She wiped her hands on her apron.

"I'm going to see Papa," I said. "But I couldn't resist the delicious smells."

"Would you like some hot bread and honey?"

"Yes," I nodded.

Giselle raised her eyebrow. "Why are you going to see your Papa at this hour?"

"Well, I'm learning more about running the winery and the estate. Papa wants me to be involved," I said.

"It's wonderful that you are so interested in the workings of the business," she said. She slathered honey over a warm, soft piece of bread and handed it to me. I took a bite.

"Thank you," I said as I chewed the bread.

"And what would Gustave say if he saw you chewing with your mouth open?" Giselle said with a smirk.

I giggled and took another bite. "I should go see Papa. Thank you again."

I left the kitchen and ventured down the courtyard to the winery, hoping to find Papa. The sun was rising over the Alsatian hills, casting rays of light down the corridor road to the winery.

When I entered the winery, Richard was already at work and preparing for the day's winemaking. The cavernous room was made of wood with high-beamed ceilings. Barrels of grapes lined the room in rows. The smells of sweet fruit were overpowering. Richard was in the process of putting the grapes into the press for crushing.

"*Guten morgen*," I spoke in my German tongue.

"Bonjour, Fräulein. You are up early." He grinned with his kind, wrinkled face as he peered over his glasses.

"I was looking for Papa," I said.

"He won't be here for another hour or so, but you're welcome to wait for him. Your uncle is usually later than that. Are you taking the cart to load the grapes today?" Richard said.

"Yes, I will be today." I knew Papa would be in his study and not in the winery. Maybe a part of me didn't want to know what he had been up to, or maybe I wasn't ready to confront him. "Can you show me how you press the grapes?" I asked.

"Of course. How is it that you're so interested?"

"Papa says I may be managing the winery one day."

"Very good. I hope you're as good as your father in the management." He chuckled. "Please have a seat," He pulled up a wooden stool.

I always liked Richard and found him easy to talk to. His mannerisms and easygoing demeanor were soothing compared to Maman's intensity and Papa's tenacity. Richard had been the winemaker at Versailles when Uncle Gustave was the Directeur de Soirées. It was a coincidence that Richard had found a position as a winemaker at Friedensthal years later. Papa persuaded Richard to further develop the winery, and together they planted new vines and cultivated a new vineyard.

Richard showed me the press that processed the grapes. The two sides of the circle were hinged, so when they opened, the grapes could be poured in and when they closed, a heavy press was cranked slowly to flatten the layers of grapes. The juice was squeezed out of them while the pomace—seeds, skins, and stems—was held back in the press.

"Thank you for showing me," I said with a big grin.

"It's time to harness your old pony and bring me more grapes! You have a way with horses like your uncle, but I know you are kinder to them."

"How do you know?" I asked.

"These old eyes see much," he said, staring over his glasses. He was always so kind to me.

"I hope we can talk again soon," I said.

"I would look forward to it, mademoiselle. Enjoy the day and bring me more grapes."

With that, I went to the barn looking to harness Schotzie, my old pony. The more time I spent outside, the less I would have to listen to Maman and Uncle Gustave tell me that I should be finding a suitor now that I was eighteen.

"Annaelise," Papa said as he made his way toward the stable in a rush. He was a tall, wiry man with high cheekbones, brilliant blue eyes, bushy eyebrows, and thick gray hair. "I must be on my way, but we shall talk later, yes?"

"Yes, Papa, as always."

Papa disappeared into the stable to saddle up his horse. It was unlike him to not be present on site on a day such as this. I waited until he emerged from the stable on horseback. He didn't look my way, just continued down the road until he disappeared once more.

CHAPTER 3

FOXHUNTING

Over the years, my uncle Gustave had taught me to ride horseback. He was none too happy about me leaving in the middle of an etiquette lesson a few weeks ago. So when he approached me on a chilly afternoon in September, he had a proposition.

"Since you feel that you have learned everything there is to know from me about etiquette—though you surely lack in it—your mother and I have decided it is time to complete your equestrian education."

I held back a smirk. "That sounds lovely, Uncle," I said with an exaggerated curtsy.

Uncle Gustave sighed. "Meet me at the stables tomorrow before dawn. Dress in your warmest riding clothes."

While I never enjoyed etiquette lessons, I did enjoy the dancing lessons, from the minuet, to the waltz, to the German polka and country dances. But my favorite were the equestrian lessons.

As insufferable as my uncle could be, he was very talented. He had been my mother's caretaker and had instructed her in the arts of dancing, dining, and proper protocol. In 1786, when he and Maman had left Versailles for Adlershof, or Eagle's Court—the Guerlain hunting villa in Alsace-Lorraine—to avoid the tension of the approaching revolution, his finest driving horses, General and Jennette, had become his bloodline for sales. He had started to earn a profit selling fine riding and carriage horses, but when Napoleon seized power in 1799; the French military soon patronized him for the purchase of calvary horses.

The Andalusian became a versatile breed, as they were elegant driving carriages and served as military cavalry horses. They were agile, athletic, fast, intelligent, and brave. Descended from the Arabian and Spanish horses of the Iberian Peninsula, these bloodlines became horses that were used in bullfights, and their tenacity was appealing to Napoleon's military officers. Napoleon's famous mount, Marengo, was mostly Arabian in breed, but Uncle Gustave swore that Marengo had some Andalusian in his veins. Uncle Gustave then moved his breeding operation from Adlershof to Friedensthal when my parents were married. My mother gained the title of countess, and my uncle pursued his talents in other areas.

Uncle Gustave was waiting for me in the stable, dressed in his riding clothes.

"Annaelise, it's time for you to learn about foxhunting. You never know when we may be invited to a hunt. We will learn the proper protocol first."

I tried to hide my excitement. I had always wanted to go on a foxhunt. Papa and Uncle Gustave went often, either together or with different parties. Every time I asked my uncle to take me, he would say, "It is no place for a lady." So I was surprised that he wanted to teach me the ways of the hunt.

"What protocol do I need to learn?" I asked eagerly.

"There are many things to learn when hunting, not just the riding."

"For instance?"

"If you are going to ask question after question, then I may rethink this," Uncle Gustave snapped.

"*Je suis désolé*," I apologized. Then I mimed shutting my mouth.

Uncle Gustave motioned for me to sit on the old wooden bench. Then he explained the protocol in an animated manner. "The hunt field consists of the elder and more experienced riders who ride behind the master of the hounds. Never pass a master, and never interfere with the hounds. You must always allow them to pass when necessary. With a larger field of persons, the field master will lead the second group.

"The less experienced riders follow behind the field master. The whipper-in follows behind to collect the stray hounds and encourages them to follow the pack. Sometimes the huntsman or the field master will turn around. When that happens, you have to stop and get off the path, then turn about-face so your horse's hind end will not face the master or his staff. This, of course, ensures your horse will not kick them. This is known as 'reverse field.' Also, if you see a hole or something dangerous on the ground, alert the rider behind you. The British say, 'Ware hole!' In French we say, '*Regarda vu.*' Whatever you do, you must follow protocol."

"What happens when you see the boar or the fox?" I asked, sitting on the edge of my seat.

"You tally-ho, take your hat off, and point in the direction of the beast. And, Annaelise, you must always thank your masters for a nice day."

"Oh, that sounds exciting. When do we start?" I asked.

"We will start riding in the ring. You can take Sergeant over some hurdles in the riding ring for practice. You will follow me, and you will experience what riding in the terrain can be like. Let's get to it."

Sergeant had large hooves, so it was a challenge to encourage him to pick them up properly to jump over poles and logs. I could extend my legs down to squeeze the horse's flanks to his sides to spur him on. I was grateful that I could ride astride and not sidesaddle.

After my horse passed that element of training, we decided to go out into the field the following morning. I braided my hair and wore my culotte skirt.

Before we mounted, my uncle said, "Now, Annaelise, you must be strong and careful. We'll be going faster today, and you must follow my lead. We'll be jumping logs and galloping in the fields."

"Yes, Uncle," I said in anticipation.

Our ride started with a fast trot through the forest, winding around twists and turns, careful to avoid the rocks. It was early morning and rays of sunlight darted through the ancient hemlocks. I had to watch the rocks on the narrow paths and managed to keep my mount's head up so he wouldn't trip.

Soon we came to a large stream with moss-covered rocks. My uncle advised me to go slow. I was glad Sergeant took his time, and his large hooves were to our advantage as he had more traction. Uncle Gustave's Andalusian, Alexander, had somewhat of a more difficult time. When we crossed the stream, Uncle Gustave turned around to face me.

"We can allow our horses to drink some water, but not too much because they could colic," he said.

Sergeant had a different idea about drinking water. Apparently, he was very thirsty.

"Kick him hard!" my uncle shouted.

With little effort, I kicked Sergeant's sides and he pulled his head up. I had worn my spurs.

We continued along the path and the evergreens gave way

to hardwood trees. The path widened and logs scattered the road up ahead.

"Communicate with your horse," Uncle Gustave said. "Let him know that you are in charge."

I leaned forward in anticipation of the hurdles. I squeezed my legs and spoke into Sergeant's ear, "Come on, boy. You can do it."

Sergeant then raced toward the logs. As we approached the first hurdle, Sergeant responded to my movement. He took the log brilliantly, lifting his hooves and legs up and over to the ground until the second log, then three strides to the log after that. A pile of brush appeared as the last hurdle.

We had never seen this before. At first, my mount hesitated, and with enough leg, I spurred him on. Sergeant flew over the brush jump with ease. I was so thrilled that I was laughing.

"Bravo, niece."

We slowed down and my uncle asked me to make sure my saddle was secure. He rallied me on, "Prepare to gallop!" Then he took off.

"Come on!" I shouted as I kicked my spurs. Sergeant raced through the forest. The trees whizzed past, the wind whistling in my ear. My horse and I became one. I felt safe and secure.

Our pace quickened when my uncle shouted, "Tally-ho!"

Even though there wasn't a fox, I pulled back on Sergeant's reins to slow him down.

"Very good, Annaelise. See what happens when you listen to me?" Then my uncle was off again. Sergeant and I followed behind.

When we returned to the stable, my uncle proudly said, "You have passed your equitation with flying colors."

"Thank you," I said, breathless. "That was the most enjoyment I've had in a while. I can't wait for the chance to experience a boar hunt or a fox hunt."

Then Uncle Gustave hugged me, a gesture he seldom demonstrated.

CHAPTER 4

AN ADVENTURE WITH MARIE

It was late September, and the harvesting was nearly complete in the vineyard. The workers had returned home. It was fortunate that we had good weather to complete the task. The grapes were in the winery, and Richard had his work ahead of him.

I still hadn't spoken to Papa. The opportunity never presented itself. He was always rushing off or busy with work. I started to think that he was avoiding me.

"Have you spoken to Papa?" I asked Maman one day.

She just waved her hand. "I do not see much of your papa when the wine is on the vine."

I convinced myself that I was being paranoid. Papa often took trips to conduct business for the estate. It was wine season. For weeks, our estate was bustling with workers from morning to night. Papa was either in his study or overseeing the work in the winery.

The autumn breeze was in the air, and the smell of spiced hazelnut and pumpkin permeated my senses. I wanted to ride again and to see my friend Marie, who lived a few miles down the road in our neighboring vicinity, yet I knew I mustn't go far from the main roads. With no one to tell me otherwise, I decided to visit Marie.

I went into the stall to present Sergeant with a nice carrot when I heard hoofbeats trotting down the road to the stable.

As I looked out, I was delighted and surprised to see Marie on horseback.

"Marie! I was just tacking up Sergeant and was going to come to see you!" I exclaimed as I led my mount out of the stall.

"The weather has finally changed, and we are getting some nice fall breezes. I took a chance that you would be here and that we could take a nice ride along the Rhine." Marie's brilliant red hair blew in the slight breeze. We had much to catch up on since I had hardly seen her all summer.

Marie was my closest friend. Her family was an old Alsatian family from France and they lived across the Rhine. We'd met years ago in Kehl while attending Papa's Lutheran church. When we were young girls, we used to pretend we were knights on broomsticks and have jousting tournaments in the Banquet Hall. Unbeknownst to my parents, we would remove the heavy armor shields off the wall from Papa's ancestral collection. One time, one of the shields was too heavy and I'd dropped it onto my foot. That was the last time we'd used props.

I tightened the girth on Sergeant's saddle. "I'm so happy to ride again after such a hot summer. I've been very busy helping with grape harvesting. We have many adventures to talk about."

It would be light for only a few more hours, and we discussed our plan for riding. We took the small path leading from the barn toward a small wooded trail that led to the main road that led along the Rhine. We only encountered a few carriages and a few wagons loaded with pumpkins along the road.

We decided to take a small path that led up to a knoll where we could view the sunset over Alsace. We dismounted so we could have our conversation and enjoy some freshly baked bread that Marie had packed into her saddlebag. To my surprise, she had also packed a small bottle of Riesling.

The conversation was enthusiastic and happy as we watched the sun descend over the Alsatian sky. Marie's family grew potatoes, and while she herself didn't dig them out of the earth, she and her sisters helped clean them.

After a moment, Marie grew quiet and stared off into the distance. It was unlike her to not fill the air with her sweet voice.

"Is something the matter, Marie?" I asked.

Marie turned to me. She had a funny look on her face. Her cheeks were blushing.

"Marie! What has happened?"

She covered her mouth with her hand. "I . . . I've been bursting to tell you. I think I'm in love."

My mouth flew open but no words came out. I gently pushed her and squealed in excitement. "You must tell me everything!"

"His name is Pierre Dumont. My father hired him to help us this summer." Marie clasped her hand over her heart. "Oh, Annaelise, he is very special. His eyes are bluer than the river. He has a smooth speaking voice. And he is such a gentleman."

I grabbed Marie's hands. "I'm so happy for you."

"We have only embraced—twice—and he has kissed my hand and my cheek. Mother and Father don't know . . ."

Marie's parents were very strict. I had gone almost six months without seeing her when we were fifteen because she and her sisters had accidentally spilled a barrel of milk. I couldn't imagine what they would think about this Pierre Dumont.

"He will be back again next harvest. I told him I would wait for him," she said.

A strange feeling came over me just then. Since we were little girls, we always spoke of love, of being princesses, of finding our knights in shining armor. But now that we were of age—and, according to Uncle Gustave, I was getting too old— we were supposed to marry and find a husband. What did it mean to be in love? To feel your heart racing just to steal a kiss from a handsome man? I didn't understand, and I wondered if I would ever be in love or if someone would ever love me.

"That is very wonderful," I said in a softer voice. "I am so very happy for you and Pierre."

At that moment, a figure on a horse rode below us, heading north. I gasped. It was Papa riding on Bravo, his Andalusian mount. He was moving quickly.

I stood up. "Hurry, we must follow him. I want to know where he's going. Then I can follow you home. I don't mind riding back in the dark. The roads are safe at this time of day. Papa won't realize we're following him," I said in a rush as I mounted Sergeant.

"Okay, Annaelise, I'm with you." Marie packed up her saddlebag.

We carefully made our way down the rock embankment back to the road. At that juncture, we galloped in the direction where Papa was heading, but he was at least a half a mile ahead. The sun was setting fast, and we couldn't catch up with him. Fortunately, we saw him turn off on a connecting road toward a small village. With any luck, he would be easy to catch up to at that point.

We slowed down and walked along the narrow path. We followed his hoofprints that led to a stone cottage with a thatched roof. Smoke was rising out of the chimney.

"I must see what Papa is doing," I whispered. "Let's wait until it's dark. If you can hold Sergeant, I will walk up to peek into the window—"

"No, Annaelise," Marie said. Her brow was furrowed. "Why do you even care? We should be going back soon. It's getting dark and I am expected for supper."

This was my chance to see what Papa was up to—his

sneaking out in the middle of the night, disappearing early in the mornings.

"Please?" I begged.

Marie stomped her foot. "All right, do as you please. But you must hurry. Your mother will be worried as well." She held the reins for both horses.

I carefully walked through some bushes that led to the back of the cottage. There was a commotion of voices coming from inside, but I couldn't make out any specific words. I pulled the hood of my cape over my head, then crouched down below the windowsill. I took a deep breath and peeked in the window.

There were two rows of men in chairs, four abreast, and an altar of some kind in front of the rows. There was no cross, so this was not a church. To my disbelief, Papa was walking down the aisle. He was wearing a Prussian blue cape, and there was a large medallion around his neck.

Was this a Satan ritual? *Oh no, this cannot be!*

On the altar was a bronze V-shaped measuring device attached to square cornerstone of some kind. Then a young man came to the altar. Papa opened a book and began to read from it, but I could not hear his words. I strained my ears to listen. His voice was muffled, but it sounded like another language, maybe Latin. Papa was preforming some type of ritual. The young man was unharmed, to my relief.

My heart was pounding so loud I thought Papa would hear it. I was afraid and needed to leave. In a crouched position, I made my way back to Marie.

"Annaelise, are you all right? You look like you've seen a ghost," she said.

"I-I'm fine," I stuttered. "I couldn't find Papa." I faked a smile. "You were right, we should be going."

The ride home was a blur. My body was shaking from the

cold, from what I had seen, from the vision of Papa in that small, cramped room. What was he doing? Was Papa involved in something evil? I was horrified by what I'd seen, and I didn't know if I could get the image out of my mind. The world felt so heavy from the secrets I carried.

CHAPTER 5

A VISIT TO ADLERSHOF

After harvesting the grapes at Friedensthal, Uncle Gustave asked Papa to assist in harvesting his grapes at Adlershof, or Eagle's Court. The Guerlain hunting villa was located near Obernai, a small French village on the other side of the Rhine. My uncle had planted grapes three years ago, and it was the first harvest of the premier season. It was decided that Papa would be instrumental in directing Uncle Gustave in the process. Papa would also transport a smaller wine press to the winery cottage. We planned to go pheasant hunting during which I would learn how to fire a gun. I was hoping to finally get a chance to talk to him.

I had good memories of Adlershof. When I was a young girl, I would play in the attic and wade in the beautiful crystal-clear streams. The caretakers who lived there, Jocelyn and René, were always so kind to me. Jocelyn would braid my hair, and I used to love the smell of her apple cake baking in the oven.

Uncle Gustave told me that when he and Maman had moved to Adlershof, Maman was horrified by the condition of the villa. Isabelle, formally her nanny and maid, testified that Maman, who was eighteen at the time, cried for days to return to Versailles. Leaving the formal high life for the countryside had been overwhelming. Maman detested the décor of the villa, specifically the animal head trophies, and she'd begged my uncle Gustave to remove them because they gave her nightmares.

After she married Papa and was settled in Friedensthal, my uncle had the trophies cleaned and rehung in Adlershof.

"After all, it is a hunting villa," he laughed.

"*Ah oui, mon frère,*" she would say, rolling her eyes.

But Uncle Gustave missed Versailles too. He had been the official horse trainer there and had developed a good reputation in France for having a sixth sense and talent for selecting fine "horseflesh" for the royal court. Maman told me his court career accelerated when Uncle Gustave prevented Marie Antoinette's daughter, Marie Charlotte, from mounting a dangerously untrained stallion pony. But then he changed his position when he was recognized as a brilliant soirée coordinator.

"I received more money and it was more fun!" he explained when I had asked him about it.

When I asked Maman why they had left, she had said, "It was our time to go." I didn't ask any more questions after that.

We left for Adlershof on a cool morning in October. The sun was bright and the leaves shone a beautiful orange and golden brown. We passed many pumpkin fields and farmers cutting hay for the winter.

Our entourage included Maman and Isabelle in the carriage with Henri driving Jennette and General, our beautiful Andalusians. Papa drove the wine wagon that transported the old wine press with Rosie and Robert, our trusty Belgium horses, while his hunting dogs, Hansel and Gretel, rocked along in the cart. Uncle Gustave was riding Alexander, while I was riding faithful Sergeant. It was a fine day, and I looked forward to this new hunting adventure and time with my family.

Arriving in less than a full day's time, we were greeted by Jocelyn and René. I remembered their faces, now aged and wrinkled from their lives of hard work in the sun and running the villa. I was surprised they were still here.

"Bonjour, and welcome back to Adlershof!" The caretakers greeted us with smiles that revealed missing teeth. Pepe, their old black retriever, hobbled out while Hansel and Gretel jumped down from the wagon, barking in delight. At that moment, another couple advanced forward with smiles on their faces.

"Herr Guerlain, this is our son, Jon, and his wife, Heidi. They will be assisting you and your family," René said, smiling proudly despite his missing teeth.

Henri drove the carriage to the stables while Papa drove the wagon to the back shed that served as a small winery. Gustave, Henri, Jon, and Papa offloaded the wine press into the charming old ivy-covered stone cottage that now served as a new small winery for Uncle Gustave.

The renovations that my uncle made on the barn were beautiful, and it seemed a shame that he'd spent so much money only to use it briefly as a breeding facility before he moved to Friedensthal. The new location was close to both Kehl and Strasbourg, and the French military crossing into Germany helped to grow his business. Soldiers needed horses. Andalusians were in high demand for both the military and for pleasure.

The barn was empty except for the caretaker's horses. All six of our horses were housed comfortably. Henri stayed with them in the barn. I was pleased and happy for my uncle and the wonderful outcome for his renovations and for his creation of the small winery. There was talk that he would retire here.

Isabelle and Heidi carried our luggage and showed us to our rooms. On the second floor, all four bedrooms had been painted in fresh bright colors. Maman stopped and laughed.

"What is funny?" I asked.

"Well, I remember when Gustave and I first arrived and

he asked me to select my room of choice. When I went into the third room, a bat flew out and chased me down the stairs."

"You know they eat insects," I giggled. "Let's hope all the insects are gone."

"Jocelyn has a beautiful dinner prepared," Heidi announced. "It will be served at six o'clock."

I wanted to take a walk, gaze at the beautiful gardens, and sit by the pond before it got dark. I asked Maman if she would like to join me.

"Of course, my sweet Annaelise. I will get my shawl," she said.

We walked around the balcony that overlooked the first floor. There was a massive stone chimney. It felt somewhat magical as I looked down on the tops of the trophy heads of wild boar, turkey, pheasant, elk, fox, and even a wolf. I loved the openness of the large room and the deep leather chairs. I was looking forward to sitting with a glass of brandy to enjoy the fire after the hunt tomorrow.

We stepped down the old oak stairs past the deck and the wide porch and headed into the garden. The last of the summer plantings were gone except for the potatoes and carrots along with some mums and pumpkins. Our path led us to a lake surrounded by lovely birch trees that held the last of the yellow leaves shimmering in the wind. We sat on an old bench crawling with grapevines.

We were lost in the silence when Maman spoke. "I remember sitting here with your papa when he proposed to me and presented me with my ring." She looked lovingly at the treasure on her hand. It was a beautiful ring with an emerald stone.

"How did you meet Papa?" I asked. Maman and my uncle were always talking about how I needed to find a husband, but there was never any discussion of love. But after seeing Marie smitten and in love, it made me yearn for something that I didn't realize I wanted.

The light graced Maman's face in a beautiful way. She smiled. "Well, as you know, your father and I met in Obernai. Shortly after Gustave and I moved to Adlershof, we went to the village square to the market. After I went shopping in the square, I joined my brother, who was tasting some of the wine from Friedensthal. It was there I met your father. He invited us to visit him at Friedensthal.

"Your uncle and I had only stayed one night at Friedensthal. After dinner, your papa and I walked in the garden, and he mentioned to me that he was lonely. He said, 'Perhaps you would not be interested in an older gentleman like myself.'"

I raised my eyebrows. "What did you say, Maman?"

"I said, 'Perhaps you should visit us at Adlershof. I would like to see you again.' I was concerned that he was Lutheran and I was Catholic; however, it hasn't affected our relationship. At first, I was dubious of our ten-year difference in age, but when I visited his estate in Friedensthal, I realized it just needed some Parisian touches and a woman's perspective.

"When we came here for a visit, he proposed to me on this very same bench. And we were married at Friedensthal four months later. After we were married, your father was so active with the winery and his scholarly studies. But I was quite content and occupied with all of the necessary changes the estate required. Besides, I loved to entertain there as well!"

It was so good to see Maman so happy as she relived the past. I had never heard this story, though I had never asked. Maman and my uncle always talked about Paris, how extravagant it was, the parties, the glamor. So it was nice to hear her speak about my father and the life they'd created.

Soon it was time to return to the villa to prepare for supper.

I was looking forward to a wonderful meal. When I entered the kitchen, Jocelyn was wiping her hands on her apron and came over to me.

"Mademoiselle, how you have grown into such a beautiful woman. You look so much like your mother, and you are tall like your father. I am so happy to see you." She kissed my cheeks.

"It is wonderful to be back," I said. "Will you be baking your apple cake?"

"Why yes, and we shall have it for breakfast before you go hunting. Now please have a seat in the dining room and join the rest of your family. We still have so much to prepare."

We were seated at the large oak trestle table, and Isabelle joined us while Heidi and Jon served us. The china depicted various animals from the forest. The Guerlain family had it in their family for generations. I'd always wanted the plate with the fox. Our first course was parsnips with a dill sauce from the garden. The main course was beef Bourgogne with potatoes, squash, carrots, and sauerbraten. The wine was burgundy and was from the first harvest of Gustave's grapevines.

"To Adlershof Winery." A salute was raised by all.

I took this opportunity to ask my uncle about his experience at Versailles. He was happy to take center stage.

"The most memorable occasion was when I coordinated and directed a celebration for King Louis XVI and Queen Marie Antoinette when Benjamin Franklin was the honored guest. The table was set with Sèvres gilded china. There were ice sculptures of dolphins and mermaids, and shells kept shrimp and clams chilled in large silver bowls," Uncle Gustave said proudly.

"How did the women dress?" I asked, taking a sip from my glass of wine.

"Oh là là," Isabelle said as she tilted her head back and

raised her thinning brows. "Women wore towering wigs with voluminous silk dresses and their bosoms on display."

We all laughed as Papa opened another bottle of wine.

Maman smiled and said, "I visited with Ambassador Franklin when we were children of the court. He visited us in his racoon hat and his frontier clothes and told us stories of America and the woods where bears, wolves, and foxes lived. He even had puppets made out of these animals, and we were all enchanted by them."

"I have learned much from Dr. Franklin's study in science and history," Papa said. "He exuded a charm wherever he went, and I understand especially with the ladies. It was no wonder he had been very successful at court in France." He rose to pour some brandy. "Dr. Franklin was quite the diplomat, and he was successful in acquiring France's alliance against the British during the American Revolution. We have General Lafayette to thank for that participation."

"Oh, nonsense!" Uncle Gustave said. "Don't you ever tire of speaking about America, Karl?" He glared at Papa.

Papa took a sip of his drink. "There is much to be learned from a country that gained its independence based on principles of equality, justice, and fairness. Unlike France that is bloated in debt, where its own people are starving and poor. Where the masses revolted against the nobility. Where you cannot even look over your shoulder for fear of being executed in the street. Emperor Napoleon exhausts our resources, and all for what? For the sake of the average citizen? For the sake of people like the Muellers, who are suffering and in debt? For the sake of France?"

The room grew quiet.

Maman burst into maniacal laughter and everyone stared at her. "Now, dear husband, let us lighten the conversation, shall we? We are having too much fun to speak of such things. This is a time to celebrate."

Everyone held up their glasses and awkwardly saluted to France and Emperor Napoleon and the freedom that we had to gather with family and friends. Maman had a smile on her face, but she kept glancing over at Papa, who looked tense and uncomfortable.

At that moment, a delicious lemon cake was served for dessert. The focus of discussion was somewhat lost. Maman was feeling the effects of too much wine and excused herself for the evening. Uncle Gustave quickly left the table, slightly inebriated and showing no interest in life in America.

I was always interested in America. My education consisted of reading and engaging in conversation in Papa's study. In my younger years, Papa taught me how to read. I would be buried in stories of princesses, and Greek tragedies, and Shakespeare. There was nothing I loved more than to read. When I turned fifteen, Papa introduced me to a vast amount of knowledge regarding the American Colonies, the Founding Fathers— Thomas Jefferson, John Adams, and James Madison—and their brilliant inspiration. Their contribution in developing the Constitution was brilliantly planned so that a government with a monarchy would never exist. America was so different from France.

As I stared at Papa sipping his drink, his brow beaded with sweat, I tried to recognize the man who'd taught me how to read, to pick grapes, to expand my mind with a wide reach of knowledge. I realized then that Papa had nothing in common with Maman, that everything he'd taught me stemmed from his own personal experiences and opinions. Maman and Uncle Gustave were everything French, even in their thinking. Papa's teachings were giving me the opportunity to choose how I wanted to view the world.

"We have our German philosophers and the movement of the Freemasons to thank, and their influence that went to the New World!" Papa exclaimed.

We raised our last toast with the remaining wine to freedom, liberty, and justice in America and not to Napoleon.

CHAPTER 6

PHEASANT HUNTING

I rose early the next day with a splitting headache, but the coffee and apple kuchen came to the rescue. I hadn't been able to stop my mind from thinking about our conversation last night at dinner. Papa had always been critical of France's governing powers, but I was surprised that he would be so vocal about it at dinner. I had many questions and made a promise to myself that I would confront Papa today.

We were to join Jon with his hunting dogs, Flash and Dash. I was excited to be able to go on my first hunt. I was to receive a hunting lesson from him on the premises before we went out into the field. All of the dogs were tethered in a double harness and collars. Hansel and Gretel were unfamiliar with the harness and became restless.

I wore long twill tan pants to protect my legs from briars in the field. I rather liked these pants, and they were so comfortable. If only I could wear them for riding. I also wore a tan vest buttoned over a blouse made of wool and cotton, a cloth I had never seen before. Leather lace-up boots covered my feet. My hat was made of felt and had a short brim that was adorned with a single pheasant feather. It reminded me of a hat Robin Hood would wear. I felt so secure and confident in these clothes, and I was warm on this crisp, cool morning. The men wore similar clothes with tweed wool jackets.

We walked east behind the villa some distance away where

a target painted in red and green sat, and bales of hay were stacked on top of each other. The sun shone lower in the sky, highlighting the tall weeds while grasshoppers darted to and fro. Jon stopped in front of the targets. His tall, handsome silhouette glowed in the early morning light that highlighted his tan face.

"I think it best you learn how to fire a gun, lest you need to use it one day," Papa said.

"Yes . . . I agree," I said.

Papa stared down out me, his eyes really studying my face. For the first time, I felt uncomfortable under his gaze. "The world is a dangerous place," he said. "I just want you to be prepared."

Jon opened the case and took out the shotgun. Then he walked over to me with the gun in his left hand, the barrel facing down. When he was at a distance of ten meters away, he turned and faced the target.

"Never point the barrel of a gun at anyone unless you intend to injure them," he said with a slight grin. He motioned me to stand beside him. He cocked the gun open and showed me how to properly load the shotgun, pulling the ammunition from his pocket.

He raised the firearm, putting his hand under the butt of the gun and raised it onto his shoulder with his forefinger on the trigger. He aimed at the target and fired. I felt as if the shot went right through me. The manly power of the way he handled this weapon affected me like none other.

Then he pointed the gun toward the sky and shot a bird in flight. He walked back over to me and handed me the gun. It felt heavy in my hand. He stood behind me, and with his arm on mine, he assisted me in raising the shotgun to my shoulder. I pressed my cheekbone firmly on the buttstock. He leaned over and showed me how to aim, that I should be squinting with my left eye. His warm breath on my shoulder and his muscular arms left me almost weak in the knees. When he stepped back, I took a deep breath and swung the weapon toward the sky, but my shot hit a tree instead.

"That's okay, Annaelise. You have to start somewhere," he said smiling, and Papa was laughing. I was so embarrassed, but it didn't take long before I was able to hit closer to the target.

Papa was happy to teach me how to use a pistol as well. I missed the target every time, but I preferred the pistol to the shotgun because it was lighter.

The dogs were getting restless, so we walked further down a path that led to the open fields to a magnificent lake. The sun was shining, casting diamonds of light onto the water and beyond the beautiful open field covered with the weeds of autumn green and gold. The last of the season's remaining dragonflies danced on the water. It was simply breathtaking.

Flash and Dash were still leashed with Jon while Papa carried the guns in their leather cases over his shoulders. At that point, Papa withdrew the firearms and carefully handed one to me.

Jon unleashed the dogs and ordered them to sit down. "*Asseyez-vous*," he commanded while looking into their eager eyes. He positioned his gun and gave the order, "*Faite-vite*, move quickly!" Though he barely raised his voice, the dogs raced forward with their noses to the ground, tails wagging among the tall grass.

Papa went right, following Hansel and Gretel. I went left behind Dash and Flash, walking tall and carefully, raising my knees among the tall grasses. In the next moment, Hansel singularly halted and gallantly pointed his nose in a direction where a brace of pheasants was flushed into flight. In the next instant, Papa timed the shot that landed his prize on the ground. Gretel retrieved the prey with a soft mouth and placed the pheasant onto the ground at Papa's feet.

"Bravo! Well done!" Jon said enthusiastically. He released Dash.

I mounted my gun with one arm and pointed at the sky with the other. After Dash stopped and pointed, I took a deep breath, took aim, and pulled the trigger. I landed a prize pheasant. Flash happily retrieved it to my feet, and I couldn't have been more elated.

We were content to hunt more than three hours. We continued on with great success before Jon walked the dogs home. Papa and I decided to take another path home, and I was happy to have the time alone with him. We paused just before leaving the lake and sat on an old stone bench.

"Thank you for such a lovely time hunting," I said.

"You are so welcome. In some ways, as strange as it seems, you are like the son I never had. I couldn't be prouder of you." He put his arm over my shoulder.

"Papa . . . I have to ask you something."

Papa looked at me with concern. "What is troubling you?" he asked.

"Please don't be cross with me, but I saw you one morning returning to the barn. I know that you are often taking care of business with the winery, but it appeared odd to me at the time."

Papa softened his eyes. "That is not what you want to ask me," he said.

"What do you mean?"

Papa took my hand in his. "Anna, you are a smart girl—too

smart, in fact. It's clear that you have been wanting to talk to me for some time now. Go on with it."

"I . . . I saw you that night . . . in the cabin in the woods."

His expression changed. "I thought I saw the shadow of a curly-haired girl in the window, but then she disappeared. That was you?"

I nodded. "I didn't mean to spy on you, Papa. I was with Marie, and we saw you, and—"

"Say no more." Papa held up a hand. "You don't have to apologize. I have been lurking in the shadows, I'll admit. But you must promise not to tell anyone what I'm about to share with you."

"I promise," I said.

"I am a member of the Freemasons. It may come as no shock to you, but I am aligned in my political beliefs and ideals with the American vision. The New World believes in freedom and justice, and my soul is aligned with the humanitarian manifesto they have set forth in the world. Emperor Napoleon is a dictator, and I believe we are no better off than we were with the French monarchy. I am telling you this because I see how smart you are, how enlightened you seem, and I trust you."

"Of course, Papa. Thank you for trusting me."

He stared at me with seriousness. "Anna, you cannot, under any circumstances, tell anyone what I have told you. Your mother—God bless her heart—and her buffoon of a brother have a lot of pride for France. *Vive la France*, and all of that. Their hearts are deeply rooted in France. They will never understand what I am telling you."

Papa's eyes softened. "I fear that Napoleon is seeking to tear down the Holy Roman Empire and create a new alliance with the regions in Alsace, Bavaria, Württemberg, and Baden, just to mention a few."

"Are you spying for Prussia?" I asked.

"Yes, but you cannot speak about this to anyone. We need to maintain our freedom from Napoleon's harsh rule."

I couldn't believe Papa was trusting me with this information. "I saw Napoleon's soldiers looting from the Muellers' farm," I blurted.

"What? How did you see that?" Then his face transformed as he realized I had been out riding. "How many times have you been riding without my permission?"

"Just those two times," I said. "I . . . saw the terror on the Muellers' faces. I saw how the soldiers just took everything from them."

He sighed. "I know. I have been working with the Lavignes to ensure that the Muellers have what they need for the winter." The Lavignes lived on the eastern side of the Rhine.

"You can count on me to keep your secret," I said. "I can help you as well."

Papa shook his head. "No, it's too dangerous for you, *ma chérie*. Your best assistance is to keep your silence. Never mention a word of this to your mother or uncle."

I took his hands in mine. "You have my word, Papa."

We got up and walked the rest of the way in silence, lost in our thoughts after the secrets we shared. But now I had an even bigger secret to carry.

I was relieved to finally learn Papa's truth. How could I have been so blind to such opposing views? I knew Maman and Uncle Gustave supported Napoleon, and I knew Papa was critical of the French cause, but to have it all laid in such a way brought everything to light. I did not align with the French cause. I did not agree with Napoleon's greed and need for France to expand her reaches to every country in Europe when she couldn't even take care of her own people. The French Empire was as corrupt as a twisted nail. How much longer did France have to suffer? We still weren't healed from the Revolution.

And there I was, Annaelise Theiss, with a French-born mother and a German-born father, stuck right in the middle.

CHAPTER 7

A SURPRISE INVITATION

Our life in Alsace changed drastically over the next several months. In the late autumn of 1805, Napoleon's campaign stepped up the occupation of troops in the eastern regions, including Germany and Prussia. We saw more troops crossing the Rhine, and soon Strasbourg became a gateway to war.

We watched our region evolve into a supply station for the French Army, and our original vision of glory for France was replaced by the increasing demands made upon us for food and livestock. When I saw what the soldiers did to the Muellers, I knew it was wrong, but now it took on a whole new meaning. Papa was taking more time to connect with envoys for the Prussian cause against Napoleon. He would go to taverns in Kaiserslautern, Karlsruhe, Heidelberg, and surrounding areas to deliver important information. Maman was worried, as his cover was to deliver wines to those areas. Of course, he was often intercepted to give some wine to the French soldiers. I was worried for him, too, yet I knew this was his purpose and passion. Papa instructed me to not discuss anything about Napoleon's advances because we feared Maman and Uncle Gustave would learn of our involvement with the opposing forces.

When we returned home from Adlershof in November, the harvest at Friedensthal was complete and Papa continued his studies with me into the winter. I now understood how Papa's influence with the British during the Seven Years' War influenced his thinking. The English were relentless in seeking colonization throughout the world. My father was sympathetic in his observation of the American colonies and their desire for a new system of government.

Being a Lutheran and disciple of Martin Luther, Papa was an enlightened thinker, especially where the German philosophers were concerned. As a student at the University of Jena, he was fortunate to have studied with Johann Wolfgang von Goethe. In return, I was fortunate to read lectures Goethe had written on logic and metaphysics. This was of particular interest for me, as Goethe had spent quite a bit of time in Alsace and Strasbourg where he gathered folk songs and wrote poetry from those stories. We also studied his plays, in particular *Faust*. His epic poem, *Herrmann and Dorothea*, was about a small family in Germany and their reaction to the Revolution.

What inspired me the most, however, was learning the philosophies of Georg Wilhelm Friedrich Hegel. He had also attended the University of Jena. He referred to spirit or *Geist* of Christianity and its influence for the human soul. Both Goethe and Hegel had no affiliation to Napoleon and his mission. "And it is its fate that church and state, worship and life, piety and virtue, spiritual and worldly action, can never dissolve into one," Hegel said.

Christmas was uneventful and rather quiet. We did not stray from our property and enjoyed a nice meal of turkey and ham, cabbage, sweet potatoes, and carrots, all from our farm. We were blessed to have food and wine, and we ate food for days. Papa went to the Muellers and gave them food. Giselle was clever in the kitchen and cooked whatever was in the root cellar. She cooked some popcorn and hung strings of it on the tree that

Papa cut on our property. Isabelle and Maman made ornaments for the tree. We all enjoyed sitting by the fire with Hansel and Gretel by our sides, sipping hot cider with wine seasoned with cinnamon and nutmeg. I read a book and Maman took to her knitting. Uncle Gustave seemed gloomy and decided to spend Christmas at Adlershof. He said he was going to meet some old friends from years ago. I felt relieved just to be with my parents.

On New Year's Eve we were fortunate to receive an invitation to visit Louis Antoine de Bourbon, the Duke of Enghien, a distant cousin of Maman and Uncle Gustave. The Bourbons were prominent French nobility and European dynasty. King Louis XVI of the House of Bourbon was overthrown in 1792, and he was tried for treason and executed by guillotine in 1793. Nine months later, Queen Marie Antoinette was also tried and executed by guillotine. The death of Louis XVI signaled the end of the Bourbon king dynasty.

The Duke of Enghien's estate, the Paix et Abondance, or Peace and Abundance, was in Ettenheim in the district of Bavaria. The name Peace and Abundance was well reflected in their position in life. The estate was only a half-day's carriage drive south from Friedensthal along the Rhine, and we all were looking forward to going in the spring. We were ready for some change of scenery.

"How exciting!" Maman said when she read the letter. "We are all invited to my cousin's lovely estate in April." She was so elated and almost jumping up and down for joy. The invitation read:

Duke Louis Antoine de Enghien
and Duchess Charlotte Louise de Rohan
cordially invite
Count Karl Theiss and Countess Louisa Theiss

Monsieur Gustave Guerlain and Annaelise Theiss
Paix et Abondance on

22 April–30 April 1806

Outdoor activities: pheasant hunting, boar hunting, fishing
Indoor: a ball and a concert

"We must waste no time!" Maman said. "We have a lot of work to do."

Maman, Isabelle, and I took to sewing garments for the event. I learned a great deal, especially on how to model a form to create a dress. I planned to sew my own dress for the ball. We utilized an old storage room where we were fortunate to have a fireplace. The three of us would sew and chatter away while watching the snow fall, creating clothing for our journey and the grand occasion in April.

The snow continued, and we were house bound. When I wasn't sewing, I passed my time curled up in the leather chairs in Papa's study, reading French literature, mathematics, and science.

One cold, dreary day, Papa came home from retrieving the mail with some good news and a document in his hand.

"Anna, I obtained a copy of a diary from my fellow Prussian friend, Alexander von Humboldt. I knew Humboldt from Jena, and we have corresponded to one another over the years." Papa held up the book. "This book is about his journey in America from the island of Cuba to Philadelphia."

"Oh, that is so exciting. Can we read it together?" I pulled up a chair to his large oak trestle table.

While reading this journal, we discovered Humboldt became known as the Prussian statesman and naturalist in America who befriended Thomas Jefferson. Humboldt shared ideals of The Enlightenment in letters across the Atlantic and wrote about his journeys from Havana to Philadelphia in 1804. He was active with the society of friends in Philadelphia. I was fascinated to learn about the city landscapes and terrains of the colonies. It was my understanding that two American explorers, Meriwether Lewis and William Clark, mapped out the western portion of America in 1804.

"I would like to visit America one day and see those cities," I said.

Papa spoke with his nose in the book, "We will see, we will see."

On January 12, 1806, we received the news of Napoleon's victory at Austerlitz. He had been successful in conquering Austria on December 2, 1805. He successfully dismantled the Austrian Empire from the Hapsburgs and Hohenzollern dynasties. This was a monumental victory for the emperor. He seized the Austrian rule and seized power from Tsar I of the Russian army in the Battle of the Three Emperors. This heralded a celebration of Napoleon's greatest victory, and we thought this to be the conclusion of his conquest. How little did the citizens know and how naïve we had become. Papa became more worried that Napoleon's next conquest would be a devastation for eastern Germany and for Prussia.

"Prussia will never be the same," he said sadly.

Our region of Germany and the various provinces, including Baden, Bavaria, Württemberg, Hesse-Darmstadt, and eleven other states became incorporated into the French Empire known as the Confederation of the Rhine. Napoleon appointed his brother-in-law, Marshal Joachim Murat, as head of the Grand Duke of Berg.

Papa's predication was coming true. Prussia was next on Napoleon's list to conquer. Napoleon's victories didn't seem to advance the quality of life for the French, Germans, or Alsatians. The French Army continued heading into the eastern regions. The surrounding provinces were optimistic with the early spring's arrival and from an illusion of peace. In Strasbourg, the French military came by the hundreds and were stopping to take livestock, food, and whatever they could take for their benefit. There seemed to be no stopping Napoleon, the unjust tyrant.

While Maman and Uncle Gustave were bustling with excitement about the upcoming ball, I felt a deep sadness in my heart for a France that could never be free.

CHAPTER 8

AN UNSPEAKABLE DISCOVERY

The birds were singing and the snow was melting with the arrival of spring. One chilly day in March, Papa returned with the mail and brought us yet another invitation to a ball at the Palais Rohan in Strasbourg. Napoleon and Joséphine had taken residency there. It was to celebrate Napoleon's victories after he defeated Austria and Prussia and now for the Confederation of the Rhine. Papa showed the invitation to me first before showing my uncle Gustave and Maman.

"Napoleon has successfully dismantled our provinces and states and into a new confederation. The treaty of the Confederation of the Rhine will be signed on July 12, 1806, and he is hosting a ball on July 14, Bastille Day. He will conquer Prussia next!" Papa was outraged.

"On a lighter note, it is the date of my nineteenth birthday, so I will be pretending that the ball is in my honor," I said.

The invitation read:

Napoleon Bonaparte and Empress Joséphine Bonaparte
request the company and attendance of
Count and Countess Theiss Mademoiselle Annaelise Theiss and
Monsieur Gustave Guerlain

A Celebration Ball at the Palais Rohan in Strasbourg, France
on 14 July 1806 at eight in the evening.

The celebration is for the formation of the
Confederation of the Rhine

When Uncle Gustave and Maman read the invitation, the excitement roared at Friedensthal. Uncle Gustave decided to venture to Adlershof to retrieve clothing not only for spring but now for the ball. With news of seeing Napoleon again, Maman became energized to clean out the attic.

When I was ten years old, my family hosted a celebration party for the marriage of Napoleon and Joséphine. That was when I first learned the art of entertainment from my uncle Gustave and Maman from their former days at Versailles. I would never forget when that beautiful carriage pulled up to our door with magnificent Friesians wearing shiny black harnesses with the letter N on their bridles. A footman opened the door and Napoleon skillfully led Joséphine from the carriage. She floated like a gliding swan whose white neck was topped with a cascade of perfectly coiffed dark curls. Napoleon was dwarfed in contrast to her regal height, but when I caught a glimpse of his penetrating dark eyes, it did not seem to matter. I found myself melting and gently curtsied, holding back a smile. In one instant, at my tender age, I felt grown, somehow seeing my life's destiny before me. Though an awkward ingénue, I knew my life after that night would never be the same.

Warmer weather was setting in and Maman was on the hunt to find the ball gown that she had worn to one of Louis XVI's celebrations. She thought to refashion the dress for me for the ball in Strasbourg. Her former gala dress was to become the ball dress for Napoleon's gala, if I liked it.

One day, when moving boxes to the attic, the attic door fell off its hinge and crashed to the ground.

"That is it!" Maman exclaimed. "Now is the time we go up there once and for all."

The attic was like a deep, dark well, and for the past two centuries it was a catchall for everything. We employed two women from the village, and they were instrumental in bringing crates up from the winery. We were able to give them anything they wanted. The men were busy in the vineyard pruning the vines, so we opened the dormer window and allowed fresh air and light to penetrate the cavernous space.

Maman, Isabelle, and I dove into the depths of the dark abyss. Maman had delayed this process ever since she married Papa, and things continued to accumulate after I was born.

The stairway to the attic was narrow. We all wore old cotton clothes and scarfs in our hair and over our mouths. Maman was sensitive to dust and mildew. She sat in a chair, and we would bring her items that she would then either keep or throw away. There were old chairs with broken seats, linens, pewterware, paintings, and dishes that were boxed and given to people in the village. The ladies were ecstatic and took the boxes to their wagon without much interception from the men, especially Papa.

We saved many things, and what remained was at least organized. The few items that Uncle Gustave and Maman brought from Paris were carefully arranged in the corner of the attic. Maman looked into her trunk and was unable to find the dress she wore to one of Louis XVI's celebrations.

"It must be in the old Banquet Hall," she said. When completing the big task, Maman gave explicit directions to leave Uncle Gustave's trunk alone. I hadn't seen a trunk that belonged to my uncle, but this aroused my curiosity.

Over the next few days, while Uncle Gustave was gone to

Adlershof, I would sneak up into the attic, sit in a chair by the dormer windows, and take my time looking through trunks of old letters and documents. It was like finding a pirate treasure. One chest contained old documents, such as the deed to the estate and Papa's declaration for the estate from his service during the Seven Years' War. I even found old love letters from Papa, and older letters from the original owners in the 1600s. On the final day, when most everything was cleaned and removed and everyone left, I discovered a trunk that was labeled "Gustave Guerlain."

I froze and listened, wondering if anyone was coming. All was silent. Maman had told me to leave my uncle's trunk untouched. I debated for a moment, then carefully opened the old trunk. There were many letters from his personal life.

Suddenly, I heard footsteps and voices. I quickly shut the trunk and shoved it into the corner. My heart was racing. The voices trailed down the hall. I exhaled the breath I was holding. If I wanted to meddle in the past, I needed to come back at night when everyone was sleeping.

And that was just what I did.

That night, tiptoeing carefully with two candles in hand, I made my way up into the attic and sat down in one of the old cane chairs. As I went through the trunk, I found a diary from Versailles made of worn brown leather. It was written in Uncle Gustave's handwriting. Even though I was up in the attic by myself, I suddenly felt like I was going to get caught doing something that I shouldn't be doing. But I couldn't stop my curiosity.

I flipped through the pages, and then something caught my attention. There was an order from a magistrate to appear in court for an accused rape and violation of a Madame Juliette Bourie, who was apparently high in ranking at Versailles. A separate document was for the release of Mademoiselle Louisa Guerlain from Gustave's custody.

I was shocked. All my life, I had been told that my uncle and my mother left France because they feared the growing revolution. Maman had said, "I had finished my schooling and it was our time to go." Now it all made sense.

They didn't leave from Paris and Versailles because of the approaching revolt and unrest, or Maman's finishing school. They left because of Gustave Guerlain's conduct and devious appetite and lack of character. They left in disgrace, their reputation in tatters.

I closed the trunk. My hands were shaking. I needed to know the truth, but for now this was just another secret I had to hold.

Since the news and invitation of the ball, all Maman could talk about was seeing Napoleon in the Palais Rohan. "The fashions have changed from the glory days in Paris," she said. "We must find silk, but we are so far from Lyon. Perhaps a shipment will come up the Rhine. Let's try to contact Monsieur de Larose in Strasbourg."

"But didn't you ever look for your dress in the Banquet Hall? You mentioned the trunk of Parisian dresses could be in there when we were cleaning the attic. Can't we remake them?" I reminded her.

I was hoping we would find the dress because time was running out before the ball, and it would be too late to go to Monsieur de Larose in Lyon.

"Well, we shall see. Let's go to the old Banquet Hall right now," Maman suggested. Papa had the keys, which were kept in his refurbished study one floor above, but Maman told me in confidence, "I had a key made." I was surprised she would go behind his back.

When Maman and I entered the old hall, I felt uneasy. There was a knight's armor standing by the door with a long spear in his hand. There was forbidden energy in the air.

The hall was the oldest structure of the estate that dated back to the 1500s. The plaster walls were covered with swords, shields, and knight's armor from the Middle Ages. Our family crest hung over every door. It was a shield with a knight's helmet with a winged horse on top. The shield was divided into quarters—the top left and lower right were red and had three crowns, and the top right and lower left were pictures in gold with an armored arm holding a sword. *Glaube and Seelenstärke*, which meant "Faith and Fortitude," was written on the shield, the Theiss family motto.

Two massive stone fireplaces flanked either end that reached fifteen feet or more with a series of old leaded glass windows that allowed light to filter through. On one end was an oak stairway with hand-carved balusters leading to Papa's study.

In the corner there were items that had no placement or use in the manor house. The trunk was not there. Maman stood for a minute, tapping the key to her lips. "Aha, I bet it's in the closet under the stairs." She walked over to the side of the room where a door was built into the wall. The key fit into the small keyhole, and we opened the door. The dust was overwhelming.

"Please, Anna, I can't go in there. I will get sick."

I moved some items out of the way and found the trunk buried on the bottom. I sneezed as I pulled the old, dusty trunk out of the closet. "It's locked," I responded as I tried to open it.

"I have a key," she quickly replied.

Maman pulled out a second key from her pocket, and without hesitation opened the old trunk. First, she pulled out a chapeau with an elaborate array of disintegrating feathers. Then she pulled out multiple silk dresses, and the last one was a cream-colored ball gown that had a voluminous skirt adorned with gold-embroidered roses.

"Oh my! This is it the dress I was looking for!" Maman exclaimed with tears in her eyes.

"We can remake it into the new empire style," I shyly suggested. The silk wasn't moth eaten. I couldn't believe it was still in such good condition. I held the dress in front of me. "How do I look?" I spun in a circle.

"*Ah, oui, très magnificent!* So beautiful!" Maman exclaimed. "I was younger than you when I wore this, and it is only fitting that you should wear this silk to the ball in Strasbourg."

Maman laughed as she waltzed around the room with the gown. Then she stopped and looked at me. "Will you have this dance with me?" she asked, gently placing the gown onto the trunk and opening her arms.

I rushed over to her, and took the lead, placing one hand on her shoulder and another hand in hers. With a Mozart's melody in my mind, I hummed as we moved around the room. I felt a kinship with my mother that I had never felt before. Maman was relaxed with no agenda, no criticism, no pretense in her mind. In an instant, I caught an impression of her in her happy days at Versailles as a younger woman. Laughing, we hugged each other in delight and gaiety.

CHAPTER 9

PAIX ET ABONDANCE

April finally came and we were all busy in preparation for the big event to our cousin's estate. Though I had never met the Duke of Enghien and his family, it was grand to know I had cousins. We were delighted to learn that many festivities were planned in our honor and for the celebration of early harvest time in Bavaria. Outdoor activities in the spectacular countryside included pheasant hunting, fishing, and a wild boar hunt on horseback. We were also informed that we would be attending lectures of famous authors and music composers, including a mystery composer from Bonn. Best of all, a ball was planned as the grand finale at the end of the week. Papa, of course, brought his finest wines, and Maman had been busy assembling the most presentable wardrobes for us all.

We made our way south from Friedensthal to Ettenheim in our Parisian carriage drawn by a pair of our younger Andalusian horses. Their harnesses were shined, including the brass buckles. Uncle Gustave had acquired a new open carriage with a curvilinear shape over the front and back wheels, and with a leather retractable awning in case of inclement weather. The frame was black with the trim painted gold. Since our trip was only a half-day's ride, we were hoping for no rain. The interior had tufted burgundy leather seats. Papa drove the wine wagon, and Hansel and Gretel were tethered to the floor. While riding in the carriage, dressed in my latest finest clothes and Parisian scarlet bonnet adorned with a silk sash that tied under my chin, I listened to everyone chattering away about the upcoming events. I tried to ignore Maman and Uncle Gustave's endless, frivolous chatter. However, truth be told, it was exciting to think about my first boar hunt and all the other planned activities.

It was a glorious afternoon when we left Friedensthal and arrived at our destination. We were met by Louis Antoine, the Duke of Enghien, and his lovely wife, Charlotte Louise de Rohan.

The duke was pleasant and seemed to have a kind word for everyone. He was dressed in breeches and boots, appearing to have just taken a ride. He had long sideburns that were mostly gray and a thick head of chestnut hair peppered with gray. When he smiled and spoke, he was jolly, his double chin wiggling. Charlotte Louise, on the other hand, was dressed in a lovely mint-green silk empire waist that complemented her soft blue eyes. Her breasts were bulging from her dress, and I thought she would lose the top of her dress and expose herself if she bent over.

"Ah, Annaelise, you are as beautiful as your mother," the duke said with enthusiasm. "Your beauty will carry you far. Make sure you find a husband worthy of you."

Uncle Gustave was in heaven in this elegant environment, lapping up every interaction and impression as a pleased kitten with a bowl of fat milk. Maman was happily talking away.

I was led to the beautiful room where I would stay. It was decorated in the high Rococo style that was prevalent during Louis XV's reign. This luxurious room was decorated with white and gold-gilded furniture and a large, ornate floral chandelier.

Mirrored paneling adorned the walls with a Chinese-styled asymmetrical design of leaves, flowers, and shells.

My next surprise took me into a bathroom, which had its very own copper tub. I truly felt like a princess. I even had a chambermaid, Yvette, who assisted me in dressing and arranging my hair, and pampered me in dressing for dinner. Since it was just our immediate family and not a formal occasion, I chose a powder-blue empire-waist silk dress that Maman had made for me. It was so much fun dressing up after wearing everyday cotton clothes at Friedensthal. For the finishing touch, Yvette styled my hair with curls galore on the top of my head, making me look suitably sophisticated, and in an instant, I felt more mature and curious of my role in this exclusive world. But on some level, I felt guilty. I attributed my new insight on knowing how the aristocrats lived and seeing how the masses suffered. If this was how nobility like the Bourbons lived, no wonder there was a revolution.

Dinner was served in a small dining room with mirrors that hung all around the walls, reflecting the light from the candelabras and shimmering silver. The servants moved like gliding ghosts, attending to our every need. I was mesmerized by the efficiency of the waiters and the beautiful crystal goblets and the Sèvres china. I was grateful for all of my etiquette lessons with my uncle. I used the correct fork. The pheasant was delicious and was paired with one of Papa's finest sparkling rosé wines. The duke spoke of the next day's hunt and the horses Uncle Gustave and I would ride. We were also informed of the pheasant- and grouse-shooting the following day, and Papa was most happy to announce his recent acquisition of his prized pointers. When hearing of a planned fishing trip to learn a new fly-fishing technique from England, I expressed an interest in attending.

"We will see," Maman spoke in a firm voice, which was not a good sign. Then she leaned over and whispered, "That is a gentleman's sport."

Duchess Charlotte Louise came to my rescue. "Why, of course she can participate. There will be an Englishman teaching a new method of fly-fishing. Other women will be there as well." I knew Maman would not counter the wishes of our hostess, and I felt pleased.

"Also, we will host a ball at the end of the week and a concert with a surprise Bavarian composer," the duke announced proudly, letting us all know he had gone out of his way to make this a special occasion for us, his friends, and the community.

"Do you think Napoleon is making a difference for France, Alsace, Bavaria, and the German states?" Papa asked.

The duke put down his fork and knife. He wiped his face on the fine linen napkin and leaned back in his chair. "Well, at least the rioting has stopped." He smiled and had a sip of his champagne.

"Yes, but the welfare of the people is not doing any better, and there is rioting still between the masses. Napoleon promised equality and harmony for France and the countries under his rule, but I'm not seeing it happening at all. I think the countries should follow the example that America has started," Papa said.

My eyes widened. I glanced around the table. Maman looked pale, and Uncle Gustave clenched his jaw.

It was true that Napoleon had rescued France after the chaos and the destruction of the French monarchy and from the horror and merciless executions that followed during the Reign of Terror in 1793. After Napoleon seized control, the original revolutionaries went into hiding, and those loyal to Napoleon made themselves known.

Uncle Gustave said, "My brother-in-law has a concern that

Napoleon could still be hunting for the members of the aristocracy, including those of the Bourbon families. The descendants of the Bourbons could be in danger, including Louisa and myself, and possibly you, sir, and your lovely wife."

"Oh, that is preposterous!" The duke laughed.

"My concern is that Napoleon has plans to break down our principalities and create a unified area for Bavaria, Baden, Hesse-Darmstadt, and eleven other states including your provinces and mine," Papa boldly announced.

Maman quickly spoke up, "My dear, we shouldn't discuss this now." She grabbed Papa's hand gently, but I knew she was agitated.

"Perhaps we can ask Madame Germaine de Staël when she will be discussing The Enlightenment philosophy later this week and her views of Napoleon's tactics and strategy. I'm sure we will learn so much," the duke said. "You know she is an enemy of Napoleon? He has exiled her from Paris!" He burst into laughter.

"I passed Madame de Staël in the hall when we arrived. I was not impressed," Maman said as she took another sip of wine.

"Well, I am looking forward to hearing her views, especially regarding John Adams, Thomas Jefferson, and James Madison in America," Papa said.

I looked down at my plate. I suddenly didn't feel hungry. I loved my father, but he shouldn't be speaking of such things. Him speaking out against Napoleon made me nervous, especially now since I knew where his loyalties lay. It wouldn't take much for someone to turn him in and he would be executed by guillotine.

"Shall we raise a toast to the welfare and future of our provinces!" Duchess Charlotte Louise said, interrupting the conversation. She demurely raised her champagne glass, and we all took her lead. "Bon appétit!"

"To our cousins and to their health and well-being!" I said and raised my glass confidently, though my hand was shaking.

We were served *pheasant à l'orange*. Aside from Papa's outburst, I was delighted to taste the champagne. When I arrived at my bedroom after dinner, I found it difficult to sleep. I couldn't stop thinking about what Papa had said over dinner—how bold he was. I was a young girl at the height of the Reign of Terror, completely innocent to the horrors of the world.

My head felt a bit dizzy, a feeling I was unfamiliar with. Deciding not to worry about Papa, I instead focused my thoughts on the boar hunt in the morning. However, the champagne released the tension, and soon I slept like a baby.

CHAPTER 10

THE BOAR HUNT

W hen the sun rose the next morning, I awoke from a deep sleep. I had a dream about dancing at a ball, but I suddenly remembered the boar hunt and the big day ahead. I stood up quickly but felt dizzy and had a little headache, perhaps from the champagne. I staggered out of bed and went into the washroom and splashed cold water on my face. I looked in the mirror—my eyes were slightly red, so I put a cold rag over my face and decided to lay down for a few minutes. At that point, Yvette knocked on the door and was able to assist me in dressing into my riding clothes.

My hunting attire was a black culotte skirt and a tight-fitting black waistcoat with a white stock ascot, which could be used as a bandage in case of injury. My chapeau was a small top hat that had a delicate veil to shield my eyes from the harsh sunlight. Delighted that the chapeau fit so well, I knotted my hair at the base of my neck. When I looked in the mirror, I was very pleased with my appearance.

I made my way down the winding marble staircase. Maman, Papa, and the duchess declined to rise early, so Uncle Gustave and I met the Duke of Enghien for breakfast. The three of us were seated in a lovely garden room that served as the home for many plants and small trees. The back wall was lined with Palladian windows that overlooked the large terrace, fountain, and garden. We were served fresh trout, hot oatmeal muffins, and apple dumplings. Very filling for a long day's ride.

After breakfast, I was escorted by one of the valets to the front of the house. Two staircases flanked either side of the grand entrance, and the elaborate brass railing seemed to cascade down to the black-and-white marble floor. I headed outside to inhale the crisp air of the early dawn.

I was surprised that there were at least fifty participants waiting outside. About a third of the riders were women. The master of the bloodhounds was assembling the whipper-in and staff members to keep the hounds in check. Uncle Gustave was dressed in a top hat with tan riding breeches that appeared too tight, accenting his large belly. He clumsily buttoned his waist coat, hoping to conceal his protruding waistline.

"Uncle, I thought you brought your own hunting clothes?" I asked politely.

"These are my clothes—too much gourmet food and fine wine," he said under his breath.

I secretly laughed to myself and knew this would be a great day.

"Welcome, everyone," the duke said. He was dressed like all the other men in waistcoats, boots, and breeches. "We're going into the forest, and if the hounds pick up the scent of the boar, we will try to run the beast into the open fields where it is safer for the members and horses to avoid narrow gaps, large stones, and brush. It is also possible the hounds will run the boar from the woods along the riverbank. Please do not enter the water on horseback, as the river has a strong current after the recent heavy rain. It can be dangerous out there. If you see the boar, stop and announce his presence by saying, 'Tally-ho!' Let the hounds and the huntsman do their job. The whipper-in will collect the stray hounds in the back, so give him space to do his job."

At that moment, the huntsman, an older gentleman with rosy cheeks, mounted his handsome half Thoroughbred-Percheron horse.

My mount was a pleasant surprise—a large Welsh-and-Belgian-cross horse that reminded me of Sergeant. It seemed as if he had been chosen just for me.

Uncle Gustave was mounted on a large Belgium draft cross. He was clearly disappointed the horse was not more refined in bone, as it was in his nature to always want to look as sophisticated and elegant as possible. However, we were told a large-boned horse was sturdier and calmer than a well-bred horse.

We were offered Vendange Tardive white wine and apple tarts from a silver tray. The apple tarts I accepted, but after last evening's champagne and my slight throbbing headache, I declined the wine. The huntsman came forward with a large pack of bloodhounds that were known for their ability to stalk wild boar. They were taller than foxhounds and very trim and fit. The huntsman sounded his small pocket horn while one of the staff blew a large French horn. We were off!

The terrain gave way from large fields while we made our way into the Bavarian woods. Gigantic pine trees engulfed us as we rode on paths covered in pine needles. My little horse was most assured of his direction and tossed his head to loosen the bit. Once I allowed and trusted him, he performed his job quite satisfactorily.

Uncle Gustave rode in front of me on the narrow path that wove through the woods. I was advised to stay behind the other horses because the boar could be quite dangerous. I didn't mind. The men, including Uncle Gustave, rode ahead as I trotted carefully behind them, feeling the cool wind on my face. As we entered the open fields, the sun was peeking over the clouds, casting a golden-yellow hue across the land. Then a strange feeling washed over me, as if I were being watched. I gazed at my surroundings but saw nothing.

"Come on," I whispered to my trusty steed, and he continued on a bit faster as we broke into a canter.

"You will get lost if you don't make that horse run faster," Uncle Gustave shouted at me. He was picking up speed, and for a moment, I worried that he would leave me in the dust.

I quickened my pace, but that uneasy feeling washed over me again. Something was watching me. I was sure of it. I looked to the left and right, then over my shoulder, but there was nothing. But I swore I was being followed, hunted.

Suddenly, I heard the squeal from a boar and saw something large dart out from the woods into the open field. Its short brown fur was matted and dirty, and it made a horrible squeal from its snout. Two sharp tusks protruded from its mouth. Everyone was ahead of me and hadn't seen the boar. My heart raced with anticipation.

I removed my chapeau and pointed in the direction of the boar. "Tally-ho!" I shouted.

Making my mount step back from the path, I allowed a few of the hounds from the back to pass in front of me. My mount was anxious to follow the field when a young whipper-in rode past me, cracking his whip to keep the lingering hounds on the path in pursuit of the wild animal. He winked at me while galloping past. He was not much older than I. He had lost his chapeau, and his long blond ponytail flapped in the wind. It was thrilling to be noticed. My mount leapt forward, and I finally allowed him to take off, following the members of the field in a hot pursuit of the wild boar. The hounds were voicing full cry.

We followed the boar with the hounds chasing the beast along the tall cliffs overlooking the riverbank. The boar was looking to escape into the river away from the steep cliffs. The race was on! When we came to an opening in the river, the boar leapt into the rushing water followed by the hounds driven by the whipper-in. The boar thrashed downstream, struggling to keep his head above water with the hounds trailing behind.

I had to move forward to see the action, careful to stop a hundred feet away from the riverbank where the huntsman and his hounds were gathered, including other members of the field. At that moment, I witnessed the enraged animal leap onto the embankment out of the river and away from his predators. The boar sprang into the trap where the huntsman was waiting with the remaining hounds positioned on land. At that moment, the hounds from the river leapt onto the bank. The terrified beast was surrounded while both packs jumped onto his back and neck, avoiding the sharp tusks.

It was a finished task, *fait d'accompli*! The large boar fell to the ground while the huntsman fired his pistol to ensure its death and safety for the hounds. The whipper-in collected the hounds and the huntsman dismounted to fire a last shot into the boar. Never in all my life had I witnessed anything so exciting and exhilarating. Being asked to dismount, I was honored to have a swipe of blood placed upon my forehead, a hunt tradition held for a newcomer.

"Well done, *bien fait*, Annaelise Theiss, on your first hunt!" the huntsman exclaimed. Uncle Gustave had to be in the limelight as well, and announced I was his prodigy.

We opened a bottle of sparkling wine, and everyone toasted the huntsman, the whipper-in, and the hounds.

Cheers went all around. I didn't know what to say. My heart swelled with pride. I knew Papa would be proud of me.

CHAPTER 11

THE ENLIGHTENED WOMAN

It was a wonderful day for fishing. About twenty of us went along, including four guides. I was excited to participate in these activities, and I hoped I was as successful at catching fish as I was at spotting the wild boar. When leaving the open fields, the fishing party entered the Black Forest. The ancient hemlocks draped down over us, and the height of the magical trees filtered the sunlight, casting spears of sunshine beams on the forest floor. The smell of the woods permeated with wet evergreens from the spring rain. We were fortunate to experience perfect weather. As we approached the river, the path was rocky and we had to take our time so we would not trip over the stones. The mist disappeared and sunshine graced the river.

We were going to learn how to fish for trout in a tributary of the Rhine. The rocks were covered in moss and were slippery. Therefore, the ladies were asked to fish from the grassy bank while the men walked into the water.

Our lesson was taught by an Englishman who spoke with a poor French accent. We all learned the proper way to cast our lines into the water from the bank. It was mesmerizing to hear the melody of the water while we focused on the casting of the line. I watched the rhythm of the river and sensed the location of the trout.

The bank was wide and not steep, so it was very safe and accessible to cast a line. Our instructor picked up his rod and showed us how to load the reel with the line. Next, we broke into groups and had a separate instructor demonstrate how to tie the fly or lure onto the line itself. It was tedious and appeared to be easier for the ladies, as we were all used to sewing and threading a needle. I observed with great interest the casting of the lightweight line that seemed to flow effortlessly and flawlessly from over the instructor's shoulder into the stream and flow gently down the rippling silver water. I tried my hand at it several times and soon I began to feel one with the river, watching the line flow and move gracefully downstream.

I was fortunate to meet other ladies who were kind to me. There were only five of us, and one woman in particular made a great impression on me: Madame Germaine de Staël. She was dressed in a beige ensemble and a wide-brimmed hat trimmed with pheasant feathers that unsuccessfully tried to keep her hair in order. Her appearance made her look as if she were on the verge of being wild, and the entirety of her passionate persona made me smile. I had never met any woman like her. She was eloquently spoken, intelligent, and her knowledge was far-reaching. Papa had taught me so much, but to meet a woman with such profound insight—a woman who was not afraid to speak her mind—was inspiring. I was enthralled and enamored when she spoke.

Her philosophy and wisdom were based on The Enlightenment. She sought to promote peace and forward-thinking to benefit the French government and society. From her observation, she was horrified that Napoleon had not accomplished these goals. She was influenced by Thomas Jefferson, John Adams, and Benjamin Franklin. Her inspiration to write evolved through her studies of Hegel, Goethe, Rousseau, Voltaire, and the Marquis de Condorcet. She was vivacious, graceful, but also humble. She was most outspoken and I loved her tenacity.

She was standing on the bank of the river by herself, so I walked over and stood some feet away so our fishing lines would not get crossed.

"Ah, Mademoiselle Annaelise, are you joining me?" she asked with a smile.

"I couldn't let you catch all the fish by yourself," I said. As best I could, I loosened my line and cast it over my head to allow slack in the fishing line as it sailed far and high and then finally touched the top of the water.

"Bravo, nice cast," Madame de Staël said as she gently reeled her line from the water.

The sun was warm on my face. "Madame, what can you tell me of romance?" I asked in a hushed voice. I didn't know why I had asked that—the words just tumbled from my lips—but I'd bet it had to do with that handsome staff boy.

She paused and regarded me with a knowing smile. "There are many things I could tell you, Annaelise, but you must learn from experience. Love is the sole passion of women. Ambition, even the love of glory, are so little suited to their nature, that very few of them turn their attention to these objects. What I can say, dear girl, is to trust your heart."

Suddenly, I felt a quick tug on my line.

"Ah, Mademoiselle Annaelise, pull your trout in!"

I quickly held my rod up to ensure the hook was steadfast in the trout's mouth. I watched as the fish leapt out of the water. I was compelled to move closer, so I went several feet into the water that rose up to my knees, drenching my skirt. The guide quickly rushed to my side with a net. I reeled the fish in, and then my left hand skillfully caught him with my net.

The fish was convulsing, and its sides were moving up

and down as it gasped for breath. Its large eyes stared at me. I removed the hook from the beautiful rainbow trout's mouth and admired his iridescent body that sparkled in colors of pink, green, and almost a violet tone speckled with brown spots. The men applauded—my prize was going to be tomorrow's breakfast.

We walked back to the carriages to take us back to our lodging. The bottom of my dress was wet and collected dirt, but I didn't care, and my spirit was elevated by this new method of fishing.

I was fortunate to walk with Madame de Staël and she shared her story. She was born in Paris and grew up in an aristocratic home. Her father was a Swiss banker and her mother was a playwright. She was a prolific writer and studied politics.

"Madame, can you tell me about your days in Paris salons?"

Madame de Staël smiled. "Well, I was fortunate to experience Paris before the Revolution. I was part of a literary group with some very enlightened thinkers. I was meeting with many writers and philosophers there, including Voltaire, Rousseau, Hegel, and Goethe. Have you heard of them, my dear?"

"Yes," I replied. "Papa knew Hegel and Goethe from the University of Jena. He was a student there, and I have been studying them ever since I was a young girl."

Madame de Staël raised her eyebrows. "Oh really? I am most impressed!"

"Goethe was a frequent visitor to Alsace when he collected stories from the local farmers and wrote poetry from the folklore. I have studied many of Hegel's essays with my father. They both believed that church and state should be separate. Hegel believed that neither religious nor political views could compete with reason. I know they detested Napoleon."

"Napoleon would not listen to reason and believed I was a threat to him with my belief in women's rights. My novel, *Delphine*, is a collection of letters written by aristocratic women and examines the limits that have been put on their lifestyles and hindered their freedom of speech—women who feel smothered and powerless with men. The Catholics are not fond of this work because I believe it is every woman's right to ask for a divorce. And Napoleon doesn't think a woman should have strong opinions and views. He would rather silence me and my writings."

I nodded. "The duke mentioned that Napoleon exiled you to your home in Switzerland."

"Oh, he did, did he?" She stopped and turned to face me.

I realized I might have made a mistake. "The duke said that you had some forward-thinking ideas about America." I lowered my voice, though nobody was within earshot. "My father also has strong opinions about the future of Germany, Prussia, and in our provinces. He thinks France should follow the American format with a constitutional government."

"Why yes, but a constitution will never happen on this continent. Napoleon has seized control, and who knows when he will be defeated? I predict the English will have to destroy him. He has already lost to the British Navy knowing that he cannot compete with their mighty ships."

"Papa sometimes mentions sailing to America and possibly living there. What do you think?

"Well, if he thinks he can leave and sell everything he owns, it may take years, but right now it will be difficult to uproot and move elsewhere until this war is over. You and your father should visit me at the Chateau Coppet Villa on Lake Geneva in Switzerland, and I will introduce you to my new Coppet group.

We have Prince Augustus of Prussia and Madame Recamier in our gathering, to mention just a few."

In that moment, the sun pierced through the trees, creating light and shadows on her face. Her dark brown hair and eyes looked lighter in the sun. Her smile was warm.

"My dear Annaelise, promise me that you'll always think for yourself. The men of this world think they know everything, but a woman holds the key to everything."

"I see why you were exiled," I said sincerely.

"I suppose it's no secret what I believe," Madame de Staël continued. "And I can tell who is of like mind, and I know you and your papa are of like mind. Excuse me if I'm speaking out of turn, but I do sense your mother may not be fond of me. She was very curt when we crossed paths."

I looked away, and I wasn't sure why.

"I'm sorry, Mademoiselle Annaelise," Madame de Staël said. "I meant no ill will. There is strength in loving those who think differently."

"I . . . yes," I said. It was the first time I felt ashamed that my mother was not enlightened. I loved her, but everything suddenly became so clear to me on my walk with Madame de Staël. For years, Papa had been teaching me philosophies and music and poetry, but I didn't understand its context or how it fit into my world. Now it made perfect sense: I was an enlightened thinker and my mother was not.

When we approached the carriages, we parted ways and she took a separate carriage to her lodging. "Thank you for the words of great wisdom! Au revoir, Mademoiselle Annaelise! I will see you tonight."

Something had shifted in me. I was so inspired by Madame

de Staël and our talk. Maman wasn't pleased, though. She'd pulled me aside after the fishing expedition and scolded me. "I see how enamored you are with Madame de Staël. How can you be inspired by that woman who believes in divorce?"

"There is strength in loving those who think differently," I said, echoing Madame de Staël. My mother just shook her head and shrugged her shoulders.

The ball was held outside the estate in Ettenheim. My confidence grew while wearing my finest silk dress and a pearl necklace, which Maman had sewn into her clothes to prevent being robbed on our journey. Yvette styled my hair with jewels, and I truly felt special and beautiful. Our open carriage was drawn by four large ebony Friesians from the duke's excellent stock. Their coats glistened from the light of the torches that lined the pathway to the estate. As we climbed out of the carriage, I waited until the door was opened for me. I thankfully accepted the outreached hand of the young footman. Together, with my family, we walked down the warm candlelit hallway that reflected the sparkle of the precious stones in my hair.

We were served a fine rosé wine from Provence and appetizers of pâté and bread. A complete string orchestra played the beautiful music of Mozart and Handel. Maman and Uncle Gustave were quietly discussing Madame de Staël, and I sensed they were offended by her radical ideas.

"Why are you discussing this now? It is not the time!" I spoke out abruptly from the influence of too much wine. I decided to mingle with the guests.

While I was surprised and pleased that so many men asked me to dance, one in particular made my heart flutter. It was the young whipper-in who'd winked at me on the boar hunt. He was dressed in a fine coat with tails and short leather boots. His hair was combed tightly back. I almost did not recognize him. He walked with long strides with a sway in his hips. His air spoke of confidence and cockiness. I took a deep breath and sensed what was coming.

"Care to dance, my lady?" he said and held out his hand. His hands were coarse and yet when he pulled me closer, I felt assured and calm.

He led me into a perfect waltz that was graceful and refined. I felt like I was floating in his arms as he led me through the movements, which were comparable to the fluidity in his riding skills. *So this is what it feels like to move with another. Not stiff like when dancing with Uncle Gustave.*

Once the music stopped, he asked if I would like to step outside onto the veranda to view the moon.

"Why, yes," I answered, feeling very mature and grown-up as he offered his arm. "What is your name?" I asked politely.

"Gunter. And your name, mademoiselle?" He looked me in the eye with interest.

"I'm Annaelise," I said.

"You are quite the equestrian, Annaelise. Congratulations for your recognition with the hunt," Gunter said enthusiastically.

We walked away from the crowd and onto the veranda. The moon was high and so were our spirits. My heart was beating wildly. He turned toward me while placing his arm around my waist and drew me closer while kissing my lips. Shocked, I pushed him away. I could still feel the wetness of his lips on mine. My cheeks flushed with embarrassment. I thought we were having a great time. I was unaware his intentions were to make advances.

"Ah, mademoiselle, are you still a child?" he asked.

Ignoring him, I turned around and made my way back to the ballroom. Perhaps this did prove him to be coarse and unmannerly. Nevertheless, I was thrilled to experience my first kiss even though it was brief and unexpected.

Our greatest surprise during the evening was a performance by a brilliant composer and pianist who had moved from Bonn to Vienna. Ludwig van Beethoven's appearance caused a stir. His hair was unruly and rose with the rhythm of the baton while conducting the orchestra for his piece, *Eroica*.

I overheard someone say in hushed excitement that he was considered the heir apparent to Mozart's brilliance. Madame de Staël informed me just before we entered the performance that Beethoven had originally dedicated the symphony to Napoleon but withdrew his dedication when Napoleon declared himself emperor. Beethoven received a standing ovation. I wanted to jump up and down, but I managed to maintain my demeanor. Completely immersed in joy, tears formed in my eyes, and I felt grateful to have experienced such beautiful music and discussions. This was the beginning to my adult life that lay ahead.

CHAPTER 12

THE HORSEMAN AND THE GIFT

When we returned home, Uncle Gustave seemed more withdrawn. He was not at the stable training his horses and he appeared to be drinking more. Perhaps he realized he might never again have a life with the magnitude of Paix et Abondance. I just did not enjoy any time with him and his moody disposition. I had always felt like he was hiding something, and after I had discovered the real reason why he left Versailles, I had lost respect for him.

With the spring flowers and warm sunshine, he insisted that we work on my sidesaddle equitation since I felt unsteady riding in the sidesaddle during the boar hunt. As much as I didn't want to be around him, I never said no when it came to spending time outside with the horses.

One morning, while working in the ring, we were interrupted by a young French corporal currier officer on a large Andalusian draft cross horse.

"Monsieur Gustave Guerlain?" the officer asked.

"Yes, you have found me," my uncle responded.

The officer handed Uncle Gustave a letter. My uncle opened the letter, read it, then handed it to me. It was from Marshal Ney, an officer under Napoleon.

Dear Monsieur Guerlain,

It is my understanding that you are a successful horse breeder and have many Andalusian horses for sale. I am in need of a stallion and possible other horses for my regiment.

Please be advised, I will be coming tomorrow afternoon to in-spect your horses for sale for Napoleon's army. Thank you for your cooperation and patronage in support for the war effort.

> *Marshal Ney*
> *Duke of Elchingen, Prince of Moskva,*
> *Marshal of the Empire*

Uncle Gustave stood up a little straighter and responded to the officer, "Thank you. We will be ready for Marshal Ney's visit tomorrow."

We watched the officer trot away until he was far in the distance. Then my uncle turned to me and said in an excited manner, "We have a great deal of work to prepare the horses."

"I will help you," I said.

"This is a wonderful opportunity. Marshal Ney is one of Napoleon's right-hand men. This encounter, should it go well, could lead to many other opportunities," my uncle said. He was very giddy in his demeanor.

That afternoon, we took the horses to a small river, a trib-utary of the Rhine some distance away from the stables. I wore old clothing and waded in the stream while we washed the horses. The water was warm, and the sun's rays beat on my shoulders and head. Henri joined us, and we took two horses at a time. I was leading a small mare to the water when Uncle Gustave stopped me.

"Oh, she is too small. I don't think Marshal Ney will be interested in her."

"But she is so pretty," I said. "I'll wash her anyway." I gently rubbed her side.

Uncle Gustave huffed. "Do as you please. As long as we get everything done."

We spent the afternoon until sunset cleaning the horses. I was exhausted yet happy we accomplished so much. It was refreshing to be working with my uncle in such a positive way.

Marshal Ney was an excellent horseman. My uncle told me he was also an accomplished trainer and equestrian, as well as an unrivaled swordsman. Two years ago, he'd received his marshal baton and was promoted to Marshal of France.

The next day, I was heading toward the stable in preparation for the anticipated visit when Marshal Ney approached the stable on his magnificent Andalusian Friesian cross. The horse was black with a long mane and tail. It was a gelded horse of considerable size. It was about seventeen hands tall and appeared to be older, with gray around his face and muzzle.

When Marshal Ney dismounted, I was overwhelmed by his handsome appearance. His military blue coat was adorned with gold medals and epaulets. He was tall and slender with a strong jawbone, and his strawberry-blond hair was tied back. He was so dignified that I actually curtsied. My heart was pounding wildly.

"Welcome to Friedensthal," I said in French.

"Thank you, mademoiselle." Marshal Ney bowed and kissed my hand.

Uncle Gustave rushed over from the barn, straightening his coat as he walked. "Marshal Ney, welcome."

"Might I watch you meet the stallion, Marshal?" I asked. Uncle Gustave flashed me a forced smile.

"Well, of course, mademoiselle. How could I refuse an offer from such a pretty girl," Marshal Ney said.

"Right this way," Uncle Gustave said.

The three of us walked into the barn.

"Your letter stated that you are interested in a stallion. But please, will you first view the other horses? We worked hard to present them to you," Uncle Gustave said.

"Of course," Marshal Ney said.

One by one, my uncle brought out the horses: three young geldings and two mares.

Marshal Ney stood in silence as he viewed the horses. Afterward, he said, "Very impressive, Monsieur Guerlain! However, my main purpose for today is to find a mount for myself, as my horse will be retiring soon. I will be back in the fall with officers to view the other horses. I am sure they will be suitable and older with more training. Now, on to see the stallion."

We walked to the other barn where the four-year-old stallion was stabled. Just as Uncle Gustave was about to take him out the stall, Marshall Ney said, "I will work with him from here, and I will see you at the arena."

"As you wish," Uncle Gustave responded. Then he nudged me forward and we walked outside toward the ring while Marshal Ney unbolted the heavy door and entered the stallion's stall.

The sun was growing hot as we stood outside waiting for Marshal Ney. Sweat beaded on my forehead and I gently wiped it away. Uncle Gustave's cheeks were blotchy from the heat. Finally, after a half an hour with the stallion, Marshal Ney led the stallion out of the barn and into the arena.

The stallion appeared to be calm but was still somewhat on edge. Marshal Ney released the stallion into the ring. The unruly horse ran circles around the marshal for what seemed like hours. Finally, the exhausted stallion, covered in sweat, slowed its pace and started walking toward the center of the ring where Marshal Ney was patiently standing. The horse lowered his head in submission. Marshal Ney then put a bridle on the stallion and climbed onto his back. He walked the horse around the ring.

"I will take him," Marshal Ney said.

Before my uncle could reply, I asked, "What is your secret?"

"He had to learn trust and respect from humans first, and we needed his permission. Using tact and diplomacy is the secret in all negotiations," Marshal Ney explained with a large smile.

As the marshal paid my uncle a handsome fee, my uncle smiled and saluted.

"For the French cause. Viva la France," Marshal Ney said.

This surprised me, and I was pleased for my uncle. We watched the marshal mount his horse with the stallion tethered behind, and the corporal following the stallion.

Once they were gone, my uncle turned to me and smiled. It was a genuine smile, something I wasn't used to seeing.

"Wait here. I have a surprise for you," he said. Then he rushed into the barn. A few moments later, he came back out leading the small three-year-old filly, the one I had bathed yesterday in the river.

"Congratulations, Annaelise. You have graduated from your etiquette school, equitation, and horse training. This filly belongs to you."

"Oh my!" I exclaimed. "Thank you so much, Uncle Gustave. I have always loved her!" I clapped my hands and jumped up and down in excitement. Then a feeling of doubt crept over me. Did he know that I knew the truth about what happened in Versailles? Was this his way of appeasing my judgment of him?

"Are you certain?" I asked.

"She is all yours. Despite your disagreeable temperament

at times, you have shown me that you are worthy of your very own project."

I thanked him again. Fortunately, the filly became my project. Because of her small size, none of the officers would be interested in her. Uncle Gustave decided she should be mine. I became the proud owner of a small Andalusian with courage and tenacity. She was my Petite Held, my very own small hero.

CHAPTER 13

LEARNING THE TRUTH

I t was a beautiful morning in June and no one saw me leave. Papa was working in the vineyards, and everyone was active with other spring projects, pruning the grapevines and burning the branches in order to spread the ashes over the rows of vines. Maman was sleeping late as usual.

All I wanted to do was ride. There was nothing like the feeling of getting on a horse and just taking off for the day. I left a note that said I went out for a ride with Marie. No one was at the stable, so I saddled up Sergeant and rode to see Marie. Fortunately, she was home.

"How would you like to ride to Adlershof?" I asked. "It's such a great day for a ride. We can be there in two hours. I haven't been there since we celebrated the harvest almost a year ago. Papa won't let me ride alone, but he never said that I couldn't ride with you."

Marie chuckled. "You always like to bend the rules, Anna."

"Come on," I begged. "It will be fun. I know the way with my eyes closed."

"But won't we encounter Napoleon's troops crossing the Rhine?" Her red hair was tousled in the slight breeze.

"It's possible. As Papa says, there's always going to be danger. But we will be back before dark. The bridge is still open." I was almost pleading at this point.

"I will ask my family and at least tell them where we're going," Marie said.

Within a few minutes she returned and went to the barn to saddle her mount. Her horse, Prince, was a draft horse like mine, only a Percheron and an English Thoroughbred horse.

I was happy to tell her about my new filly, Petite Held. I had been working with her and would be retiring Sergeant by the end of the summer.

"Oh, what wonderful news. And you can train her yourself!" Marie spoke with enthusiasm. "You have the time and the know-how."

We headed out toward the main road where we would be safe. There were travelers there, so we felt safe and were able to see the budding blossoms of the trees along the way. There was a slight breeze and our horses seemed happy to escape the heat and to be on a journey.

I told Marie everything about the document I'd found in my uncle's trunk, the stress of the etiquette lessons, and my uncle's attitude of still treating me like a child. She knew how much we didn't get along.

"Well, you got a horse out of it. Just avoid him as much as possible. Your lessons are already complete," Marie said.

"Avoiding him will be hard to do!" I shook my head.

As we approached the bridge that crossed over from Germany into France, we were halted while a renegade of French troops trotted on their horses toward us. I became nervous and apprehensive. There were maybe twenty soldiers carrying flags, packhorses loaded with supplies, and wagons undoubtedly filled with weapons.

They asked of our destination. "Adlershof Hunting Villa," I responded.

"Length of your trip and your purpose?" the guard asked.

"To visit a relative. We will return in three hours," I said.

"What are your names?"

After giving the guards our names, we crossed the bridge slowly and soon turned to the left along the road that ran parallel to the Rhine that would lead to Adlershof.

Upon entering France, we headed south. When the coast was clear, I said, "Well, that has never happened before. I guess Napoleon really is continuing to go east into Germany."

It was alarming to witness firsthand what Papa had spoken about. Napoleon was invading Germany, and his mission was to conquer our area and the eastern regions. This would probably be the last time we would be able to cross into France for a while. Anxiety swept over me at the thought.

The road was open, and we set our horses into a gallop and raced for fun to relieve the tension. Marie's horse passed Sergeant and we were laughing. It must have been the thoroughbred in her horse that loved to race. We slowed down to cool our horses before we got to Adlershof. Since Sergeant was getting older, I had to keep in mind not to overdo it with him. When we approached the barn, no one was there. I thought it was strange, however, that Uncle Gustave's horse, Alexander, was there.

Dismounting, we put our horses in the stalls when we heard voices coming from the house.

"Marie, be quiet," I said. "I need to make sure no one has broken into our house."

We crept by the side of the house and peeked in the window. To my horror, I saw Uncle Gustave kissing Philippe, our stable boy. We ducked down from the windowsill. I couldn't believe my eyes. Their voices were still audible. They were in the process of lovemaking and the sound became louder.

"Come on," I whispered, and we left quickly.

Once we were out of hearing range, Marie exclaimed, "Oh my! I have heard of men like that, but to see it!"

My uncle wore such colorful clothes and his gestures bordered on the feminine side. I just thought that was characteristic of men from Versailles. I thought him peculiar and strange at times but never suspected him of a different sexual preference.

"Marie, please be quiet." I was shaking. "I believe he likes women as well based on the letter I discovered. He is such a pig!"

We rode away quietly. I was determined to ask Richard more questions about my uncle since he knew my uncle from his days in Versailles.

As we got closer to our road, I said my goodbye to Marie and apologized for my uncle's behavior. "Please keep what you saw to yourself," I said.

"I will," Marie said, and she blushed. "It was still a fun adventure. I love spending time with my dear friend."

I raced home. When I arrived at our barn, Henri, our barn manager, took Sergeant.

"Where is Philippe?" I asked.

"Oh, he and your uncle went to Adlershof for a few days. They will be back tomorrow," Henri replied.

I nervously pushed my hair under my riding cap and led Sergeant to the stall.

"Thank you for attending to Sergeant. I must speak with Richard."

When I arrived at the winery, Richard was tasting the last vintage of wine before it was bottled.

"Ah, Annaelise, what a nice surprise. Would you like to sip our most recent vintage?" He was a gentle soul, and I knew I could trust him.

"Oh oui." I needed a glass after today's shock. "Richard, I must ask you a question. I must know the truth about my uncle."

Richard's eyes grew wide. "Whatever do you mean?"

"I . . . I know some things that I probably shouldn't know."

Richard shook his head. "I should not tell you what is not mine to say."

He became silent for a moment, torn between loyalties and decency, but our friendship triumphed. "I will tell you now that you are a grown woman, but it must be our secret. What I relay to you could be for your own protection." Richard looked intently into my eyes.

"I promise to be discreet, and it is a blessing that you have always been more of an uncle to me than Gustave," I replied. "Today, Marie and I went riding to Adlershof. I saw my uncle kissing Philippe. I cannot repeat the rest, as it was too shocking!" I quickly gulped down a glass of wine.

Richard's jaw dropped. "Come sit down here at the table. We may have to have another glass or two," he responded in dismay. "As you know, before the Revolution, I had worked at the winery near Versailles where rumors flowed like the wine. Gustave was at the winery coordinating the delivery of wine for the palace parties."

Richard further explained that Uncle Gustave, as Directeur de Soirées, was popular with the ladies of the Court, and they sought his advice on fashion and decorum. Whether he liked ladies over men was uncertain. Gossip was always flowing at the winery.

"I know that my uncle was petitioned to court. I found the document when we were cleaning the attic. Please tell me what you know," I said.

Richard went on to say that my Uncle Gustave was awakened

one morning by a magistrate who issued a summons for him to appear in court. There was an allegation from Madame Bourie that my uncle had violated her, and shortly thereafter a court order was petitioned to remove my mother from his custody. The magistrate told my uncle, "You will appear in court or be thrown in prison and your sister will be seized.'"

Richard offered me another glass of wine as he continued his story. "Gustave put down the bottle and decided to leave Paris that night with your mother. All they took with them were a few family portraits, some silver pieces, a trunk of Paris gowns, jewelry, and the clothing on their backs."

"I found that trunk filled with documents in the attic," I said.

Though shocked and saddened by this news, I was glad to know the truth. After what I had seen today and what Richard confirmed had happened in Versailles, I didn't think I would be able to look at my uncle Gustave the same way again.

CHAPTER 14

A CONFESSION

O ver the next few weeks, my relationship with Uncle Gustave was even more strained. Whenever I heard his voice carrying down the long hallways, I made sure to turn the other way. Whenever he entered the room, I'd make an excuse to leave. I didn't think he knew that I had seen him with the stable boy, but his eyes would linger on me when I scurried out of the room, and I could feel them burning a hole in my back.

But then I couldn't avoid him any longer. It was a quiet morning and I had risen earlier than anyone so I could tend to the horses. I had just finished a quick breakfast of eggs and warm cream when Uncle Gustave's figure darkened the doorway. I gasped when I saw him.

"Up early, I see," he said in a dull tone, as if he were bored. "Did I catch you doing something you shouldn't be doing?"

My eyes widened. *He knows I saw him with Phillipe.* He was blocking the doorway and there was no one else around. For the first time, I felt frightened of him. "Just filling my belly before I tend to the horses," I said. My voice was a little shaky but I held my ground.

Uncle Gustave stepped into the room. He didn't take his eyes off me. He was wearing a short sleeping gown. It was unusual for him to be up at this hour. It was clear that he knew something was wrong. He had been drinking all night.

"You have been avoiding me," he said bluntly.

"W-hat? No . . . I haven't. I've just been—"

"You have been avoiding me," he said again. He grabbed a chair and sat opposite me. The sound of its legs scraping against the floor raised goosebumps on my arms. He plopped down in the chair and stared at me.

"I haven't been avoiding you," I said. "I've been busy with my studies with Papa. Now if you will excuse me, I am off to see Petite Held." I arose quickly and went out the door.

"You are up to no good, mademoiselle! I know!" my uncle shouted.

Horseback riding outside our farm was prohibited to me, as it became more threatening with Napoleon's soldiers crossing the Rhine into the eastern regions of Germany toward Prussia. Papa and Uncle Gustave strictly forbade me to go riding alone. Being unable to ride on my own took away a large part of my freedom and happiness. But I wasn't the only one who felt the effects of war coming closer and the world becoming less secure. It was, however, the perfect time to train Petite Held in the riding ring. I found joy training her. She was a quick learner and very smart. We started walking over poles or *cavaletti* on the ground, then we graduated to jumps, and she took to the fences like a duck took to the water. In no time I would be able to ride her with other horses on the trails and road.

As I was heading back into the house, I encountered Papa near the stable. "Come on up to my study when you're free and we can discuss Napoleon's ball."

"Can I come now? I need to talk to you on a matter too," I said with a little trepidation.

"As you wish," he said. "Go tend to your horse. I will wait."

After I put Petite Held away, Papa and I ventured toward his study. I loved this old building. When we walked up the stairs to his study, I always looked down and visualized knights and lords and ladies seated at a banquet table.

I sat down in one of his comfortable chairs and gazed about the room. The walls were filled with books. When it was warm enough for a fire, this was the coziest room in the house.

I cleared my throat, wondering how I would broach the subject. "I . . . I . . ." I began.

Papa sat in his large leather chair, peering over his glasses. "I know my daughter well enough to know that this is a serious manner when she is having difficulty expressing her thoughts. So . . . what is troubling you?"

"I saw Uncle Gustave kissing the stable boy some time ago," I said in a rush. I chose not to disclose I had seen him at Adlershof because I was not allowed to travel far off the property.

"Oh, you now know." Papa leaned back in his chair. "Well, as you know, Gustave lived at Versailles, and apparently it was quite acceptable there. Does this upset you?"

Leave it up to Papa to always get to the root of the matter. It was an interesting question that I hadn't really thought about. Of course, I was shocked and appalled when I'd seen my uncle with the stable boy. But it was more than that. It was finding that document in the attic. It was knowing that my uncle could be capable of violating a woman in such a horrific manner.

"I am shocked at what I'd seen, but there is more. I . . . I found—"

Papa raised a brow. "Reveal what you know," he said. "There is no sense in hiding secrets."

"I found a document in the attic. It was about Uncle Gustave behaving in a dastardly manner, and he was—"

"Who knows about this?" Papa snapped.

"Um . . . I confided in Richard about what I'd found—"

"Does your Maman know about this?" His hands were clenching.

"No, Papa. I haven't told anyone but Richard," I said. My face felt hot.

"Good. And keep it that way. Your mother must never know that you found that document, do you understand? Your Maman has never been able to get over that her brother's actions are the reason they've been exiled from the home that she loved. She would be disgraced once again if she learned that her daughter knew of her family's dark secrets. You must promise me that you will never speak of this again."

"I promise," I said with my head down.

Papa rubbed his hand through his hair in frustration. "Does Gustave know?"

"I don't know . . . I mean, I think he knows that I saw him with the stable boy and is becoming angry with me. Also, he is drinking too much. I'm frightened of him." I wrung my hands.

"Yes, I understand. And he certainly can be a mean drunk. I will have a talk with him. Maybe this summer he can move back to Adlershof. I have noticed his drinking has worsened. Please do not worry, Annaelise," he said.

"Thank you, Papa. You always know what to say to make me feel better."

Changing the subject, he said, "Are you excited about the ball in Strasbourg?"

"I'm very curious about the ball. In truth, I enjoyed my time at the Duke of Enghien's estate," I said.

"Good, as it should be. I know your mother is very eager. Just remember, we cannot reveal or give any indication that we are not loyal to France, you see? Do not let any wine loosen your lips. I will be there as a silent observer," Papa said with authority. "You will show no emotion when you go down the receiving line, and you must bow down, not curtsy, for Emperor Napoleon and Empress Joséphine."

With that, he rose and kissed me on the forehead. "You are everything to me, *ma chérie*. Now, go see your mother and focus on getting ready for this ball."

I smiled and wiped the tears from my eyes. We were kindred spirits.

CHAPTER 15

THE BALL IN STRASBOURG

J uly was hot and dry in Alsace. On the day of the ball, tensions rose with all of our focus on our appearances, along with the heat. Fortunately, we were blessed with a heavy rainstorm that afternoon, which brought a huge relief from our heat exhaustion and weary spirits.

Maman and I were dressed in her Louis XV boudoir. All the furniture was white and gilded in gold, and a Fragonard painting hung over her bed. Her room was decorated in a different manner to the rest of the house except for her salon addition on the main floor. Isabelle assisted in our coiffure. It took hours to wash and curl our long hair. Maman was complaining about her gray locks.

"Why can't you just wear a wig?" I asked.

"The age of wigs is gone. I once had beautiful hair like yours," she remarked, unwilling to hide her age under a wig just yet. We were able to arrange a silk scarf into a turban with a plumage of peacock feathers that covered her gray and rested primarily on the top of her head. Her dilemma was resolved when we curled her longer brunette tresses and pinned them at the base of her neck.

"Oh, how chic, Maman!" I exclaimed.

After my hair was done, Isabelle slid the beautifully altered cream dress over my head. It flowed over my youthful body, and the new corset bodice hugged tight, enhancing my breasts. The skirt had intricate embroidery. Blushing, suddenly embarrassed by my silhouette, I smiled at my reflection in the mirror.

"Now for the finishing touch." Maman then carefully placed a necklace around my neck and a bracelet on my wrist. "I will let you borrow these because it is your birthday, and this is a special night for you!" She kissed my cheek. "They match the emerald engagement ring your father gave me." The necklace was of gold that held a beautiful and rather large emerald, which was flanked with diamonds.

"Maman, are you sure? You should wear them."

"This is your nineteenth birthday, and you should wear them with pride. One day they will be yours," Maman spoke with a bright smile.

Although the necklace was magnificent and enhanced my green eyes, it sent a chill down my back, as if it had the spirit of an aristocrat's guillotine-severed head who had once worn it around her neck.

When our family assembled in the vestibule, we were amazed at each other's elegant transformation and our spirits were high. Henri had groomed our Andalusians so their coats were glistening white in contrast to the black leather harnesses adorned with the polished brass buckles that reflected the setting sun. Our drive took us through the winding hills across the bridge over the Rhine to Strasbourg. My heart beat rapidly to the rhythm of the horses' hooves, somehow sensing this evening would be life altering. My excitement was soon replaced by a sense of fear as I watched my father wipe his forehead and wring his hands in his handkerchief.

I knew what he was tense about. Napoleon was going to be there. I told myself it was going to be a beautiful evening and all should go well. The night was alive, and the evening breeze whisked the dreadful heat away. But I couldn't get the image of Napoleon out of my head.

As we approached the estate, we saw at least twenty torches and many carriages that stood alongside the canal of Strasbourg. The Palais Rohan shined like a jewel sparkling over the canal.

Upon Napoleon's coronation, the new emperor claimed the property for his use and pleasure in the same manner as he chose Versailles outside Paris and the Palais Schönbrunn in Vienna. I could not understand how the people were free and how Napoleon had established a new government when masses were still starving in the streets and anarchy was still prevailing. It was all my father could do to remain silent knowing that we could not be loyal to Napoleon. I experienced the same feelings when I had to be quiet around Maman and Uncle Gustave when Papa went off on his reconnaissance missions.

After our carriage pulled up, an elegantly dressed footman assisted Maman and me down the steps of the carriage. The gazes from so many men made me feel as though I were royalty while Maman basked in all her glory. Upon entering the magnificent ballroom, we were overcome by the scent of roses, which wafted through the open doors as a gentle breeze from the river swept through the entire room.

At the entry of the majestic ballroom, our names were announced and then we were led to the receiving line. Seeing them from a distance, Napoleon appeared a bit heavier than I remembered. He was clothed in his blue French military jacket trimmed in large amounts of gold and very large epaulets adorned with a red velvet sash, including medals from his latest victories both abroad and for Austria. Joséphine also appeared heavier, and her aura was filled with fatigue. Her neck was adorned with the most opulent diamond necklace I had ever seen. Tiers of diamonds and rubies coordinated with her scarlet velvet dress. The latest fashion from Paris, no doubt.

Upon my curtsy, Napoleon touched my chin to raise my head. "My lovely Mademoiselle Annaelise, how you have grown into such a lovely woman." He spoke with a seductive smile. His face was puffier and lined with many wrinkles from age and no doubt from little sleep. I was now taller than the emperor. Strange that I was swayed by his charismatic smile when I was a young girl, and now the mere sight of him made me feel ill.

Overwhelmed, my stomach fluttered when I curtsied and bowed once more for the regal Joséphine.

"My dear, you must be cautious of the handsome officers here," Empress Joséphine said. "Be careful you do not lose your head!"

In an instant, all I could see was an image of a guillotine. Maman must have sensed my sudden urge to run away and hide. She quickly reached for my elbow and promptly escorted me to be introduced to some of her friends and dignitaries. I felt foolish. I didn't feel like I belonged in this world. While I had enjoyed my time at the Duke of Enghien's—getting a taste of the lavish lifestyle, eating delicious food, and dancing and listening to beautiful music—this felt different. Here, I was among the elite. The women laughed and gossiped without care. The men spoke of politics and business. And my mother and my Uncle Gustave were enamored with this world that felt fake and shallow.

I looked over at Napoleon and Joséphine. A line of well-dressed men and women had formed to pay their respects to the emperor and empress. Napoleon was shaking the hand of some dignitary, but he was staring at me. I froze as I held his gaze, unable to look away. His dark eyes were piercing, even from this distance. He nodded his head, and for some reason I nodded back

"Annalise," Papa whispered in my ear. "You must be famished. You need to eat." He quickly pulled me off to the side, his fingers digging into my arm. "Try to be invisible," he said. I was thankful for his intrusion.

Nervous thus reluctant to eat, with Papa's persistence I managed to consume some of the elaborate food. Although many gentlemen approached me, they were significantly older. Their appearances, wealth, or titles left no impression on me. Wanting a moment to hide, I went to the back entry on the veranda to get some fresh air. A nightingale was singing, and the wind suddenly changed direction, creating a chill on my shoulder.

Suddenly, I could sense a presence of someone nearby. I turned to the unmistakable sound of military boots on the cobblestone walkway that led from the street to the veranda, and in that instant the full moon shined on his face while he walked up the stairs. He stepped closer, and I could see his well-defined cheekbones and handsome face. He had wavy black hair and long sideburns. In an instant the moonlight captured the brilliance of his bright blue eyes.

He approached me and I felt rooted in place.

"Pardon, mademoiselle. I did not mean to alarm you. I am Captain Hans Roster," he spoke elegantly.

"Do you always ambush strangers?" I asked.

"Only by horseback," he replied. Based on his attire, he was a high-ranking soldier in Napoleon's army. His uniform consisted of a blue breast coat with tails trimmed in red. His jacket was trimmed with some gold cording, buttons, and shoulder epaulets. Although he wore a white sash, no military medals were apparent.

"I see you are a cavalry officer serving Emperor Napoleon," I said. "Tell me about your trusted steed. What is his age and breeding? Is he bold, brave, and loyal as all cavalry horses should be? What is his name?"

Why did you ask those questions, Annaelise, I chastised myself. It was as if I had no control over my own voice.

"His name is Excelsior, mademoiselle. His sire was Friesian, and his dame was Andalusian. He can jump the moon and requires a light touch, and he knows my every command by my thoughts."

"My family breeds and raises Andalusians," I responded.

"Mademoiselle, would you please tell me your name?" The dashing captain took a step closer.

"Annaelise Theiss. Today is my nineteenth birthday," I replied nervously.

"I certainly hope this has been a great birthday for you." He looked deeper into my eyes.

"Thank you. I was asking about your horse because riding is my passion."

"Are you then of German or French descent?" he asked.

"Why, both!" I exclaimed. "My mother is French, and my father is German and was born in the Pfalz where the Theiss family is from. Papa fought in the Seven Years' War, and so was granted land on the east of the Rhine. We have a brewery and a winery in Friedensthal."

"Your father must be a very intelligent man," Captain Roster said while the moonlight illuminated his brilliant blue eyes. "I would like to meet him."

"I would be happy to introduce you to him, Captain Roster," I offered while stepping toward the ballroom.

He gently took my arm. "Please, call me Hans. There is time for me to meet your father, but first I want to learn more about you," he spoke softly. "The music is playing, and it is time to dance." He extended his arm in a graceful invitation.

In that moment, I was utterly swept away as he pulled me inside and onto the beautiful black- and white-marbled dance floor. All I could feel was the incredible sense of weightlessness as I glided across the floor with Hans. Moving in circles, my vision became blurred, yet I felt all eyes were upon us. I was swept away by his strength and coordination. In my state of euphoria and elation, time felt suspended as I exhaled when he guided my body, leading me in a perfect waltz.

Following his every lead, I relaxed and had never felt so connected with anyone. My doubts and fears melted, and we were lost in a timeless, eternal moment that kindled a sense of destiny and wonderment that linked my soul with his.

My waltz dancing lessons with Uncle Gustave certainly proved to be beneficial. I could see in my dizzy vision that all eyes in the ballroom were watching us. The minuet, a social dance, had become less popular, and Napoleon had described it as stiff and had expressed that it represented the aristocratic taste. The waltz was derived from the German *ländler* dances similar to the polka dances, which were smoother and more flowing in rhythm, similar to the dances that were new from Vienna.

Hans was smiling, and we continued with two more dances, including our German contra dance beautifully orchestrated to Mozart's music. Although I had never heard him perform in person, Uncle Gustave had heard Mozart at Versailles, and he often hummed Mozart's music. Mozart was born in Salzburg and they spoke of his brilliance. Hans smiled as the music played, knowing not only the dance steps, but also the importance this music represented to our culture.

Uncle Gustave watched with intense focus, and I knew, of

course, that introductions were expected. I wished the music could go on forever. I didn't want to introduce him to my uncle. Maman and Papa were intently watching from across the ballroom. I could tell that Maman was pleased, but I couldn't read Papa's face. Hans was proficient in dancing, which led me to believe he must be very accomplished in his riding skills.

After our dance, Hans led me off to the side. My uncle applauded. "Ah, *très bien*, well done! Where did you learn to dance so gracefully as a soldier?"

"I was taught in Vienna at the Academy," Hans answered.

"But I thought you were French?" my uncle asked firmly.

"Oui. I am from Provence, and growing up as a boy, my family visited a distant cousin in Vienna. We received waltz lessons there," Hans explained, nervously wiping his brow with a handkerchief.

"Well, that is interesting. You will have to tell us more," Uncle Gustave said with a raised brow.

At that moment, my mother approached us. "Maman, I would like to introduce Captain Roster," I said while he politely bowed to kiss Maman's hand. She asked him questions in French, and of course she commented on his French accent.

"Ah! I have not heard that accent in years," she demurely spoke while looking up at him.

"I am from Provence, and my mother is from the Pfalz in Germany," Hans said.

"What is your father's full name? I know some families in Provence."

Before he could reply, a lieutenant with bright red hair from the regiment stepped up and said, "Pardon, Captain Roster, but we must be going." He politely bowed and introduced himself as Lieutenant Wilhelm Ferré.

"You must come visit us during your regiment campaign

here in Alsace-Lorraine," Maman spoke while elegantly cooling herself with her feather fan.

Hans nodded. "Oh oui, we would like to visit soon. We are camped not far from here, and I would also like to ride with Mademoiselle Annaelise. I understand she is quite the equestrian."

He gazed at me with those intense blue eyes and then bowed, kissing my hand with his sensuous lips. "Happy birthday, mademoiselle. I look forward to seeing you soon."

For the rest of the evening, I could only think of Captain Hans Roster. The ride home was magical and I was elated. The last of the moon's glow was upon us, and my mind was racing with excitement. Maman was quite chatty as she and my uncle discussed their encounters with Napoleon and the many dignitaries, and of course they pressed me with many questions. In stark contrast, Papa was distant and spoke little. Perhaps he was concerned I had met a French officer.

All I could think about was riding with Hans, showing him the overlook to the Rhine, and meeting his magnificent mount, Excelsior. *Who knew if he would really come?* I needed to let go of the thought, but all I saw were those piercing blue eyes and felt his sensuous kiss upon my hand. My head was spinning from the dancing and excess of champagne.

As we approached Friedensthal, the eastern horizon was beginning to blush with the coming dawn. We crossed the Rhine, its waters flowing fast, and I found my eyes closing, suddenly feeling very drowsy. By the time my head finally hit the pillow, the sun was coming up over the Alsatian hills.

CHAPTER 16

LOYALTIES OVER TEA

I awoke late the next morning with a splitting headache, *mal à la tête*. My mind was in even more of a tailspin as I remembered waltzing with the dashing Captain Hans Roster. How could my feelings leave me so overwhelmed by a man I barely knew? Was this what it felt like to be in love? My heart was drumming in my chest. *Pull yourself together, Annaelise.* But visions of the captain swirled through my head— his smile, the sound of his laugh, how strong his arms were when they held me as we danced. I had never been in love. Since I was a young girl, Maman had always talked about me finding a handsome husband with titles and land, just like she had found in Papa, but I'd always brushed it off. Now I began to understand her sentiments. Being wrapped up in the aura of something larger than yourself and wanting to know his every thought and delve deeper into his soul, finding the core of his being and heart. It became all-consuming for me.

But he was French, and he was a captain in the French Army.

Papa had inspired me to align my heart with the ideals of The Enlightenment and of the American Founding Fathers. I groaned in frustration and rolled over in bed.

I decided to get some fresh air and bypass my family's in- terrogation. A ride on Petite Held seemed to be the perfect diversion, and hopefully my family would be none the wiser sleeping away the night's gaiety.

I headed down to the kitchen for a bread roll in the hope of settling my stomach.

"Miss Annaelise, any tea this morning?" Giselle asked politely. She leaned in closer and smiled. "How was the ball?"

I quickly grabbed the roll and shoved it into my mouth to avoid saying anything. "Thanks, I need to check on Petite Held," I mumbled with my mouth full and raced out toward the barn.

It was late morning and Henri was not present. This was the perfect time for a quick ride to visit Marie and discuss last evening's episode. I was greeted by the whinny of my small hero, Petite Held, her head hanging over the stall door. She had been in training, and I felt she would be ready for me to take her out alone. She sensed my excitement when I saddled her, pawing the stall floor with her dainty hoof. I decided to use a pelham bit with the double rings and longer shaft for more control as per Uncle Gustave's suggestion. Having two reins added braking power, which was safer.

I looked around to see if anyone was watching, remembering Papa's warning not to go riding alone in these dangerous times. With Napoleon's soldiers in surveillance of everyone, a woman riding alone was frowned upon. Even so, I just had to tell Marie about Captain Hans Roster.

Tucking my hair tightly beneath my chapeau and raising my long skirt to accommodate my riding breeches, I decided to take the wooded trail by the road that led to Strasbourg, hoping the leaves would conceal us. Our pace was slow leaving the barn, but once on the wooded trail, Petite Held shook her head and broke into a canter. Her muscles tense beneath my legs, she sped forward into a gallop. I was glad I had chosen the stronger bit.

When we came to the open meadow that went uphill to the cliffs overlooking the Rhine, the wind suddenly rose and blew off my chapeau. Petite Held shied, swerved, almost knocking me off, scaring me as we both noticed the cavalry regiment of four only fifty yards away. Thank God they were French and were serving to protect the citizens of the new Confederation of the Rhine.

"Pardon me, mademoiselle, I hope you are not hurt. I am Lieutenant Wilhelm Ferré. I met you at the ball last night," he said as he gallantly removed his military helmet to reveal a brilliant head of red hair. He dismounted and retrieved my chapeau and continued to talk while walking toward me with my hat.

"We have a letter from Captain Hans Roster requesting a visit tomorrow at three o'clock in the afternoon as per the kind invitation from Madame Louisa Theiss." The lieutenant handed me a letter.

I thought my heart would pound out of my chest. Hans had actually followed through and was true to his word! I was elated.

"That will be acceptable, and I will respond for my mother," I politely replied, trying my best to contain my excitement.

Lieutenant Ferré smiled, and I noticed a scar on his left cheek. Despite this slight disfigurement, his kind hazel eyes shone brightly in the morning light.

Although confirming confidently for Maman without knowing the plans of the rest of my family, I knew she would be thrilled with their visit. Then my heart jumped to my throat when I realized that I would have to convey to Papa the truth about my lone departure from the estate.

"Thank you, Lieutenant, for my hat and the letter." I smiled while he politely tipped his military helmet. I took an about-face on Petite Held in the direction of home, carelessly stuffing the letter into the side pocket of my culotte skirt.

Startled with the encounter, sharing my experiences with Marie would have to wait. "*Allons-vite*, move quickly," I commanded. Petite Held took off.

When we arrived back at the stable, Henri held my horse and asked, "Where have you been, Fräulein? Your horse is covered in sweat, and your parents don't know that you left the estate. I am tempted to tell them."

"Don't worry. I will tell Papa now. I met some members of the French cavalry officers who intend to visit us tomorrow."

Henri tilted his head. "Your father is in his study," he said, nodding. "I will watch you walk across the courtyard. You know I am responsible for your safety. I will rub Petite Held down for you." His voice was firm.

I remained silent as I reached for the water pump to rinse the sweat from my face and hands. My throat tightened when I gulped the water down from the tin cup Henri handed to me. He was only trying to look out for me since I was a little girl. But I was more worried about what Papa would say about my disobeying him. Brushing the hair back from my face, I took one more deep breath while Henri watched me walk across the courtyard to face the likely punishment from Papa.

As I approached Papa's study, I was more afraid than I had ever been, but I sensed that this *tête-à-tête* would be enlightening somehow. Gently knocking on the door, Papa commanded in French, "*Entre.*"

"Bonjour, good morning," I said nervously.

"*Guten morgen,*" he responded in his native German, looking up from his old table desk. His bushy gray eyebrows half hid his eyes peering over the wire spectacles that were clinging to the edge of his bony nose. Hoping the punishment would be less severe, I connected to Papa in his native tongue. As I spoke nervously in German, relaying my morning adventure and encounter with the French officers, he cut me short.

"Have you been riding this morning after such a long evening at the ball?" he asked. "Did Henri go with you?"

Nerves danced in my stomach. "I met French soldiers on the road, and they relayed that Captain Roster and two in his regiment would like to come to tea at three tomorrow afternoon.

I accepted the invitation, knowing Maman would be thrilled if Captain Roster came. I did ride alone and promise never to do it again, Papa."

Papa rose from his desk and raised his voice. "Wait, wait, Annaelise!" I'd seldom heard him speak this loudly. His temper rose and his face reddened as he bellowed, "You know you will have to suffer the consequences of this!"

"I know I was wrong, Papa, and I will not ride alone again," I replied.

He clenched his jaw and glared at me. "Once again, Annaelise, let me remind you there is a serious war going on and your life is in danger. I can't explain the severity of the war, and you don't know the consequences that may affect you and this family!"

Clearly, he was not yet consoled. I wanted so much to embrace him, but instead I bowed my head, curtsying while speaking sweetly to him. "I love you, Papa, and will obey and respect your wishes."

He softened and that familiar twinkle in his eye returned. "I will relay this news to your Maman, and we will receive the soldiers tomorrow. This will be our little secret, *ma chérie.*" He kissed my forehead and pressed my head to his shoulder. "Never do this again," he said, raising my chin to look me in the eye. He held my hands in a firm grip. As I stared into his eyes, I realized that I possessed more Germanic traits in my soul than French.

Maman was thrilled when I told her about Hans's visit. "We must find a proper dress for you to wear!" she said.

I chose a simple cotton gown adorned with silk ribbons, and the empire waist was garnished with satin appliqué roses. Maman had selected a gold chain that had a single teardrop pearl pendant, which fell between my breasts to complement my cleavage.

"I am elated that Captain Roster took a liking to you. He's such a handsome young Frenchman!" Maman said.

My cheeks grew hot—something that happened every time I thought of Hans.

"Oh, my dear, look at you. You deserve all the happiness in the world, and I'm so proud of the woman you're becoming. Now you understand what all the fuss is about. We could not be happier for you!"

She was looking forward to the possibility of romance for me. And for the first time in my life, I was also thrilled with the prospect.

I had asked Papa if I could meet the captain at the barn when he arrived because I wanted to see his lovely horse, Excelsior. Papa agreed, adding, "As long as you don't soil your dress. Henri will want to attend to his horse, and I am sure he, too, is looking forward to seeing this magnificent stallion as well."

The next day, punctually at three o'clock, I heard the French officers approach the stable. I was suddenly aware of how I looked. *Will the captain still find me appealing? What if he sees me in this plain dress and is no longer interested?* Thoughts raced through my head, and I broke into a sweat.

Papa, Uncle Gustave, and Henri rushed to my side while Giselle held a tray of brandy and apple tarts for the officers. Lieutenant Ferré and Major Fischer accompanied the captain.

And there was Captain Hans Roster, sitting atop a magnificent horse. Excelsior was champing at his long-shanked bit while his muscled haunches pranced in place, sensing the excitement of this meeting. Hans looked at me, and his eyes looked even bluer in the daylight. I wasn't sure it was possible for him to be any more handsome. My breath was taken away as I watched him dismount Excelsior.

"What a magnificent stallion! Was the dam Andalusian?" Uncle Gustave inquired.

Hans nodded. "Yes, she was, and a descendant from Babieca, El Cid's horse from the Spanish line."

"Ah yes, the same bloodline as our stallion!" Uncle Gustave spoke in excitement. He signaled for me to stand back while he stepped forward to take the reins, watching the horse champ at the bit. The beautiful copper bit shone in the afternoon sun and was highlighted against Excelsior's black coat. The four-inch bit was adorned with a round medallion sunflower on the top of the shank, something I had never seen before. I gathered it was used for precise control during battle to keep his head down.

Uncle Gustave bowed while giving the reins to Henri and said, "Welcome, Captain Roster. Your mount is as intelligent as he is large and powerful, is he not?"

"Yes, Monsieur Gustave. He is my rock and castle in battle," Hans replied. Then he turned to me and our eyes locked. We gazed intensely at each other, and it felt like a divine light of fire and ice. He bowed as I curtsied. From the corner of my eye, I could see my uncle watching us with a cool stare.

"Mademoiselle, it is so wonderful to see you again. You are far more beautiful in sunlight than you are in moonlight," Hans said with a smile.

Finding myself speechless, my face turned crimson. Smiling, I managed to say a simple, "*Merci*, thank you."

Tea was taken in our newly remodeled salon a step down from the older section of the manor house. We crossed through the old manor section of dark walls and Alsatian art viewing the old oak mantle. I noticed Hans glancing at the wall where two swords were crossed over the Theiss family motto written in German, but I couldn't tell if he was impressed with my heritage or merely appreciated my father's military experience.

We stepped into the bright, sunny salon that was strictly of Maman's creation. The furniture consisted of a new Aubusson French rug from Paris and a collection of gilded Louis XV and Louis XVI chairs and settee. A Bombay chest and large gilded mirror graced the wall opposite the series of three French doors overlooking the patio and fountain outside. Geraniums lined the stonework and summer was in full bloom.

Giselle served us tea from Maman's family Louis XV silver teapot, ornate in detail with cherubs. I stayed quiet while Maman and Uncle Gustave discussed their former lives in Paris. I felt slightly embarrassed as they recounted their Parisian lives and the splendor that existed in the aristocratic regime. Yet I knew this was important for their background. Napoleon was all about ultimate elegance, but the French citizens were still starving.

Our conversation took a slight turn when Hans asked, "Countess Theiss, have you heard of any other conquests that

Emperor Napoleon has planned? Being in the field, our cavalry is the last to be informed."

"Well, possibly for Sweden, but I learned that from a very remote source," Maman said while fanning herself.

Both my mother and uncle spoke with their knowledge of Empress Joséphine's family and the residences of Malmaison, Fontainebleau, and Palais Rohan in Strasbourg where the ball was held.

"As you know, Captain Roster, the Emperor and Empress have taken residence at Palais Rohan," Maman said.

"Yes, I know as some of our troops are positioned there and at Fontainebleau, and Joséphine's prime residence is Malmaison."

They also explained Napoleon's plans to influence the eastern regions of Germany and Prussia and his great plans for the future of France.

"I am well aware of our emperor's plans since he was victorious in the Battle of Austerlitz and his achievement of developing the Confederation of the Rhine," Hans said.

Lieutenant Ferré chimed in, "His next expansion will be in eastern Prussia and on to Russia, and we are positioning ourselves for that future expansion."

I remained quiet as Hans spoke about Napoleon's conquests, and I felt conflicted. I did not believe in Napoleon's cause to expand France's reach throughout Europe when France's own citizens were suffering. A feeling of dread washed over me, and I wanted to burst into tears. Hans had captured my heart, but we were on two different sides of a coin. I thought about Madame de Staël and what she had told me: *There is strength in loving those who think differently.*

"Will you be going to the front, Captain Roster?" I blurted out. My voice sounded loud and foreign. Maman gave me a look that said, *What's gotten into you?* I resolved to ask no more questions.

"It is possible I will be going to Prussia," he spoke with trepidation.

A lump rose in my throat. Papa was against Napoleon invading Prussia. Before the discussion could go any further, Uncle Gustave changed the subject. His focus was business to secure more sales of horses to Napoleon's army. "Captain Roster, have you heard of Marshal Ney?"

"Why yes. Napoleon called him the 'Bravest of the Brave.'"

"We know him personally, as he recently purchased a horse from us," I said, sitting up straight.

Uncle Gustave said, "Ah oui! We know Marshal Ney. He has a way of training horses."

"He is a renowned horseman and swordsman, is he not?" Hans said.

"Yes, and we are using his technique in our training. We can try to notify you upon his next visit," my uncle replied.

"We would be very interested in meeting Marshal Ney. As you may know, he led the Battle at Austerlitz. Our regiment was in Italy at the time, so I haven't met him because we were not under his command. It would be very interesting to observe his training methods," Hans replied with an approving nod.

I quickly changed the conversation to the philosophy of Hegel, Madame de Staël, Goethe, and Voltaire. "Captain Roster, are you familiar with the teachings and philosophy of The Enlightenment?" I asked.

Maman nervously fidgeted in her overstuffed bergère chair.

Hans raised his brow. "Why yes, indeed. And how is it that you are so enlightened?"

"I am very lucky and grateful to have a father who has given me a well-rounded education." I looked over at Papa, who seemed nervous. I knew I should keep my mouth shut, but I couldn't stop thinking about Madame de Staël. She was so outspoken and confident, and I wanted to be the same. "Many of these ideals and philosophies were incorporated by George Washington into the development for the Constitution of the United States of America. They have achieved the goals of liberty, equality, and justice for all. I fear that Napoleon's promise of this for all French citizens has not evolved as such. What do you think, Captain? Is Emperor Napoleon achieving these goals? Are his regiments taking from the poor? I heard a rumor that they are," I said defiantly.

Papa was glaring at me to stop this topic.

"Annaelise!" Maman exclaimed. "I'm sure the captain and lieutenant didn't come to tea to talk about such radical things." She turned to Hans. "Captain, I assure you that we are grateful for our emperor's efforts to strengthen France."

Uncle Gustave interjected, "He saved France from ruin after the Revolution and the Reign of Terror. Certainly, things are better now and we have to keep the faith!"

"We are leading forward, and I certainly believe the emperor has this vision as well, and his goal is to unite the nations toward that goal," Hans said. He looked straight at me. "To my knowledge, I haven't heard about the poor being asked to give food."

At that point, Hans rose and quickly and announced, "We must return to camp. Soon the roads will be getting dark, and we must be safe from ambush."

I swallowed a lump in my throat. *Why couldn't you keep your mouth shut?*

Hans quickly exchanged handshakes with Uncle Gustave and Papa, and bowed to kiss Maman's hand. Reaching for my hand, he looked deeply into my eyes while asking Papa,

"Might I have the pleasure of your daughter's company within a week's time for a ride?"

"Of course, as long as you don't ride on the main roads. You will be safe in the woods, and be sure to have Annaelise back by dark. This could be the last time she can leave the estate for quite some time," Papa said.

Although happy that we would ride, I was confused. I was sure that I had offended Hans. *He must focus on his own mission, the troops, and the battle strategy*, I told myself, yet I could feel the knot in my stomach again. Things that could have dire consequences were moving behind the scenes, and I didn't understand what they were.

CHAPTER 17

A PICNIC OF PASSION

T he July heat was relentless and everyone seemed irritated, but I felt like I was floating in anticipation of seeing Hans again. He preoccupied my every waking thought. The week passed quickly, and the day arrived for my ride with Hans. I had gone over our conversation when we had tea countless times. Maman and Gustave scolded me, and Papa barely talked to me. I learned my lesson. I couldn't be so outright with my views. As much as I wanted to be like Madame de Staël, I was just a naïve girl from Alsace.

Hans arrived at two in the afternoon, and we were fortunate to have a beautiful day with a cool breeze. Henri groomed Petite Held and had her saddled before the captain arrived.

I wore a culotte skirt and tucked my hair under my chapeau. Uncle Gustave was dressed for the part as well. He wore rose silk pants with a formal waistcoat that was too tight, accentuating his bulging belly.

"Now, Annaelise, please remember all of the instructions regarding riding sidesaddle, and no jumping logs. It can be too dangerous."

"Yes, Uncle," I said.

I could hear the approaching hoofbeats of Excelsior drawing near.

"And try to keep that pretty little mouth of yours shut,"

my uncle seethed. "No man wants a woman with silly ideas floating around in her head."

I glared at my uncle.

"You will never attract a man with that pouty face," he said.

Hans approached, looking as glorious as ever.

"Bonjour, good day," I greeted him while witnessing his muscular leg swing gracefully over the saddle as he dismounted. He was dressed in his finest military uniform with a blue waistcoat trimmed with red cuffs and a collar, a white vest with brass buttons, and gold epaulets on his shoulders. His bicorn hat, trimmed in a blue cording, was his crowning glory.

Hans complimented my appearance as well as that of Petite Held while gazing steadfastly into my eyes. I was simply speechless.

"Monsieur Gustave, you have a fine stable here, and the architecture is very French in style—quite different from any other structure in Alsace-Lorraine," Hans spoke with enthusiasm.

"Oh yes," my uncle responded. "We had the original structure fortified with plaster and archways, very similar to the Parisian stables."

"Very well done!" Hans exclaimed.

Hans lifted me by my waist while I put my left foot in the stirrup, and then I swung my right leg around the pommel of the sidesaddle. Mounting was effortless, as our motions were synchronized.

"Mademoiselle, all cavalry horses are trained to trust us at a slow pace," Hans said. "We must walk our horses together first while they learn to know one another. I want to know everything about your ideals, the food you love, the favorites in your world, and your fears and passions in life."

I managed to speak shyly, "I would like to show you my

favorite spot in all the world where we could ride, but you must trust me to lead the way and set the pace."

"Is it off the main road, Mademoiselle Annaelise?"

"Yes," I replied with a bright smile.

Having obtained that approval, I set Petite Held into a fast pace through the woods. The path was sandy, having been recently flooded by one of the creeks feeding into the Rhine. Over time, the rock had washed away or been buried, and the footing was perfect for the horses. Trotting faster, squeezing Petite Held's sides, we advanced into a canter. The path revealed a recently fallen tree.

Disregarding my uncle's advice, without hesitation or fear, we approached the obstacle quickly, and I swung my right leg over Petite Held's right side, needing both legs for security to jump the large fallen tree. She knew instantly it was time to jump, and Excelsior was close behind. Although we both executed the jump with ease, it did not lessen the exhilaration. We were laughing while galloping to the bluff that overlooked the Rhine, and our spirits connected in those few moments of time.

"Mademoiselle Annaelise, your Petite Held is magnificent beyond my greatest expectations for such a small horse," Hans said, revealing his handsome smile.

Struggling to catch our breath, our voices laughing in the rapture of the moment, I looked at Hans and again witnessed the intensity of his bright blue eyes shining hypnotically in the sun. Assisting me off Petite Held, he grabbed my waist and held me near. It took all my inner strength to back away.

After we dismounted, Hans set out a blanket. As a surprise, he had brought a bottle of his father's vintage wine, a fine rosé from Provence, a good cheese from Luxembourg, and a loaf of fresh bread.

"*Danke schön*, thank you. I mean, *merci*," I corrected myself back to French.

"Why did you correct yourself, mademoiselle? Your German is lovely."

"Papa has taught me so many things."

"Such as the philosophies you were speaking about over tea?" Hans prompted.

How stupid was I to think we wouldn't talk about what had happened? I regretted speaking my mind, but I also thought that maybe Hans wasn't angry after all. He did invite me out for a ride, so he couldn't be too upset with me. Maybe he genuinely wanted to learn more about me, and I didn't know how to express myself without expressing my love for learning.

"I . . . um . . . I have learned many things from my papa," I said.

"Please, go on," Hans said.

I told him about when I'd met Madame de Staël while visiting our cousins at Paix et Abondance, and how impressed I was when she spoke of philosophy and the plays she had written.

He poured some of his wine into a military tin cup and handed it to me. "I am so impressed with your knowledge." He lifted his cup to mine. "To your quest and journey as a friend. I hope to know you until the end."

Hans set down his cup and removed his hat, revealing his raven-black hair. He reached out his hand, touching mine, staring into my eyes while he gently leaned forward. Eyes locked, our lips met, breaking my trance. It was everything I had ever dreamed about. I felt as if I would float away with the feeling of his lips on mine. He gently touched the side of my face, cupping my cheek in his hand. The tips of his fingers gently caressed my skin, and his touch sent sensations of hot and cold down my spine.

I pulled away, stunned. I didn't want to pull away—I wanted our kiss to deepen—but some unknown force pulled me back.

"Mademoiselle, I'm sorry if I approached you too quickly," Hans said. "However, I must tell you that I have never met a woman as beautiful, intelligent, and so aware of the new movement for true freedom and equality for mankind. I am completely and utterly enchanted by you."

My lips tingled, and I was sure I looked like a frightened deer. He was a skilled equestrian, he was well educated, and his family knew about the production of wine. I couldn't have asked for a more suited match. But there was something nagging at me. Could he really fall in love with me? I'd just expressed how influenced and inspired I was from The Enlightenment. But all I wanted was for the captain to kiss me again.

"Captain Roster . . . Hans . . . please. I am overwhelmed and need to know you better," I answered, my voice shaking. "I am still so naïve, and I have my family's reputation to protect."

"Mademoiselle Annaelise, I could never hurt you," he responded sincerely. "My intentions are honorable. I assure you I want only your happiness and protection."

Calming my breath, I decided to let reason guide our conversation, lest passion push us too far. "I want to know more about you and your family," I suggested with a smile.

"As I mentioned to your mother, I was born in Provence and my mother is from Karlsruhe in the Pfalz."

"Why, how interesting," I interrupted. "My grandmother—my father's mother—lives in the Pfalz at Leisel. How is it that you are fighting with Napoleon?"

Hans stared at me. There was something behind those blue eyes. "I hope to make my fortune serving Napoleon. My family acquired land in Provence from serving in the military. When my father passed away, we moved to my mother's small winery, Glaubenstrung, the Leap of Faith Winery, in Karlsruhe. This is why we're so blessed to have found one another. Also, my desire is to acquire additional land there for my military service with Napoleon."

"Ah, I understand. So, what are your goals and passions?"

"To flourish, love, have a family, develop the vineyard in Karlsruhe, and breed horses. I would love to see the new regime born and live in peace and prosperity."

"Your passion and idealism thrill me, sir," I responded with enthusiasm.

"Mademoiselle, you must believe the glories of the new age that are coming."

"Do you really believe Napoleon will fulfill his promise?" I said hesitantly. "He has not improved the lives of all his people. The poor are suffering, and the government has taken over the independence of the German provinces."

"We must continue to believe the Emperor's vision! By uniting the states under one government, we can have a better government," Hans exclaimed.

At that moment, thunder rumbled in the distance, drawing our attention to the heavy clouds beginning to darken the sky. I felt grateful for the distraction. I couldn't believe I was speaking so openly and freely with a member of Napoleon's army. I had to watch what I said because he was for the French cause. Perhaps I had been too outspoken on my beliefs and those of Papa's.

"Mademoiselle, we must leave for now and savor the rest for another time."

He took my hand and looked deep into my eyes while

kissing my knuckles. I knew at that moment my future was now interwoven with his, and there was no turning back.

Making our way through the forest, silence fell between us, leaving only the sound of the hoofbeats from our trotting mounts. Hans led the way, and I was able to fully appreciate his evident equestrian skills. He became very vigilant of the road, minding the rocky condition as well as the impending storm.

Within minutes, the thunder clapped and lightning hit close to the river. Petite Held, startled by the thunder, raised her hind legs in a buck and surged forward into a gallop. I passed Hans and Excelsior, and the race was on! Petite Held had met her match and we rode on with wild abandon. She loved the challenge and, while small, she had some English thoroughbred blood in her veins.

Hans and I were laughing wildly as Excelsior sped forward, leading the race with unmatched power and strength. And then my vision grew fuzzy and I was suddenly watching Hans as if in a dream, feeling suspended in time and moving in slow motion.

He was in a battle, leading his battalion and commanding a charge while drawing his sword toward the approaching opposition. A flank of the opposition approached his battalion from the right. He was soon surrounded. The sound of piercing horns, screaming horses, and men dying filled the air. Cannon fire rumbled so loud, and then it morphed into the sound of thunder.

The horrific vision quickly passed as soon as it had come, and I was again aware of our thrilling race. Though Hans was still laughing, I couldn't share that laugh with him.

When we returned to the stables, I felt icy cold.

CHAPTER 18

DEPARTURE TO THE PFALZ

The Theiss vineyard had a good season with an abundant yield of grapes despite the hard times and war effort. However, it was a challenge to hide this production from the French, German, and Prussian armies who were endlessly looking to procure wine for the French cause. It was decided that Papa would arrange a trip to transport some barrels of wine from our vineyard, which would conceal heavy artillery for the Prussian cause, to the farm owned by my grandmother, Lisolette Theiss, in the Pfalz at Blumenthal, the Valley of the Flowers. My grandmother's vineyard had produced only a small yield of grapes, and she needed more wine to increase sales. She was in need of a winemaker, and Richard's brother, Albert was perfect for the position. He was also included in our entourage. Papa had to rely on his trained staff at Friedensthal to carry through the harvesting at home with Richard, Uncle Gustave, and the additional help from the village while we traveled north to the Pfalz.

Papa called upon Hans and the officers—Lieutenant Ferré, Major La Fond, and Corporal Fischer—to escort us to the Pfalz, a three-day journey through the Black Forest. Papa explained that Hans and his men were planning to go north to meet another regiment to build forces for Napoleon. My thoughts and feelings were conflicted. Hans was an officer in the French army, and I shuddered at the thought of him finding out that we were smuggling weapons for the Prussians.

"Aren't you concerned that Hans or his men will find the weapons?" I asked, panic setting in.

"Captain Roster is fond of us, and the wagon of wine is needed in the northern campaign to serve the French cause, *n'est-ce pas*, right? He is unaware that we are also transporting artillery. We will be crossing French lines, so we will conceal the weapons under the barrels of wine. There should be no problems," Papa said with a wink.

Despite possible danger, Papa had given me permission to accompany him. I had not seen my grandmother in seven years. As her only grandchild, I would inherit her entire estate, thus my presence would serve as a decoy should anyone stop us.

"A young woman going to see her dying grandmother would hopefully not be seen as a potential smuggler of weapons," Papa explained. Then he gifted me a pistol. "This is for your own safekeeping. You remember how to load it and use it?"

"Yes, Papa," I said. The gun felt heavy in my hand.

"Keep it near at all times," he said. I promised to pack it in my saddlebag.

I had not seen Hans since the summer, so I was even more thrilled to have Hans as an escort, and so was Maman for obvious reasons. She had a sense for romance and a keen sense of knowledge of who would be a good match for me.

But how can I love a French officer and be aligned with Papa's beliefs with the Prussian cause?

I decided not to dwell on my conflicted thoughts and instead be happy at the prospect of inheriting my grandmother's estate, the site of so many joyous memories of my childhood. I vividly recalled summers playing in the beautiful streams and meadows. I remembered the dairy cows and the delicious cheeses made from their fresh milk. Grandmother Liselotte was an amazing cook. She would prepare breakfasts that included egg soufflé, apple tarts, and freshly baked bread with trout. With her kindness, patience, and her simple ways, she had been more of a mother to me at times than Maman. She was much older now, and it was Papa's hope that I could learn from her as I helped her run the estate.

We chose the time of our journey to coincide before the harvest festivals, hoping to be less obvious to the military. We spent a week getting ready while Richard was selling beer for the festival. I was elated about traveling with Hans; however, Papa's thoughts were more on the practical side, so he advised me to restrict my clothes to my winter clothing and coats. To my surprise, Maman insisted I take her finest fur, wanting me to be warm and beautiful as well.

Fortunately, the weather stayed mild during the early morning in September when we departed. All were gathered to say our goodbyes, and Maman unsuccessfully tried to hide her worry. Papa assured Maman that time was in our favor and that we had soldiers to protect us.

I did feel optimistic that Hans would keep us safe, and I focused on my purposeful mission with my grandmother and my future. After all, land was wealth, and if it would be mine, it could be my stronghold for future security. At least that was my hope.

Our new trusty Percheron draft horses, Dàrtangan and Dominique, pulled the wagon while Petite Held was tethered behind the wagon carrying my belongings on her back. I embraced Richard, Giselle, Isabelle, Henri, and then Uncle Gustave and Maman. Tears welled up in my eyes. Maman was crying, too, and I could tell she was genuine in her feelings. I would miss her frivolities, her laughter, and her piano playing. I was grateful in that moment for her influence and polishing me off as a fine lady. Even though we would be gone for two months, I was touched by her sentimentality. Despite my agitations with Uncle Gustave, I was appreciative of his etiquette training and teaching me how to train horses, especially the gift of Petite Held.

Uncle Gustave was giving me final instructions for Petite Held's care and feeding. I wished to express my appreciation, but his embrace was cold. He looked up at Hans and exclaimed, "Take care of her. You know well what I mean!" His words gripped me like an icy hand, and the hair rose up on the back of my neck.

The mist lingered early that morning, and when the sun came up on the Alsace hills, a brilliant light filtered through the golden leaves. I was instructed to ride in the wagon with Papa and Albert. Hans was riding far in front of us, keeping vigil. Lieutenant Ferré kept pace next to me while Major La Fond rode beside the wagon next to Papa. Corporal Fischer brought up the rear. Hans was distant, both physically from the wagon and emotionally from me. I realized, however, that he was concentrating on the task at hand, and I was witness to his tenacity and military discipline.

When heading uphill, we had to walk alongside the wagon because of the weight of the wine barrels and weaponry, but our pair of Percherons were loyal and steadfast. We made our way north on the rocky roads that led us through the enchanting Black Forest and away from the main road to Karlsruhe, Hans's home. I was seeing another side of Papa that I hadn't witnessed before. Having ventured in times past on this journey, he was pensive, knowing the difficulty of getting safely through the rocky terrain.

We decided to make an early camp to avoid a fire that

could be viewed at night. Hans circled back on Excelsior and dismounted while offering me a hand so I could get down from the wagon. I could see the exhaustion in his eyes. His regiment tended to the horses, and he suggested I join him by the river while he caught fish for our dinner. We were just east of the Rhine near Karlsruhe next to a tributary where Hans knew the trout were plentiful. Being very tired and hungry, Hans gathered his rod, reel, net, and basket as he asked Papa for permission for me to accompany him by the stream. Papa set up our camp with our tent close to the wagon and started a fire.

"Annaelise may catch more fish than you!" Laughing, Papa pitched his fishing bag toward me, and I picked it up and smiled. It was a welcome relief from the tensions of the travel.

"Mademoiselle Annaelise fishes too?" Hans asked with a surprised look.

While we walked toward the woods, Hans tossed his equipment over his shoulder and reached for my hand. When we approached the rushing water, he released my hand and focused on rigging his reel, line, and rod. He set his intention and concentrated on the water while walking upstream.

Stretching my legs, I removed my boots before wading in the cool water. Closing my eyes, I felt the warm sunshine on my tired body. While filling some water sacks, I splashed my face with the refreshing water. Then I looked up and saw Hans remove his shirt. I was frozen in awe, watching the golden light from the late afternoon sun highlight his well-chiseled torso. He was ever so balanced while wading barefoot into the water. I recalled that same agility and dexterity he demonstrated while we were waltzing. I became mesmerized, witnessing the sunshine casting diamonds on the water while he skillfully caught a large trout from the river.

His focus was not lost when I rushed over, running on the

sandy shore to meet him with a basket, pulling my skirt up above the water's reach at the same time. He placed his prize in the basket and quickly rose to take note of my bare calves and knees.

We both laughed. Then he wrapped one arm around my waist and pulled me tightly to him. Our lips met and our tongues engaged in a sweet exchange of passion. I never knew a kiss could feel like this. This time I didn't pull away but longed for more, yet Hans politely pulled back. We paused and our eyes met.

"Ah, Fräulein, the best is yet to come, but we must catch more fish."

I assembled Papa's fishing equipment to cast my line upstream in an exhilarating rapture of joy and excitement. Feeling connected to the river, to my life, to my passion, in that same moment, I felt the tug of a large trout that took my line just as surely as Hans had taken my heart.

The entire traveling company enjoyed the delicious trout with potatoes and turnips that we brought from our garden. Albert opened a bottle of Riesling. We ate earlier than usual so we could extinguish the fire. Papa had set up our tent as well as Albert's, and I was instructed not to leave except for obvious reasons. Hans and his regiment set up their tents and took turns guarding our camp.

All I could think about was Hans and myself by the river, and I longed for another time just like it, envisioning a future place where we could all live in peace and plenty. I thought of a future with Hans and our children residing in Karlsruhe at Leap of Faith Winery, Alsace at Friedensthal, and maybe at my grandmother's estate in Leisel at Blumenthal.

Despite these dreamy desires, part of me was perplexed by

Hans's allegiance to Napoleon. His beliefs seemed to contradict the vision of freedom that Napoleon appeared to represent. Papa had studied Rousseau's *Social Contract,* which described a new order for society and leaders who deferred to the general will of the people. I could not see how these views represented Napoleon's values and vision. Perhaps we would discuss this at another time, if only we could connect again as we had done by the river.

We rose before sunrise. Although sleep was difficult, I did not feel exhausted. The thrill of romance and anticipation of seeing my grandmother and Blumenthal were first and foremost on my mind.

Our journey changed from the Black Forest to open land along the Rhine toward Karlsruhe. It was wonderful to see a bright sky with plenty of sunshine. Papa informed us that we could be intercepted by Prussian troops, now an enemy of the French cause and of Napoleon. Papa was also nervous about the possibility of the troops taking some of the barrels of wine, thus exposing the hidden artillery. Soon we were met by a file of Napoleon's French soldiers, so we knew we were safe with Hans and his officers.

"Bonjour, good day, Captain," one of the guards said. "What is your destination, and what is your cargo?"

"We are traveling north to the Pfalz, to Leisel, to deliver wine to the Theiss village estate of Blumenthal. We are escorting Monsieur and Mademoiselle Theiss who reside in Kehl and are loyal to the Confederation of the Rhine. They are visiting family and requested an escort from my regiment. We are traveling the roads to spot out the Prussian Army," Hans said. "We will later connect with another regiment and venture east to join Napoleon and his campaign to Jena."

"We are ordered to take a third of all produce and materials for the French cause," explained the guard. "How many barrels do you have?"

"There are six," Papa said.

Hans's officers quickly dismounted to unload the wagon.

"We must inspect the load, and that is an order!"

I could see the fear in Papa's eyes. Albert and Papa climbed down from the wine wagon, and I jumped up into the seat and held the reins. The soldiers stood by the back of the wagon while Papa and Albert carefully rolled two barrels of wine to the ground.

From my position, I could see the glare from the sun reflecting the bright metal of the hidden guns. Fortunately, Hans kept talking to the guards and it distracted their attention. I decided at that moment to lean down to distract one of the guards with a good view of my cleavage.

It worked, and I spoke kindly and enthusiastically to the French guards, saying, "*Vive la France,* long live France!"

"Ah oui, mademoiselle!" replied the guard as he waved us through. I was happy and proud that I had used my feminine charms so the soldiers didn't see the guns.

When Papa climbed back into the wagon, he whispered, "Thank God we are safe."

CHAPTER 19

VALLEY OF THE FLOWERS

As we made our way closer to Leisel, I was thrilled to see the lovely silver birch trees lining the stream along the dirt road. Their golden leaves gently waved in the wind. The smell of freshly cut hay and harvested pumpkins aroused my memories of baked pumpkin pie with the scent of cinnamon and spice. The sky was brilliant blue with white wisps of clouds that feathered the heavens. The village's many dwellings with thatched roofs and stucco and timber walls were still present from medieval times. The small stream flowed steadily with shimmering rocks along the narrow road where I'd waded in my earlier years. As we made our way up the winding road past dairy barns to the knoll, the steeple of the Lutheran church reached high in the southern sky. There stood the massive graveyard embraced by stone walls surrounded by magnificent oak trees veiled with hanging lichens that gently blew in the wind. The Theiss name was prominent on most all of the stones. Opposite the church and graveyard was a clear open pasture with neatly stacked hay awaiting collection from the hay wagons.

Suddenly, the breeze blew out of nowhere as if to say, "Welcome home, Annaelise!" In the next moment, Hans rode next to me and smiled. My heart was fully aligned in my being. I felt like this was home.

We went down a small decline and in the distance was

Blumenthal, the Valley of the Flowers. Golden flowers danced in the wind. My excitement rose as I recalled those joyous times at Blumenthal. I could not wait to see my grandmother and smell the scent of lavender she always wore.

Hans rode forward down the slope and past the wagon. He didn't catch me staring at him, but I couldn't help it. He was handsome, charming, and he seemed to like spending time with me. The thought of him leaving for the next battle made me sad, but my worry quickly went away as we trotted down a long path that led to a large house. There it stood, rising in the distance with the white stucco walls graced by the red roof and the bell tower rising toward the clear blue sky.

Just then, a black Bouvier dog ran up to us, barking wildly. I couldn't believe my eyes. I remembered Jacques when he was a puppy. We rode closer to the garden in front of the house and there was my grandmother. Her hair was grayer than I remembered, but her radiant smile was the same. She was holding a lovely bouquet of flowers in her hand, and she waved to us.

We stopped our caravan, and I eagerly jumped off, rushed over, and embraced her in a warm hug.

Her tired, pale blue eyes were filled with happiness. "Ah, Annaelise, you are such a beautiful young woman!" She kissed me on both cheeks. "Please come in. I have cooked a large meal in anticipation of your arrival. It has been far too long! We have so much to talk about. We have so much to discuss, and we only have a few weeks."

"I can help you with many things," I exclaimed. "It's wonderful to see you, Grandmother Liselotte."

Frederick, the farm manager, introduced himself, while Papa unloaded the wagon and directed the stable hand regarding the care for the horses. Alfred was happy to meet my grandmother. Papa led Hans and his men to the old barn and found their quarters in the guest house. I watched Hans lead the horses to the stable until he turned and looked at me. I blushed and then smiled, my thoughts running wild. I looked forward to talking with him privately.

Papa embraced his mother with open arms.

"Oh, my son, how I have missed you! We will have much to discuss." She looked lovingly into his eyes.

"Don't worry, Mama. We are here now to help you. Let us get settled in and we will address all of your concerns."

We were all exhausted, and I hoped Hans and his regiment could stay the evening.

Upon entering the old villa, I could see how much the house had deteriorated over the years. The massive stone fireplace appeared strong and untouched, and the Theiss coat of arms—Faith and Fortitude—hung over the old oak mantle. The room was dark and dreary and had grown tired like its owner. Old window curtains darkened the space and needed removing to allow light to brighten it up. *I will have plenty to do here, and I can make this beautiful again.*

Gretchen, my grandmother's housekeeper and cook, met me at the front door. "Ah! Fräulein, you are so beautiful! Please let me help you take your things upstairs to your bedroom. Supper will be served at six o'clock, and I know you would like to rest a bit. The table is set for eight people, so we can have the officers join us for dinner."

I was elated by the thought of sharing dinner with the officers.

"We will have a bath drawn for you in the pump room," Gretchen added.

The pump room was off the kitchen and had a fireplace to heat the room and warm the water for the bath. The walls were covered with old plaster that was peeling, and the beams were covered with cobwebs, but I didn't mind. It was cozy.

I sank into the water and allowed my tired limbs to feel weightless. I leaned my head back and closed my eyes. I almost fell asleep when I heard the loud noise of the barn doors opening in the courtyard. Curious to see what the noise was from, I craned my neck and parted the covering on the small window over the tub and observed Papa enter the old vineyard barn to unload the four kegs of wine we had brought to Blumenthal. In recent years, the production in Pfalz was down, so Blumenthal Vineyard sold grapes to the surrounding vineyards. My grandmother was not only glad to receive more wine to sell, but she was looking forward to having Albert as her new winemaker.

Relaxed from the hot bath, I left the pump room wearing a long gown and walked up the old, hand-carved oak steps and went to my room unnoticed. I loved this small room that had a double window with old leaded bottle glass made by our ancestors who were bottle makers. Fairy-tale pictures covered the walls. I remembered when my grandmother read fairy tales to me when I was a small child.

There was a knock on the door, and Gretchen greeted me with a welcoming cup of hot cocoa. The journey was tiring, and I was grateful for the gesture.

"I brought you a surprise from your grandmother," she said while handing me a large faded box.

When I opened the box, I discovered a German Pfalz dancing dress with an apron. It had a black bodice embroidered with brightly colored flowers. The skirt had stripes of red and gold, and a red velvet sash was tied under the bustline. The ruffled white blouse was worn under the dress. I looked at it curiously, apprehensive of such a strange dress. How would my corset fit into this?

Gretchen came to my rescue. "Oh, Fräulein, may I help you?" And she pulled the dress over my head.

It was then that I realized the corset was built into the dress with lacings that could be adjusted in the back to fit one's figure. To my surprise, the dress was very flattering. I truly resembled a German Pfalz Fräulein and was delighted by how it complemented my womanly figure.

"You look magnificent!" Gretchen exclaimed.

I hoped Hans would be pleased with my dress as well.

I headed down the stairs, looking forward to getting to know my grandmother again and her connection with me on our German Pfalz heritage. This really felt like home, and I knew it was where I belonged.

Papa, Hans, and my grandmother were waiting at the bottom of the stairs. Papa was dressed in his Pfalz clothing with leather lederhosen, suspenders, and a shirt with a ruffled collar and cuffs. My grandmother was dressed in her finest traditional dress. Hans was in his military uniform without the white collar. His eyes were on me as I descended the magnificent stairway. I could feel my cheeks blush crimson that matched the red velvet trim on my dress.

Papa came forward and kissed my hand. "You are a real Pfalz princess," he said. I curtsied.

Hans came forward and bowed to kiss my hand. He then stood tall in a military stance, raising a salute with the other officers. "To the beautiful Fräulein Theiss."

Grandmother set an attractive table with an array of duck, venison, sauerkraut, carrots, and potatoes. Papa opened the Blumenthal's finest wine from the cellar, an aged Edelzwicker

Riesling, one of Pfalz's finest. The table was adorned with the traditional Pfalz cornflower-blue pottery. I recalled loving these dishes as a child, and I loved them still. The simplicity of the design of the Bavarian china appealed to me more than the very formal china we had in Alsace. The stucco and timber walls were decorated with trophy heads of wild boar, deer, and pheasant. Portraits of our ancestors who fought in various wars hung on the walls.

The first fire of the season crackled and popped while we took our seats. Grandmother sat at the head of the table with Papa on her right while I sat to her left. Hans sat next to me with Albert across from him, and the three officers were at the other end of the table. We discussed the future of the winery and the challenges Albert would face with the increasing warfare. Albert asked Hans about Napoleon's plans in this campaign.

"Napoleon's goal is to conquer Sweden and then Russia, as he views these countries as the last frontier. With Sweden's alliance, Russia could be won and become an ally against England," Hans explained.

It was confusing to me that Hans relayed so much information. The Confederation of the Rhine never grew or developed as a new Germany. Napoleon recruited more German soldiers from those states, such as Bavaria, Württemberg, Baden, as well as the provinces of Alsace including Strasbourg and our region in Offenburg. Although Hans and his French officers provided for our safety and passage to Leisel, I was in doubt about the entire campaign.

Taking a sip of wine while looking at Hans, I asked, "So, you are headed east to build armies against Prussia?"

"Fräulein Theiss, I can only state that we are building support for liberty and freedom. That is the general plan."

"Oh!" I said sharply, clearing my throat. "It just seems that Germany and the provinces have been doing fine before the Confederation of the Rhine. I can't comprehend how improved our provinces will be when so many people seem desperate."

At that point, Papa gave me a look and I knew to be silent.

Grandmother then brought out the pumpkin pie. I felt nauseated and had a headache. *How can this be? Napoleon doesn't want freedom and equality forever. He is a devil in disguise!* I was utterly disappointed that Hans trusted and believed in Napoleon. It felt like my heart was being pulled in two separate directions.

"If you will excuse me, I am getting a headache. Thank you for the lovely dinner, Grandmother, and for the lively company, gentleman." Then I quickly stood up and left the room.

I stormed down the hallway as fast as my feet would allow. I was so angry that I had let myself get so wrapped up in Hans. I knew from the moment I saw him that it could never be—the handsome, dashing French soldier—but I had pushed those thoughts away because I had been swept up in his charm. It was clear to me now that he and I couldn't share dreams of building a family and a life together. It all felt so hopeless.

I decided to visit Petite Held. A breath of fresh air to clear my head seemed like a good escape. I picked up a shawl that hung by the back door and walked out the into the crisp, cool air.

The moon was nearly full, and a bright halo illuminated the lake behind the barn. It was also the night of a lunar eclipse. The horses seemed restless as I approached the barn. I always felt the high energy from a lunar eclipse, and my emotions were in alignment with the event. I had a premonition that something terrible would happen and that Napoleon—France's new dictator—would lead us to poverty and ruin.

My thoughts were interrupted when Petite Held whinnied. I spun around and saw Hans standing there. I quickly wiped my wet eyes with my apron.

"Annaelise, I must talk with you."

"Why, to encourage me to be your lover? How can I love you when you are a traitor to the welfare of the people? Napoleon wants to conquer and destroy more people for equality and justice," I spoke in rage. I was my father's daughter, and I didn't care anymore to hold back my views.

Hans sighed. "Fräulein Theiss, I must speak to you alone." He gently gripped my hand. "Please, let us sit by the lake."

My heart was pounding, and I was feeling tension in my chest as I sought to take a deep breath. I nodded, and he led me down the path toward the lake. We sat on a bench and stared out at the vineyard. The light of the fading eclipse shimmered on the surface of the water. After a while of silence, Hans turned to me.

"I need you to know something about me, and you must understand my hesitancy of revealing such sensitive information. I realize that we haven't known one another for very long, and it's important that you can trust me."

He tenderly reached for my hand, but I rescinded his gesture. I was suddenly worried. I was out here all alone with a man I was not married to, a man I didn't really know but wanted to know.

Hans looked away. I could see the tension in his jaw. Then he looked at me again. "I am not a French officer, nor are those of my regiment," he said. "I am for the Prussian and German cause, and I have known your father for some time. We are spies against Napoleon. We have kept this a secret from you so your mother and uncle would never know."

Spies? I felt dizzy, as if the world was spinning. I gripped the side of the bench to hold myself steady. I couldn't believe what Hans had revealed. Dozens of thoughts raced through my head. *How could he be a spy? And he has known my father? How did I not know?* A feeling of dread and excitement whirled through me.

"Oh my!" I shouted. I was in shock. I stood up. "Why was I not trusted to keep your identity? How can I trust you now?"

"Please, Annaelise, sit. I will explain everything," he said.

"How can I trust you?" I demanded to know. "You have already lied to me." I felt betrayed and hurt and confused.

I felt myself drifting backward, my feet crunching over dead leaves, but Hans grabbed my hand and pulled me toward the bench.

"Annaelise," he said. "Please, let me explain. If you no longer wish to speak to me after I have said my peace, then so be it."

Every fiber of my being wanted to trust this man. So I sat down.

"We had to wait until we were out of danger," Hans said. "Russia has guaranteed our alliance, and we have promised not to provide Napoleon with any troops to attack Russia. We must form forces now as the French move to the eastern regions. To make matters worse, the sovereign states of the Confederation of the Rhine under Napoleon do not honor the provinces of Alsace on both sides of the Rhine in France and in Germany."

As I sat there listening to him, trying to piece together what he was saying, my grip on the bench relaxed.

"Your father has been very dedicated and has shared his political views from Hegel and Goethe, and he has attended meetings with the Freemasons. His Prussian friend and comrade, General Steuben, influenced him during the Seven Years' War. My father and your father got to know one another during the war. Your father is passionate about creating equality, justice, and freedom for all mankind, just as the Americans have proved possible," Hans further revealed.

"So, Papa has known you for a long time? And he arranged for us to meet at the ball?"

"Yes. He sensed that we would be perfect for each other, and I had gotten to know your father at many of the Freemason secret meetings. We have been working together for over a year now," Hans explained.

"I know the truth about my father," I said. "I knew his allegiance was with our German states, Alsace, and Prussia. We had made a pact to keep our secret between us and away from Maman and Uncle Gustave. I have never believed in Napoleon's cause to unite the countries while ravaging the people through war and devastation."

It felt like a weight had lifted to finally reveal the truth I had kept secret for so long. Now it all made sense that Papa was heading this with Hans and his soldiers posing as French officers. All those secret outings, the things he taught me . . . everything finally made sense.

"General Steuben fought under General Washington and has trained soldiers for the Battle of Valley Forge during the American Revolutionary War. He influenced your father with his correspondence from America, and your father has been very instrumental for our cause in the Alsace, the German states, and Prussia," Hans said. "Your father has been a disciple and has attended many secret meetings. That is how I met him."

"I can't believe you are a spy," I said. "And that you've known my father all this time."

"Well, your father believed it would be better for you to discover whether you loved me on your own. He knows you're stubborn, and if he told you about me, you may not have believed that my feelings for you are genuine. Also, it was safer to get the ball behind us. I was instrumental in obtaining information from the other French officers when I was there," he said with a big grin.

"Yes, my father knows me! And you're right—I wouldn't have believed your feelings toward me to be genuine," I said.

My emotions felt like they were being tossed around in a wild river. On the one hand, I had fallen for Hans so hard, but I had also been hesitant with my heart because of his French views, which were a lie. And my father was behind it all. My head was spinning. Then the intensity of the situation hit me all at once. Hans was a spy, my father was a spy, and I knew sensitive information about them both.

"Hans, you are in great danger," I said. "I'm very worried for you. When are you leaving?"

He pulled me closer. "I leave the day after tomorrow. Annaelise, I must go to the eastern areas to rally our troops. I will be gone for a month or so, but I want us to marry in a church near Rothenburg. I will send a message to you. I love you so!"

I felt like my heart would stop. This amazing, brave, and wonderful man was in love with me, but a few moments ago he told me he was a spy. I felt so conflicted in my feelings. I wanted to love him and trust him, but suddenly I was worried for his life. This was all too much to understand in the moment.

"I don't know much about you or where you are from. I don't know the real you!" I gasped in disbelief.

There was desperation behind Hans's blue eyes. "I will tell you everything you need to know. I was born in Provence, and after my father, Stefan, died, we moved to Karlsruhe where my mother, Millicent, is from. Both my mother and my sister, Mary, live on the old estate, which is not far from here. I would truly love to develop their estate and increase the land for the winery, as well as work with you here at Blumenthal. When I return, we will meet them."

"Yes, you spoke of this when we had our picnic," I said, "but I need to know more about your character. Oh! This is happening too fast!" I touched a hand to my feverish brow.

"Annaelise, I love your family, and your father is allied with our cause. He knows my family and that I am of good character. I was excited to meet you in Strasbourg at the ball. This was all planned. We must create a new life for us all," he spoke tenderly, holding my hand.

I arose quickly from the bench. A shadow of doubt embraced me as the eclipse extinguished the light from the moon, mirroring my heart's confusion. *That wonderful, beautiful night when Hans had swept me off my feet had been planned.* Anger swirled through me at the thought. *No, what we had was special,* I reminded myself. Nothing could take away the pure magic of the night. *Did he even love me?* But as I stared into his eyes, I felt love there. While it might have been planned for Hans to meet me at the ball, there was no denying that our connection was pure.

I felt like I could finally let go and be free of my emotions. Hans brought that out of me. Hans allowed me to feel love, kindness, and tenderness. I never felt so happy as I did when I was with Hans.

After several minutes of hesitation, I said with resolution, "I will wait for you. My love is steadfast and strong."

Our lips kissed, our bodies falling into each other, becoming more passionate with every moment. I wanted to kiss him forever, to never leave his arms. He pulled me closer until I felt I would suffocate, but I didn't care. I wanted him to take my breath away. I embraced him without restraint. Hans pulled back and stared into my eyes. I couldn't tell if he was holding me up or if I was floating.

"Come, let us walk in the vineyard and look at the stars," Hans spoke softly, leading me by the hand.

While we whispered promises, dreams, and goals to one another, shooting stars sailed through the heavens, intensifying our love. The stars twinkled brighter than I had ever seen them. We strolled between the rows of grapes and found a comfortable spot to stargaze. We could envision Blumenthal growing into a prosperous business while raising children and horses together. We kissed passionately and swore allegiance to one another. Our plan was to marry near Rothenburg in a month's time. It was all happening so fast, but a peace came over me knowing that my destiny was clear.

And then, in the distance, we heard cannon fire. The once magical night suddenly turned sinister. At that moment, the moon was totally eclipsed by the sun, casting darkness all around. A chill ran up my spine.

Was this a warning sign? I looked over at Hans, and his face was covered in shadows.

CHAPTER 20

PREPARING FOR WAR

Early the next morning, I got up and quickly dressed. I needed to find Papa before he started the day's work, otherwise I wouldn't have any time alone with him because he and Albert would spend hours harvesting the grapes. Luckily, I caught him leaving his room.

Before I opened my mouth, Papa said, "Well, you now know about the captain?"

"Yes! And you put me through the aggravation of being fooled!" I said in anger.

Papa pulled me inside and shut the door.

"It was too dangerous, and we just had to let it play out," he said. "I was protecting you. If I'd told you before the ball, you could have been nervous and perhaps not have been as elegant for Napoleon and Joséphine. And besides, you might not have fallen in love." Papa waved his hands in a dramatic gesture.

Papa was right, though. I probably wouldn't have fallen in love. But I was still somewhat upset that he hadn't disclosed his plan to connect Hans and I together at the ball. I realized Papa was a master of his work in espionage.

"So, you have known Hans's family for years?" I asked.

"Yes. Stefan Roster and I met during the Seven Years' War. We worked together, he in the battlefields and I in espionage. Unfortunately, Stefan passed away just a year ago."

"Is that why you went to Karlsruhe so often?" I asked.

Papa nodded. "Our families were also involved in the winery business, and I delivered wine to Millicent after Stefan's death. Millicent and her daughter, Mary, have been struggling with the business, and I like to help them when I can. We will have to visit them on our way back to Alsace."

"I look forward to that. Hans has mentioned them, and I so long to meet them," I said.

"Please, Annaelise, know that I couldn't tell you because I had to protect you. You are my shining sun, and I would never forgive myself if something were to happen to you."

I embraced him in a hug. "I know, Papa. I love you."

"I love you too," he said. "Now, run along and help your grandmother."

I went down the stairs to the kitchen where Grandmother was baking rolls with Gretchen.

"Ah, you are baking rolls for the men, I see." I grabbed one garnished with smoked ham. "I have been up so early and I am hungry."

"Have another roll," Grandmother said, and I complied. "So, Captain Roster is quite handsome and very knowledgeable with horses. His family lives here in the Pfalz near Karlsruhe?"

"Yes, that is what Papa was telling me," I said with a mouth full.

"Annaelise! Slow down. You will get a sick stomach with your mouth filled with a bread roll," Grandmother said with a smirk. "We will have to ask Captain Roster more questions regarding his family."

"Now is not the time to discuss this with him. His troops are leaving tomorrow for the eastern front," I said.

The conversation became a mute issue. I packed a picnic for Hans and myself. We planned to ride out to a quiet place by a tributary of the Mosel River. I walked to the barn carrying a saddlebag packed with some bread, cheese, bratwurst, pickles, and smoked trout. The other side of the bag contained some of Blumenthal's finest Riesling.

Petite Held whinnied as I approached the barn, as she knew I would bring her a fresh apple. As I entered the stable, pigeons were cooing and flying between the rafters. A light shined down through a loft above where the hay was stored. Hans's hair was ruffled, and his tan, muscular arms were grooming Excelsior. He was humming a tune I didn't recognize. His clothes were plain, and his appearance was earthy, and I thought I would float away at the sight of him. I loved seeing him in his everyday clothes.

He turned and grinned, walking toward me. I stood motionless, and he embraced me passionately as I rose to kiss his sensuous lips. His musk overwhelmed me, and I wanted more and more as my tongue searched for his. We fell to the ground and were emerged in the freshly cut hay. The weight of his body on mine felt heavy, and my body tingled. It felt so right and so wrong.

I heard something faint, and I knew someone was coming, so I quickly pushed him off and rose quickly. I adjusted my dress.

It was Albert. "*Guten morgen*. I'm here to hook up the cart, and Bella and Bernard are going to pull the wine wagon to load the grapes." He smirked at our appearance—hay in our hair and clothing.

Embarrassed, I replied, "Yes . . . yes, it is a fine day for harvesting the grapes! We are going on a picnic by the Mosel."

Papa entered then, and spotted us with the saddlebag of food. "Ah, I see you two are headed for a picnic."

"Yes, and we should be helping you with picking the grapes," I said as I pulled more hay from my hair. My cheeks burned from embarrassment.

"We have the help from the townspeople from Leisel, and both of you must enjoy this gorgeous day. Hans will be leaving tomorrow, and your grandmother will need your assistance in the house when he is gone." Papa averted his eyes; it was clear he knew what we were up to.

We saddled our horses, and Hans secured the saddlebag on the back of Excelsior. He assisted me in mounting, and I admired his strength once more as he hoisted me up onto the horse.

We went north on the road along the river lined with birch trees. The breeze picked up and Hans slowed down. He motioned me to move behind a barn just off the road. It was there where we saw the French troops heading south. Hans motioned me to me stay quiet as he suspected that there would be many more troops coming. It seemed like there were hundreds of soldiers, and it was all we could do to keep our horses calm and quiet. Hans opened the back of the barn door and we slipped inside to hide.

"Napoleon has been active in the north recruiting forces. They are coming south to prepare to fight in the eastern regions. That is why we are preparing to go to Jena," Hans whispered.

"I don't want to lose you," I said. I wanted to be with Hans for as long as possible.

"I must go back to alert my men. We'll leave tonight when it will be dark, and we must take the weaponry to the front. I will have Lieutenant Ferré come for you when it's safe." Then he gently kissed my lips.

"I will be so worried," I said.

"We must return to Blumenthal. My heart lies with you, my love." He took the horses out of the barn.

My heart was soon clouded with fear.

That evening after an early supper, Hans and his three men were leaving in disguise to take the artillery loaded in the wine wagon. Dàrtangan and Dominique were hitched to the wagon. Major La Fond was to bring the wagon and horses back in a few weeks to deliver an update to Papa. I packed some food and other supplies for the men.

I was devastated. Before he left, we dodged around the corner of the barn for one last embrace.

"I will see you after we deliver the guns near Rothenburg, and we will marry within a month's time," he said. "Have no fear. We must conquer Napoleon. It is for our future." Hans held both of my hands to his heart. I didn't want him to let go.

Papa and Grandmother came outside to watch their departure. I gently stroked Excelsior to say goodbye. "Take care of him, good fellow," I whispered into the horse's ear.

The new moon was on the rise. As I watched them ride away, I couldn't control my tears any longer. Grandmother placed her arm around my shoulder for comfort.

I decided to keep our impending marriage a secret. I knew Papa would want us to wait until the war was over. All I cared about was Hans making it back to me safely.

CHAPTER 21

SHARING SECRETS

Working with my grandmother in the garden kept me from worrying about Hans and made time pass quickly. Since it was fall, we began pickling cucumbers and beets. We also pulled turnips, potatoes, and carrots for winter. It was an opportunity to bond with my grandmother and learn the workings of the estate. After all, this was going to be my future home with Hans. Although I missed my mother, I knew this was the life I wanted. The questions of the past were answered, and my focus was clear.

We took our baskets loaded with the vegetables toward the kitchen.

"So, I see that young Captain Roster looking at you," my grandmother said. "I think he's rather fond of you. How do you feel about him?" She flashed me a big smile.

I didn't know if I should tell her about my love for Hans, and since no one knew about his proposal, I decided it was best to be discreet. "I do miss him, and I worry that he is danger," I said.

Grandmother stopped and turned to me. She rested her hand on my shoulder. "I know love when I see it. I also know about Hans."

I gasped. "What . . . do you know?"

"Well, it's about time that we share our secrets. It is not good for the soul to keep things to ourselves for too long. I know your father and Hans are Prussian spies. You have to stop worrying. No good will come of it." She pulled me into her embrace. "Hans is in God's hands and fighting for a noble cause."

"How do you know all of this?"

"I am a mother, aren't I?" she said. "I know more than I let on. Everything will work out the way it should."

"Thank you, Grandmother," I said. What a welcomed surprise to learn that my grandmother felt this way. I didn't feel so alone in my secrets.

The housekeeping at Blumenthal became of interest to me as well, and I was eager to get the house in order. One afternoon, I explored the elaborately carved wardrobe at the end of a hall where I found many fabrics suitable to make curtains to replace the battered and torn window coverings. At the bottom of the chifforobe, to my good fortune, I discovered a lovely cream silk fabric suitable for my marriage day. I located an old wooden dress form bodice in the attic. I made an elegant empire-waist wedding dress. I would go up to the dusty attic by candlelight late in the evening to work on my dress. I really missed my mother on those nights. She would have loved to help me make my dress. Keeping secrets was beginning to weigh on me.

I organized the closets, removed the old curtains, washed the windows, and opened up the rooms for more sunlight and fresh air. I spent quality time with Grandmother. She told me funny stories about Papa being a snoop and spying on people and being a tattletale on his sister when they were younger.

"I remember Papa mentioning he had a sister, but he never talked about her much. What was her name?" I asked my grandmother one day.

"Elsa. She passed from smallpox at age six. Your father was very sad for her loss—they were close. Your grandpapa also passed from smallpox." Her eyes filled with tears. "That was a long time ago."

"Maman's parents passed away from smallpox too. You have been brave to stay here all these years alone. I should like to reside here and help you. I am so happy here, and Hans's family lives nearby," I said, then quickly hushed up.

Grandmother smiled. "Ah, so I see that you are thinking about your future with Hans. Time will tell," she said with a wink.

While waiting for news from Prussia, one evening at dusk, Major La Fond returned the wagon with Dàrtangan and Dominque with his mount in tow. He delivered two letters from Hans: one to me and one to Papa. Earlier, we had learned that Prince Friedrich Ludwig of Hohenlohe would lead the Prussian Army with the Duke of Brunswick and General Blücher under his command. Prussia had requested that Napoleon withdraw his troops from Southern Germany and restore the territory taken by France's General Joachim Murat. Prince Ludwig asked permission for the Confederation of Northern Germany to become a part of Russia. Napoleon denied this request, and war seemed imminent.

My letter was an invitation to come to the Church of Our Lord at Creglingen near Rothenburg on October first.

My Dearest Annaelise,

We successfully delivered the supplies, and I will have a few days to see you outside Rothenburg. I so look forward to being with you, my dear!

All my love,
Your devoted Hans

I knew he could not speak about the weapons or the war plans, so I read it one more time before throwing it into the fire.

The church was remote and off the main roads. With the threat of war so close, I became doubtful of my decision to marry Hans. Lieutenant Ferré was to accompany me to the church. I would leave the night before on Petite Held. My thoughts ran wild.

Is this a good time to marry? Is it dangerous to travel? Will Papa be disappointed in my making such an important decision without involving him? What will Maman say? Should I wait? However, I had to respond. To give myself some time, I told Major La Fond to come in for some cold cider. As I gathered my thoughts, I penned a response: "Yes, I will marry you," and handed the letter to the officer. Whether we were to be married or not, I had to see Hans.

Hans relayed to Papa that the French cavalrymen were in Jena and Auerstädt. His letter only stated, "We need supplies in Karlsruhe." I became worried about Papa's involvement. It was decided that Albert would go with Papa to deliver the kegs of wine with more guns concealed to Karlsruhe. He would also deliver more wine to Hans's family winery and surrounding villages.

My resolve was to do what I could for the Prussian and German cause. Somehow, this also helped me work up enough courage to be confident in the most burning matter at hand. Over the next week, I tried to remain calm while working the details of our elopement. I wrote a letter to Papa and Grandmother about my forthcoming plans:

Dear Papa and Grandmother,

As you may know, I have fallen in love with Captain Roster.
He has asked me to marry him, and I will leave on the night
of September twenty-ninth to meet the captain in a church
outside of Rothenburg. We will be married on October first.
Lieutenant Ferré will be escorting me, and we will stay one
night at the Fox Fire Inn in Heidelberg. I just have to see my
Hans before he goes to war. I hope you understand and will
support me on this decision.

All my love,
Annaelise

After dinner one evening, I summoned Gretchen to my
room.

"Gretchen, please sit down. I must tell you a matter of great
importance," I said.

Gretchen sat on the chair next to my bed. I sat in the chair
opposite her near the fireplace.

"You know I am deeply in love, and it is my greatest desire
to see Captain Roster before he goes to war," I said. "The captain
has asked me to be his wife. Lieutenant Ferré will be escorting
me to a church close to where the captain is camped, and there
we will be married."

Gretchen gasped. "You are to marry the captain?"

"Please lower your voice," I said. "Yes. I know it is soon,
but it feels very right in my heart. I must see him, do you
understand?"

Gretchen nodded. "I'm so very excited for you, Fräulein."

"You must not speak of this to anyone. I have written a letter
for Grandmother and Papa, and I would like you to deliver it to

them the morning after I have left. You understand?" I handed her the letter.

"Yes, I understand." Gretchen had tears in her eyes. "I will be so worried for you," she said as she embraced me in a hug.

"We will be fine. 'Faith and Fortitude' is my family's motto, and I will live up to that."

"You will make a fine wife," Gretchen said. "You are always so gentle of heart."

A wave of guilt came over me then, and I ached to be sharing this moment with Maman. But I knew she would approve of the man who stole my heart.

CHAPTER 22

DEPARTURE FOR HEIDELBERG

Lieutenant Ferré came for me on the evening of September twenty-ninth. I had prepared and packed two saddlebags: one for my clothing and one that contained bread, trout, and cider. I kept the faith that this was what I had to do. The journey was a two-day ride; the first night would take us through the Black Forest, and we would ride the following day to Heidelberg, staying outside of town at the Fox Fire Inn.

Around eleven o'clock, I quietly went to the barn and saddled up Petite Held. It felt like a rock was in my stomach. Leading my horse quietly away from the barn, my path was fortunately highlighted by the magical moonlight. Lieutenant Ferré met me at the edge of the Black Forest. He was dressed in civilian clothes; however, his presence shined like a knight in bright armor. His face beamed with a smile as he dismounted his horse and gently assisted me onto Petite Held as she softly whinnied.

"Have no fear. We will be fine, but we must be silent until dawn," Lieutenant Ferré said. Hans and Lieutenant Ferré had been loyal friends for many years. This was evident witnessing the lieutenant's devotion in his polite gestures.

A feeling of great peace overwhelmed me as we rode along the soft pine-needled path through the dark woods. The moon darted in and out of the clouds, and the only sounds were the soft hoofbeats and the occasional breeze softly blowing through the long boughs of the ancient trees, sending wonderment and magic through my soul.

It was just before dawn when we came to a brook where we dismounted and filled our canteens with water. As I splashed some water onto my face, Petite Held took a long drink from the rushing stream. The lieutenant spread a linen cloth under a large hemlock tree, and I was impressed by his attention to detail. Weary from the ride, I brought over my basket, sat down on the cloth, and placed the bread and smoked trout on a pewter plate.

The lieutenant took a piece of the bread and spoke openly, "You know, I am from Heidelberg, and my family has an apothecary shop there." He chewed the bread vigorously.

"Hans did relay that to me. You have a farm as well?"

"Yes, I share the farm with my father, brother, and sister. We could have stayed there on this journey, but the location of our farm is out of the way, and we must leave soon to arrive at the inn before sunset on the outskirts of Heidelberg."

We quickly finished our meal, then packed everything up and continued on our journey. We passed a large open field, and then suddenly a dozen French soldiers blocked the road to Heidelberg. They held guns with bayonets. A lump formed in my throat.

"Halt! Who goes there?" a soldier demanded.

"We are attending a family wedding in Rothenburg," Lieutenant Ferré responded.

"Whose family?" the soldier asked.

"The Theiss family from Leisel," Lieutenant Ferré said sharply.

"You may pass. However, you will find more officers on the road ahead. They might not let you pass so easily."

Thankfully, the rest of our journey to Heidelberg was

uneventful, and the sun shined brightly as we rode from a trot to a canter on dry turf and open roads. We arrived at the Fox Fire Inn just before dusk, and after settling the horses in the stable, we were assigned to the two separate rooms Hans had reserved for us. The innkeeper looked surprised when we asked for two. I was not amused at her question because my hunger had really set in. We had a wonderful meal of roast lamb and potatoes with a bottle of local pinot noir wine, Cuvée Exceptionelle. It was such a surprise for me to have a pleasant conversation, and I learned more about Hans and Lieutenant Ferré's friendship of many years.

"Please tell me a story about Hans," I said with great curiosity.

"I got to know him when we were in military school in Karlsruhe. I remember when he was having difficulty riding one horse. I had observed his riding and noticed he was pulling his mount's mouth too tightly, so the horse tumbled backward with him hanging onto him. When I got on the horse's back, I sat back in the saddle and really loosened the bit. The horse relaxed and we had a fine ride. Hans was humiliated, but soon we became good friends," Ferré said with a smile. "He is like a brother to me."

I laughed. "I will never mention that I heard the story, I promise."

Afterward, we retired to our rooms. My room was rather small but clean with a simple bed and a small window that opened up the busy street below. I lay on the soft bed. My thoughts wandered to my parents, family, and friends who I wished could be at our wedding. Would I regret this elopement later? Was I doing the right thing? But as much as I questioned the timing of it all, I really felt deep within my heart that Hans was my one true love. I knew this was meant to be. Being away from him was tortuous on my soul, and although I felt sad that my family couldn't be witness to my marrying the man I loved, I couldn't wait another day to call myself Hans's wife.

CHAPTER 23

TAKING A LEAP OF FAITH

The Lutheran Church of our Lord at Creglingen was magnificent. As I stepped inside, my vision was drawn to a large, beautifully hand-carved wooden altar. It was so intricate in detail I felt compelled to kneel and ask the Lord for our protection and blessings. In a world of uncertainty, I was feeling the discord and upheaval from the devastation from the war, and love was the only promising force. This step forward had to be right on all levels.

The next moment, the late morning light cast a sunbeam that shined through the stained-glass window, illuminating the hand-carved altar that depicted the story of the Virgin Mary and the Annunciation. Like Mary, I felt a divine purpose in a time of uncertainty and was once again reassured this marriage was the right step for both of us. I had chills all over my body and felt blessings that replaced fear and doubt. Suddenly, with the thunder of approaching hoofbeats, butterflies rose in my stomach.

"Stay here, Annaelise," Lieutenant Ferré said. "Let me be sure it is Hans."

I was wearing the silk dress I had sewn and the pearl necklace Maman had given me for the ball in Ettenheim. What a happy and carefree time when my family visited our cousins.

I adorned my hair with the fading red roses that bloomed outside the church and tied my hair up with many hairpins.

I had packed my silk slippers that I had worn at the ball in Strasbourg. I wished Marie were here. She would be so upset to learn that I got married without her being part of the festivities.

The door suddenly opened and Hans stood tall, silhouetted in the backdrop of sunlight in his Prussian blue uniform, more handsome in contrast to his former French uniform. His bright blue jacket was adorned with white cording across his chest with a red collar and cuffs. His height was taller from his black helmet trimmed with white cording topped with a brass Prussian eagle. He held flowers in his hand. He took my breath away.

Hans rushed forward and was breathless while speaking. "Annaelise, you are so radiant, and I am so blessed that you are mine. We will wait for the priest. Ferré, will you ride to Rothenburg to find if he was detained and to collect a few more supplies? It is only a short ride," he asked.

Lieutenant Ferré took note of the supplies and rode to Rothenburg while Hans told me of his month of negotiations and gathering of forces with General Blücher. He was so handsome, but his puffy, sunken eyes indicated little sleep. We discussed the future for Blumenthal and his mother's winery in Kaiserslautern. We became excited talking about both wineries and breeding Andalusians and Friesians. To speak of future dreams and hopes brought some comfort to the strange situation in which we had put ourselves.

As we sat there chatting, we ate some ham and smoked trout that I had brought for the journey. I was eager to learn more about his mother and sister.

"How old is your sister? What does she like to do, and is she as handsome as you?" I asked, taking a bite of a ham biscuit.

"Mary has blue eyes like me and blonde hair like our mother. She is more German and has fairer skin. She likes to garden and sometimes she will ride with me. We have some ponies, Percherons and an old Friesian mare named Chérie."

"That is the pet name my father has given me," I said, laughing.

"I can see why your papa named you that! You are a dear," he said, tweeting my nose.

"So, you take after your father, Stefan?" I asked.

"Yes, as you know he was from Provence and had the influence of the Italian culture, and perhaps I inherited his darker skin and hair." He lovingly looked down at me.

"Then I guess you inherited your mother's lovely blue eyes," I said as I gazed into them.

"Yes, that is correct. We will have beautiful children, and smart as well!"

It felt so freeing to speak with Hans with nobody watching. With every passing moment, I longed to be his wife and lay with him and feel his warm breath on mine.

By mid-afternoon, Lieutenant Ferré returned without the priest. "The priest was called out to hold a funeral for young soldiers who were recently killed in action near Rothenburg," he explained. "It is not advisable to stay at the inn in Rothenburg tonight."

Hans grimaced. "Tonight, we will stay at the Heidelberg Castle that is not far from here. It was built in the thirteenth century as a fortress and expanded over the centuries as home and court for many different regimes and ruling parties. My father and your father found refuge in this castle during the Seven Years' War, as we will too," he said confidently.

Hans took two golden rings from his uniform pocket. "Annaelise, we can kneel before the altar and exchange our vows with Ferré being our witness. There is a bible at the altar, and we can read to one another. If you like, that is."

I hesitated. None of my family was here, and now there wasn't a priest. Was this God's way of saying that this union should not happen? Hans smiled at me and held out his hand, and I followed him. I couldn't resist his enchanting smile.

"We don't have to do this," he said. "We can wait for another time when I return, and we can have our families together in their church with a feast to follow." He softly squeezed my hand.

Approaching the magnificent altar, my feeling was one of disappointment and discouragement as I realized the wedding would not be legal because an ordained priest was not here to officiate the ceremony.

"God will provide and I will keep you safe," Hans reassured me, drawing me closer. "You deserve a proper wedding with family and friends. There is no pressure from me to have our ceremony today."

I felt lost in his blue eyes. It meant so much to me that he could sense my disappointment, and without me even telling him, he knew it was because my family wasn't here.

"I want to wear your ring and feel protected. I don't know when I will see you again," I said.

"Then let us have our own ceremony. And when I return, we shall have a formal ceremony with our family," Hans said. I kissed his cheek and agreed.

Lieutenant Ferré stood before us and read from St. Paul's first letter to the Corinthians. Facing one another, Hans spoke with strong affirmation as he looked into my eyes. "With this ring, I give you my heart and soul, for better or worse, for richer or poorer, and in sickness and health, till death do us part."

He took my hand and gently slid the gold wedding ring onto my finger. To my amazement, the ring fit perfectly. I felt the Holy Spirit come through me, and there was no question that Hans was my true intended. I was resolved, and therefore confident, repeating the vows.

Lieutenant Ferré then proudly announced, "You are now husband and wife."

Hans wrapped one arm around my waist and the other around my back and pulled me to him. Our lips tingled as we kissed. I was locked in his embrace in a timeless dream.

As I looked deeply into his eyes, he spoke to me in German, "*Ich liebe dich, mein Schatz*; I love you, my treasure."

Even though I was not Hans's legitimate wife, I felt a joy just knowing that one day we would be married with a priest, family, and friends. After the ceremony, we had a glorious late afternoon ride from Creglingen as we headed toward Heidelberg castle. As a child, Hans and his family often visited the castle when Prince Karl Theodor was ruler of Baden. Hans's father was a friend of the prince, and they would visit in the summer to hunt stag and wild boar.

We traveled through a wooded section south toward the city and away from the main roads. Hans and I rode on Excelsior with me in front and Hans holding me tight. Lieutenant Ferré rode beside us. Petite Held was tethered close behind, carrying my belongings securely on her back.

The castle had been struck by lightning in the 1500s and again in 1764. The prince had planned to take full-time residence in the castle, but prior to moving in the summer of 1764, a lightning bolt hit the main tower, causing fire destruction, so he was forced to set up court in Munich. Did this somehow signal a warning or haunting of an unseen premonition?

Sensing my apprehension, Hans held me even tighter, and when he turned toward me, he said, "Do not worry, my love. It is our destiny to be here."

The afternoon turned to night. When we finally arrived, the forest opened up to the main road and the magnificent castle rose high into the sky. The climbing harvest moon silhouetted the glorious structure. The magical light shone brightly, highlighting the ravaged turrets and spires. I truly felt like a queen being escorted by my king, my forevermore man of principle, passion, and fortitude. This had to be God's will.

We crossed the mighty brick archway bridge over the Neckar River into Heidelberg. The gate was open on the old bridge and ascended the rocky road toward the castle. Excelsior was surefooted and steady climbing the steep incline.

The castle had deteriorated because the entrance was open and had eroded over the years. The structure had gone into deterioration and the stones had been robbed for other constructions elsewhere in Heidelberg. Hans assured me it was abandoned. The moonlight illuminated the courtyard, and we could see broken wood and several extinguished torches.

We finally came to a stop at the entrance. The massive twenty-foot stone archway was still standing, with very little deterioration of the masonry after three hundred years. I imagined what the large wooden oak doors might have looked like with enormous iron straps welded together to hold the wood together. The expansive courtyard was mostly intact with a working well and old lumber that was dismantled from the interior. Old torch sconces were welded to the stone walls. Leaves scattered the cobblestone floor. The towering walls surrounding the courtyard felt ominous as if a thousand eyes were peering down on us.

Lieutenant Ferré quickly lit the torches in the courtyard. We dismounted while Hans led the horses to the barn, and we were fortunate to find hay in relatively good condition. The barn smelled of rotted manure and straw. The mold was a strong stench, but fortunately the stalls were near open windows peering down a thousand feet to the Neckar River below and the bridge we crossed earlier.

After returning to the courtyard, we went through a main door. Hans said the enormous double oak door had been replaced when he was a boy. It seemed odd that the mighty door did not have a lock, and he explained that looters shot off the lock over and over.

We walked into the old banquet hall. The large beams were still mighty in structural integrity. The stone walls and floor made it dark and cold, and it smelled of musk from centuries of banquets, celebrations, and perhaps sword fighting. The smell reminded me of our old Banquet Hall at Friedensthal, and in some sense I was comforted and felt more assured. There was one trestle table, and benches remained in front of the magnificent fireplace. The mantle had been stolen, but the Tudor-shaped arch above the hearth was still visible. Lieutenant Ferré made a fire in the fireplace. It was clear this expansive room had housed many celebrations and feasts in centuries past.

"When I was a young boy, I witnessed the prince honor my father for his bravery in the Seven Years' War," Hans said proudly.

I gazed around the room and imagined it filled with dozens of people cheering and eating at the long tables. I saw maidens wearing simple crowns of flowers while the princesses and queens wore crowns of gold. I saw pewter chalices and large platters of wild boar, turkey, and pheasants with wine flowing like water. Perhaps the ghosts from the time would attend my wedding reception.

"Ferré, take this torch and enter through this hidden door," Hans said as he pointed to the oak paneling to the right of the fireplace. "Hopefully you will find bottles of wine in the cellar for us to celebrate this special occasion."

Ferré pushed open the door to a narrow stairway that led to the old wine cellar. After he disappeared into the wall, Hans turned to me. "I am so sorry this was not the proper wedding with a wedding feast that you deserve. We can wait until this war is over—"

"No, Hans!" I said a bit too loudly. "When the war is over, we can celebrate again, but I cannot contain my passion for you any longer."

He pulled me into his embrace—his strong arms wrapped around my waist—and once again I was lost in his love. As we kissed, the flames from the fireplace grew hotter.

"You are mine forever," I said, breathless. "But who knows when I will see you again? I have your ring and you have my heart. I only want you."

At that moment, the lieutenant entered the room with three bottles of Vendange Tardive Pinot Gris. I quickly pulled away from Hans, as if I had been caught doing something I should not do. I wasn't used to physical touch, let alone someone catching me in the act.

"I purchased provisions in Rothenburg—bread, cheese, and smoked venison and trout," Ferré said.

"It looks like we can have a small feast," I happily exclaimed. "I will retrieve the dishes and cups from my saddlebags."

"Wonderful!" Hans replied as he began to wipe off the table and chairs.

Before he could say another word, I stepped out into the cool night. I was having trouble catching my breath. The musty smell of the room was making me dizzy. I was excited but very nervous. I knew what happened to a bride on her wedding night. Marie and I used to talk about it—always giggling and squealing with laughter and embarrassment. But a few years ago, I had asked Maman about it and she merely said, "It is about conjoining together the way God made it sacred between a man and a woman." I only knew from watching our horses breed.

As I approached the barn to retrieve my saddlebags, Petite Held whinnied at me. "Tonight, I will become a woman. Someday you will foal many colts and fillies at Blumenthal," I said to her.

Someone laughed behind me and I quickly turned around. Hans was standing there with a big smile on his handsome face.

"You have to stop sneaking up on me like that!"

"Do you think I would let my future wife be alone in the dark night? You ran off without me."

"I-I'm sorry," I stuttered. "I just—"

Hans grabbed my hand and kissed my ring. "Tonight is going to be wonderful, I promise. We will have many colts and fillies of our own," he added with a smile.

"Yes, my dearest," I replied, laughing with embarrassment. There was no mistaking my nerves and the butterflies dancing in my stomach, but I loved and trusted this man with every bit of my heart.

"Now we will have our wedding feast," he declared. "But first we must find my knife to open the wine."

By the time we entered the dining hall, the old oak trestle table was dust-free, the wood still in good condition. The fire was magnificent, its warm orange flames reflecting on the stone. At the sight of this grand hall, I felt a little more at home. I placed the dishes on the table and Hans opened the wine. We were pleasantly surprised to find the wine was still good.

Lieutenant Ferré said Vendange Tardive Pinot Gris would age as well as a fine white Burgundy. The taste was divine and complemented our meal with a touch of richness. Lieutenant Ferré toasted us; we could not have had a finer best man. It was sad that our families were not here, but I hoped we would all be together again soon. The harvest full moon shined on the old gothic window above us, illuminating Hans's handsome face and intensifying his brilliant blue eyes.

He rose to salute me. "To my future wife, Annaelise Theiss Roster."

We didn't talk about the war, our families, or the doubts we had in our minds. The wine kept our spirits high, and we spoke of the future for mankind, for Germany, and for Prussia. We had finished two bottles of wine, and as we saluted Prussia, Alsace-Lorraine, and the future of our German states, Hans put the mug down and lifted me in his arms.

"Good night," he nodded to Ferré.

While we were ascending the bright, heavenly-lit stairs, the sound of cannon fire blasted in the distance.

"We cannot succumb to this fear of warfare," Hans said in a determined but reassuring way as we proceeded down the long dark hall.

"Why, of course not," I agreed, smiling with great enthusiasm.

When we approached the large suite, Hans kicked open the door with his boot. It was a nice surprise to see that the lieutenant had already made a fire in the bedroom. The bed was magnificent and dressed in fresh linens.

"I had Ferré purchase these linens in Rothenburg in the event that we might have to reside here for safety."

"It's perfect, all perfect, as my love is for you," I replied.

He tenderly kissed me. "Are you ready and sure about this?"

"As sure as the sun will rise tomorrow," I replied.

Hans gently put me down and we stood side by side while the lunar light shined upon us.

"*La luna, la luna, la bella.* How beautiful the moon has kissed you as I have," Hans said.

There was no stopping when I dropped my gown to the floor, exposing my corset, garters, and silk stockings. Turning my face toward the brightness, his lips were running down my neck to my exposed breasts. He carefully removed my undergarments as his eyes gazed over my naked body in the moonlight.

"Ah, more beautiful than all the princesses in the world, my queen."

Unafraid, I stepped forward and said, "Now, I must see you."

Hans removed his shirt, exposing his well-chiseled chest. Somehow, his torso was even more magnificent in the bright light of the moon. As my heart beat wildly, I unbuttoned his trousers and let them fall to the floor. My eyes widened at the sight of his naked body. His muscles were strong and defined, and he looked powerful, like some type of god sent down from the heavens. He was strong, like a stallion, and the hardness of his muscles was beyond my wildest dreams.

He lifted me onto the bed and gently laid me down. His lips kissed my neck, peppering kisses up and down my breasts, and his hands sought my maidenhead. The angels in heaven sang as he entered the gateway of our divine union. I suddenly felt the joy from a thousand summer days, riding by the Rhine, that feeling of freedom.

Cannon fire exploded in the distance, echoing the excitement of our passion and promise. Witnessing all the power and strength in his passionate being and soul, my heart smiled, bursting into tears of ecstasy and exhilaration.

CHAPTER 24

SAYING GOODBYE

I woke up the next morning feeling elated and overjoyed. My king was sleeping still, his hair ruffled and the musk of his body intoxicating. I didn't want to go anywhere, and the thought of him leaving me to go to war was cruel beyond anything I had ever known. His eyes were dancing, and his body trembled. *Was he dreaming of war? Riding Excelsior?* I found myself jealous of his departure from me in the dream world. I longed to be wherever he was.

Then he rolled over toward me and opened his eyes. "*Guten morgen*, my queen." He gently pulled me closer for a sweet kiss.

"You were dreaming. I didn't want to wake you, my love. Were you in battle?" I hated to ask, but the words slipped from my mouth.

He stared at me. "Yes, and I don't want to go. My life is nothing without you, and my heart is breaking that I must leave." He ran his hands over my face, and he pulled me toward him until our lips met, soft and slow. Our souls locked in love forevermore.

When we descended from the castle, the view of Heidelberg was magnificent. In the distance, we could hear explosions of fire. Despite my looking forward to being home in Leisel, I knew Papa and Grandmother would be upset with me. I was so wrapped up in Hans that I didn't think about them worrying about my safekeeping. I had just left without telling anyone.

Surely they would have read the letter I gave to Gretchen and be happy for me. I hoped they would be glad I was safe. But now that I knew Hans and I would part soon, and I would have to face the reality, a feeling of dread threatened to overwhelm me.

As we entered the forest, we heard rapid hoofbeats approaching. We quickly went down a ravine and dismounted under a wide stone bridge to hide from the French soldiers who we were heading our way. We had no idea how many cavalry regiment went over our heads. The thundering of hooves was deafening. It felt as if the bridge would collapse over us. Our horses were almost uncontrollable, and we had to hold on to keep them from breaking loose from our grasp. I could only hope that their whinnying was muffled under the sound of the calvary's passing and the hoofbeats on the bridge. Fortunately, the soldiers were going toward Rothenburg, opposite my direction; however, they were heading east to prepare for battle.

My heart sank. My worry was all-consuming for Hans and his men. Feeling blessed to have escaped this encounter, we waited until the men were long gone before we emerged. Before we mounted, Hans had made sure I had the pistol that Papa had gifted me. It was tucked in the holster under my skirt.

We traveled for the next hour in silence for our security. As the old evergreens gave way to the hardwood forest, my heart sank. This was where I had to separate from Hans and Lieutenant Ferré.

"I will make it from here to the outskirts of Heidelberg and then take a coach home. You men have a war to fight, and I know you must return to your regiment as soon as possible."

Tears filled my eyes. Hans dismounted and gave Excelsior's

reins to the lieutenant. I dismounted as well. We embraced and I inhaled his scent, his hair tickling my neck. He pulled me close to him with his strong hands. Our farewell kiss was one of heat and desire without the security of knowing when we would see one another again.

"I will send word to you, my love. Remember, Faith and Fortitude. We will always be together." He lifted me back onto Petite Held. I saw the same tension in his eyes that he surely saw in mine.

"May God protect you and bring you back to me," I managed to say as I stared down at him, memorizing every inch of his face. I had to look away; I didn't want him to see me grow weak with my emotions. "Many thanks, Lieutenant Ferré, for your devotion and kindness. Godspeed to both of you."

I pulled the reins and spun Petite Held around to take off at a fast gallop, and I didn't look back. I couldn't bear the sight of seeing Hans still standing there. I knew he was going to watch me until I disappeared from his sight.

Petite Held was strong in her gallop, as if she were sensing the long distance that lay ahead to Leisel. We galloped most of the way to the coach station while my tears dried in the wind. Everything rushed by in a blur, and I didn't know if I was awake or dreaming.

The coach station lay west of Heidelberg. It was an old station that had been established during the medieval times. I could see the curling smoke from the chimneys in the distance as I approached. The forest-green coach was of substantial size, and there were six horses driving. We arrived just in time to meet the departure.

"Hello, Fräulein," a large gruff coachman greeted me. "Where is your ticket?"

"I will go to retrieve it in the inn, but first I must tie my horse up," I panted, out of breath.

"Well, be quick about it! And the horse is extra!" the coachman shouted.

Petite Held was cooperative as I secured and tethered her behind the coach. When I went into the station, I could hardly see from all the tobacco smoke. I pushed my way through the crowd to the booth and quickly obtained my ticket. I rushed outside, slapped my ticket into the coachman's hand, and upon entering the coach, my skirt caught in the steps and tore at the bottom. I must've looked a fright with my hair that had come loose and my ripped dress. I sat down to catch my breath.

Fortunately, we started out at a slow pace, allowing Petite Held to cool down after our long gallop. We were to stay the night at the White Horse Inn in Karlsruhe. A long silence ensued within the coach during the journey to the inn among five other traveling companions. However, I was pleasantly distracted watching a Papillon dog sitting on the lap of an elderly lady. For obvious reasons, I didn't want to converse, but she was persistent and I responded to her inquiry about the purpose of my travel.

"I was visiting my husband in Heidelberg before he was off to the battle at Jena," I said.

"Ah oui, the French will win. Napoleon is getting stronger. Your husband will be fine," she said confidently.

"Yes, Napoleon is most masterful," I responded. *If only she knew my husband was fighting for the Prussian cause.* Suddenly, I burst into tears, and then her dog jumped into my lap and licked my tears away. Surprised and happy by the gesture of the canine, I unexpectedly broke into laughter. What a welcome relief from the tedious time and emotions of the last two days.

We approached the top of a small mountain that overlooked the valley of Karlsruhe. It was another quarter of an hour before we arrived at the White Horse Inn. Pulling up front, there appeared to be quite a bit of chaos outside. I took a deep breath. I just needed to stay safe. I would get something to eat and then retire to my room.

While leading Petite Held to the stable, I glanced over and saw a beautiful horse. I stopped in my tracks. *"Dàrtangan?"* I rushed over and couldn't believe my eyes. It was our faithful Percheron from the Pfalz. That could only mean one thing: Papa was here!

I embraced the large horse around his neck and Petite Held whinnied. She was fortunate to have a stall next to her stable companion. I remembered Papa saying that he would travel to Karlsruhe on business, but what were the chances that he was here? Then my stomach felt upset thinking about how he would react upon seeing me. I could only hope that he wouldn't be too angry.

Running inside, I looked around the tavern. Every table was full. My eyes scanned the crowd, and sure enough, Papa was seated at a large table in the corner with three gentlemen. I exhaled in relief, yet I knew he would be shocked, and relieved, to see me.

The tavern room was dim. Curls of tobacco smoke rose in the low candlelight. I made my way over, pushing people out of the way, and stood in front of the table where Papa was engaged in a conversation. He looked up at me, then looked away. Then he snapped his head in my direction.

With his mouth open in shock, Papa said, "Annaelise?" Then he spoke wildly, knocking over his chair when rising. "Annaelise! You are safe!" He hugged me and it felt like he wouldn't let go.

Then he grabbed my arm and practically dragged me deeper into the corner. "What in heavens were you thinking?" His eyes were fiery with rage. I had never seen Papa this angry. "How dare you leave! I received your letter. Did you forget that we are at war?"

"Papa, I'm sorry," I said, and I meant it. "Hans and I—"

"Thoughtless, careless Fräulein!" he interrupted. "You cannot go running off like that!"

My eyes burned with tears, and my bottom lip quivered. Papa's expression softened.

"I'm glad that you do truly love Hans Roster, but this was selfish!" Papa said. "So, you are married? I see your ring."

"No, Papa. The priest could not come, but we exchanged rings." My cheeks burned at the thought that Hans and I had lain together.

"Let's go upstairs," Papa said in a low voice.

His room was small but clean with a small window of bottle-leaded glass. He shut the door behind him and sat on the small down mattress. I sat in the small chair next to an old wobbly desk.

Papa recounted that his journey took him to Leap of Faith Winery, the home of Millicent Roster, Hans's mother. He delivered wine there, as well as weapons for the Prussian front. Even though he was still angry with me for leaving without permission, Papa was elated that I was in love and would become part of an honorable family in the Pfalz. We shared several laughs regarding the woes of running a winery.

"We will have more time to discuss your fiancé's home and family when we are traveling on the road," Papa spoke with a big yawn.

It was late and time to turn in with our long journey home ahead of us in the morning. We eagerly anticipated our return to the Pfalz. I retired to my small room, and Papa brought me a plate of bratwurst and hot soup of potato and cabbage. It was soothing and so nourishing, just what I needed after the stress of the last several days.

"Get a good night's rest," he said and kissed my cheek. "I'm so glad you are safe."

As I drifted off to sleep, visions of Hans danced through my mind, and I spent the night dreaming of my true love. When would I see him again?

Our journey the next day was uneventful. The wine cart was lighter without a heavy load. Petite Held trotted behind the cart and we made good time. We were fortunate to have arrived home just before sunset at Blumenthal, and Albert saw us approaching the barn.

"Ah, Fräulein Annaelise, are you all right? What a nice surprise to see you both returning. Your grandmother has been so worried."

The tears in my eyes interrupted Albert, and he refrained from asking any further questions. "I will attend to your horse, Fräulein," he said.

While Papa unharnessed Dàrtangan, Dominique whinnied to welcome her stablemate home. I headed into the house to clean up in my room and was thankfully met by Gretchen at the back entry.

"Annaelise! You are safe! We were all so worried. I gave them your letter, and they were going to have a search for you. Your papa was going crazy with worry and fear," she relayed in distress.

"Shh!" I replied. "I must clean up. Please help me. I don't want Grandmother to see me like this."

"Of course, I understand," Gretchen said as she led me to the pump room.

I washed up while Gretchen went to my room to fetch clean clothes. "You must be starving," she observed when she came back in. Then she gasped. "I see a ring, Annaelise. So you were able to marry the captain?"

"You must keep a secret! The priest could not make it, and we exchanged vows in the church. I may have made the mistake of laying with Hans, but I do not regret this. I am in love with him," I said.

"Oh, but surely he will marry you when he returns," Gretchen suggested. I couldn't tell if she was hopeful or just being sweet.

"He is off to battle in Jena to defend the Prussian front. Please pray he will return." I began crying uncontrollably.

"Ah, Annaelise, all will be well. I will keep your secret," Gretchen promised, hugging me. "Your grandmother is so worried for you."

"Yes, I will go down now. Help me change."

Walking slowly down the old oak stairs, I saw my grandmother coming through the front entry. When she saw me, she dropped the basket she was carrying and ran to embrace me.

"Oh, Annaelise! Thank goodness you are safe! We have been so worried for you. I wish you hadn't run off like that." My grandmother took my hand and gazed at my ring. "I read your letter, and I see this ring on your finger. Congratulations, my dear! I approve of your choice. I know the Roster family from Karlsruhe."

Taking a deep breath, I told her the truth. "The priest could not come because he was attending to the dying Prussian soldiers, but we will be married as soon as Hans returns."

"How did you get home?" Grandmother asked.

At that moment, I turned around to see Papa coming from the rear of the house.

"We met at the White Horse Inn Tavern in Karlsruhe," Papa explained.

Grandmother nodded. "We must keep what has happened to ourselves. We mustn't tell your mother or Gustave. There is more at stake here. We are not supportive of Napoleon, and we want the old ways in government without the doctrine set forth in the Confederation of the Rhine. Your captain is brave to fight for that cause."

I expressed my grave concern for Hans in battle, as well as his intention to marry me.

"He will honor his word. As I've said, I know of his family and they are honorable," Grandmother said.

I was so relieved that my father and grandmother approved of my decision to marry Hans even though I had gone behind their backs. All my caution went away, like a bubble bursting and floating off in the distance.

"We know he will honor you," Papa spoke with a knowing smile. "It was my desire for you and Hans to be here at Blumenthal and at Leap of Faith Winery. Your roots are here in the Pfalz, Annaelise, and we will wait for him."

"Thank you, Papa. Please pray for his safe return."

CHAPTER 25

THE WOLF WOMAN

The cold was settling in. I continued to help my grandmother prepare for the winter. She often encouraged
me, "Keep the faith, dear. God has a plan." Staying busy
helped keep my mind occupied. I helped Grandmother pickle
beets, cucumbers, and we made jam for the winter. Maman had
never taught me how to do these types of domestic chores and
I was learning a lot.

Once again, I found refuge in riding. Petite Held sensed
my sadness, and she obeyed my every command one brisk
afternoon while we went down a small forest path encased
with leaves of red and gold. The sun shined on a small building
that was overgrown by weeds and thick brush. Smoke rose
from an old stone chimney. I was curious to see who lived there,
and I dismounted nearby and tethered Petite Held to a birch.
The building had a thatched roof and an old door. Curious, I
knocked on the slightly open door with no response, and then
pushed the door fully open and stepped inside. There was a
beautiful stone fireplace that showed evidence of a recent fire.
Apothecary jars and mortars with pestles sat on a long wooden
table. Dried herbs hung everywhere. I turned to leave when
suddenly the old door opened from the outside.

"Are you a thief or are you here for a reason?" a slightly
hunchback woman in ragged clothes snarled at me. She shook
the stick she was holding in her bony hand. Her wiry gray

hair was as unkept as her entire persona. Her face was more wrinkled than anyone I had ever seen, and her old gray eyes were clouded. I could tell her vision was less than adequate.

"Why, neither," I replied calmly, though she had startled me. "I am from Blumenthal and have never seen this cottage before this morning. I apologize for not knocking."

"So, is Liselotte still alive?" the woman asked with a softened demeanor. She lowered her hand and pointed the stick toward the floor.

"Yes, she is," I said. "I am helping her store food and prepare for winter with the vineyard."

"Oh, I see. Then you are here for a reason. There are no mistakes and no lost causes. You have a heavy burden, do you not? Come, sit. I will make you some peppermint tea," she said.

The woman was peculiar but I was curious. I readily agreed to a soothing cup of tea.

While she laid out the cups, I noticed more objects in the room: branches, bones in strange shapes, and feathers. There was even a stack of cards with intricate characters on the table. I recognized them as tarot cards, used to tell fortunes by people who claimed to see things others couldn't see. I had never had a tarot reading. It appeared the woman could perhaps be a witch. I was not afraid, however. She seemed harmless enough now that she was no longer snarling at me.

I sat down at the old oak trestle table that showed years of hard use. The chairs were missing most of their caning yet were strong enough to support me with a sturdy back.

While pouring the tea, she asked, "You are here because of this war?"

"Yes," I responded.

She grabbed the stack of tarot cards. Then she sat across

from me, breathing heavily with her mouth open. "Let's look deeper into this," she said.

"Yes, please. I must know," I said. My mouth suddenly went dry. *Do I want to know?* I remembered my vision of the battle scene when Hans and I took our first ride together. "What is your name?"

"*Wulf Weib*, the Wolf Woman," she replied while gazing at me with her faded, glazed blue eyes. The Wolf Woman picked up the cards and gently shuffled them. She drew seven cards and laid them in front of me. Then she turned them over one by one. The cards were the Tower, Queen of Pentacles, Nine of Cups, Nine of Swords, Knight of Wands, the Empress, and Death.

My stomach dropped, covering my mouth in surprise. When I saw the Death card, my thoughts cried out to Hans.

"You're shaking, my dear. Drink more tea," the Wolf Woman said.

I picked up the tea and tried to steady the cup with my other hand. The tea tasted like peppermint and sage, and was somewhat bitter, but it soothed my throat and calmed my nerves.

"Do you want me to continue?" she asked.

Did I want her to continue? My heart raced at the thought that this woman—this stranger—could tell me something I didn't want to hear. I hesitated a moment as visions of war and darkness flashed through my head. I always wondered if there was anything to my visions or if they were just a figment of my imagination. Could this strange woman give me answers? My stomach fluttered in anticipation.

"Y-yes," I stuttered. "I'm ready to hear."

The Wolf Woman smiled, revealing missing teeth. Her

crooked finger pointed to the Tower card. "You have torn down something of value. You are passionate about the new politics, are you not?"

"Oh yes," I said. "Napoleon has made many promises, and they have all been broken. I am fearful for the region and the Prussian cause."

"We will talk about that in a minute," she said, and then pointed to the Queen of Pentacles. "You are a powerful woman in your own right. See, you hold the grapes. You will have inheritance of your grandmother's vineyard. You can manifest anything you want. You are also very clairvoyant. You have visions and dreams and sometimes know when things are going to happen before they happen, yes?" She looked directly at me.

My mouth dropped open in shock. I nodded.

She then pointed at the third card, the Nine of Cups. "You have a brave knight in your life, do you not?"

"Yes. He is in Jena at the big battle." I paused. It suddenly felt very hot in this stuffy cabin. "Is he all right?" I asked.

"I cannot see that as of yet." Pointing to the Nine of Swords, she continued, "You are guilty over some action?"

"Yes," I responded. I had lost my maidenhood as an unmarried young woman.

She hinted at an insight with a slight smile, turning her gaze to the cards. She pointed to the Knight of Wands and said, "I see sudden changes for you. A move perhaps?" Then she reached for my hand with her bony fingers and pointed to the Empress with her other hand. "You are with child, my dear."

"W-what?" I was in shock. *I'm with child?* My hands instinctively touched my belly. I was suddenly angry at myself for being so foolish. I started to cry. I didn't know if they were tears of joy or sorrow.

"What if my knight is slain? Is this Death card for him?" I asked.

She grasped my other hand, and suddenly there was an unexpected kindness in her pale blue eyes. "No, my dear, it is for your mother."

I stood up quickly, knocking the chair over. "That cannot be! You are a charlatan! A witch! Do not trick me with your sorcery!" Tears flowed down my cheeks.

"I have read the cards for aristocrats in Paris before the great fall of the regime. Joséphine was one of the ladies. I knew what was coming and escaped in time, perhaps as your Maman did as well?" the Wolf Woman replied.

I took a step back, regretting that I had ever set foot in this cursed place. "How could you know about my mother? I do not believe you! I must go!" I shrieked in disbelief.

"In time you will believe," the Wolf Woman remarked as she assembled a bundle of sage, peppermint, and ginger, and wrapped it with a cord. "This is tea for the morning sickness," she explained as she gave me the tied herbs. Angrily, I turned away from her.

"One more thing: beware of the man who can harm you. When you return here, bring me a bottle of your finest Blumenthal wine."

"You are nothing but a miserable witch," I screamed, slamming the door behind me. Not until I reached Petite Held to mount did I realize I held the witch's bundle in my hand. Hesitating just a moment, I dried my tears with the backside of my hand and placed the herbs into the saddlebag.

Despite my efforts to keep busy with farm work, I was beside myself with sorrow over my love and became restless, finding it difficult to sleep.

Over the next few days, I felt like I was in a daze. I didn't want to believe the Wolf Woman's prophecy. Then I woke up one morning and felt sick to my stomach. I felt hot and cold at the same time. I was panicked. I couldn't be with child, not now with Hans gone. This wasn't the way it was supposed to be. He was going to fight for the cause and come home to me alive and in one piece. Then we were going to get married with my family as witness. We would start our own family here or at his family vineyard in Karlsruhe.

I made myself some of the tea the witch had given me. I woke in the middle of the night, nauseated. My menses was late. *What will I do?* How could I face Papa and Grandmother? Maman would be so disappointed. Would I stay in the Pfalz? I waited with nervous anticipation for news of Hans while each day the realization of my state sank deeper into my being.

CHAPTER 26

THE SOLO SOLDIER

My dreams were becoming more frequent and vivid. I had a recurring dream of a soldier riding a horse, but his back was toward me and I couldn't see who he was. The soldier was racing toward an unknown destination. At one point, he was riding in an empty field, the sun shining over him, making his hair glow red, and then he suddenly entered a battlefield and the sun disappeared behind the clouds. The horse continued on, faster and faster, until the man pulled on the reins. That was when I always woke up.

One night, I woke up from the dream and couldn't go back to sleep, so I went to the kitchen to make the tea the Wolf Woman had given me. It had been helping me feel less ill. When I entered the kitchen, Gretchen was sitting by the fire sipping a glass of Riesling.

"What are you doing up at this hour?" I asked.

"I could not sleep; it is a full moon, you see." She took another sip of wine.

"Oh, no wonder. Maybe I should have some wine instead of tea." I pulled a chair up to the blazing fire.

"I know the waiting is so hard for you. Being in love can be torturous at times." Gretchen got up and poured wine into the hand-blown glass made by my ancestors.

"If I may speak boldly, Fräulein, are you with child?" She handed me the glass of wine.

"Oh, I hope not!" I took a slug of the wine. Then I lowered my voice and said, "You have a child . . . when do you know when you are with child?"

"After you miss your monthly menses. Has that happened?"

"Only a few days," I responded nervously.

"Hasn't your mother taught you these things?" Gretchen asked in surprise.

"In her society, they do not explain about lovemaking until the night before the wedding."

"A woman as beautiful as you should know these basic fundamentals of life."

I held my head in my hands and cried.

"No worries, my dear, it is too soon, and I'm sure it will all work out. I am here for you. Now go to sleep and have no worries." Gretchen pulled me into a hug. I was grateful for her loyalty and friendship.

One evening, I went to the vineyard barn to talk to Albert. I wanted to ask him for a bottle of wine to take to the Wolf Woman, my fear creeping in that all of her predictions would come true. I needed to know more. My plans were disrupted and even forgotten when I noticed two horses coming down the road. The setting sun in my eyes made it difficult to focus on the moving figures. Coming closer, I observed that one horse was chestnut and one was black. I could not yet make out the riders. The wind picked up as I started running wildly toward them.

My bonnet blew free and my hair came unpinned. My excitement turned to dread when I finally saw there was only one rider. It was Lieutenant Ferré leading a riderless Excelsior.

The sight hit me right in the chest and took away my very breath.

Hans is fine, I told myself. *Think about his smile.* I tried to conjure up a vision of his face, but I couldn't. A heavy feeling settled in my body and my limbs felt like lead, and I realized I had to be careful running down the grassy hill although my heart went running in wild abandon.

"No, no, no!" I shouted as I ran faster, my vision becoming blurred with tears. When I got closer, Lieutenant Ferré dismounted. Trying to catch my breath, I stopped a few feet in front of him. His red hair flew loose in the wind, and his weary hazel eyes were raw and red-rimmed.

"No, no!" I cried, falling to my knees. "Tell me this did not happen!"

Lieutenant Ferré held me while I sobbed uncontrollably, my tears soaking his tattered uniform. He pushed me away to look into my eyes.

"Hans saved so many men, Annaelise. You would have been proud."

I pulled away from him and hugged myself in shock crying all the more. My Hans was gone . . . forever. My grief was too much. I closed my eyes and saw a smoky landscape of gunfire. I could hear men screaming. I could see bodies, bloodied and broken, young men lying on the dirt. But not Hans. I couldn't see Hans.

"How can this be? Please tell me my Hans is alive."

Lieutenant Ferré shook his head. "I'm so sorry," he said. "Hans led our battalion. Napoleon's soldiers surrounded us. We sought to break to the front of the line, and Hans ran to the front with his saber out. He was yelling. Everyone followed him. I ran from behind to be next to him, but there was a cannon blasting from the right and Excelsior swerved left. The cavalry came out of nowhere. Hans was stabbed in the back through his left shoulder."

"Hans . . . my Hans," I said weakly. "What . . . why did this happen?" I was at a loss for words. My body felt numb.

The lieutenant continued, "Excelsior fell to the ground with his master. I directed the rest of the regiment to run left as the cannon kept firing from the right. Excelsior followed my horse. We escaped, but we were totally outnumbered. We sought to find a clear space to rejoin the troops and retaliate. It was such a massacre and we were outnumbered. The Duke of Brunswick was also mortally wounded. There was nothing we could do, Annaelise. There was nothing we could do," he repeated sadly, looking down at the ground.

It hadn't occurred to me to blame the lieutenant for what happened, but when his voice broke and the pain and guilt overflowed his eyes, it was clear that he blamed himself for his friend's death.

The lieutenant took a deep breath and hid his emotions under military discipline and continued in a low voice, "We were trying to be optimistic for months. There was fire everywhere. Hans Roster was a brave man, and he loved you more than life itself. I was able to retrieve his body for a proper burial and to return his wedding ring. The war isn't over yet. Napoleon is a tyrant, and the English will defeat him, mark my words! You must believe in the promise of a new world and the ideals for liberty and justice."

The lieutenant then placed the ring into my palm. I stared at it, not knowing what I was looking at, not wanting to believe that this was real.

This isn't happening. Hans couldn't have died in vain. "So,

Prussia as we know it is destroyed?" I asked, feeling defeated in spite of his courageous words.

"Yes, Prussian forces were slaughtered. But you must be strong now, Annaelise. We must tend to Excelsior—his leg was injured, and I sprained my ankle. Excelsior needs you. He is a gallant steed, the best of the best cavalry horses. We must honor him."

I threw my arms around Excelsior's neck. The battered stallion whinnied. He knew my sorrow as I knew his. I leaned my head on his strong body, feeling so weak. I needed this horse to hold me up. What I really needed was Hans in my arms, assuring me he was fine.

Lieutenant Ferr rested his hand on my shoulder, then pulled away. "We must tell your father."

Somehow, I found the strength to move my legs. I took the reins to walk toward the barn with Lieutenant Ferré. Both Excelsior and the lieutenant were limping.

"We will get you into a bed and you can prop your foot up," I said in a quiet voice.

As we approached the barn, Petite Held whinnied, recognizing Excelsior was in close range.

The lieutenant and I went into the house. Gretchen drew him a bath and offered me a steaming cup of hot cocoa without asking any questions. The weather had cooled rapidly and the first frost was setting in. I sat by the fire in the salon, saying nothing. Though the cocoa was a simple gesture, it strangely offered some comfort with its ingrained memories of easier times.

Papa and Grandmother came down the stairs, embracing me while I cried.

"Oh, my dear, I am sorry for this loss," Grandmother cooed

as she cradled me in her embrace. "Annaelise, this is nothing new to mankind. You will go on and Hans's memory will always live in your heart. You will find happiness again. You have your life, his horse, and his ring. Life is full of changes, and death will always be a part of life. After Lieutenant Ferré has cleaned up, Gretchen will bring us some cake and tea."

Papa sat next to me. He spoke slowly, with emotion. "He fought a battle. Hans was such a brave, honorable man, and he loved you. His father, Stefan, would be proud. He honored his family and his country."

Lieutenant Ferré entered the room and sat down in a nearby chair with a heavy sigh. He was clean and freshly shaven, with his brilliant red hair tied in leather. We made sure his leg was propped up on an ottoman with ice from the icehouse.

"His body was buried two days ago in Rothenburg. We were unable to bury him in Karlsruhe." The sadness in the lieutenant's eyes reflected so much misery and pain. "A letter of his death has been sent to his mother and sister in Karlsruhe."

"What will you do now?" I asked Ferré.

"I will return to my family home in Heidelberg. My sister, brother, and father need me now that winter is coming and supplies are low," he spoke wearily, holding his head down in sorrow.

"We will send you off with food from our garden and some salted venison, including wine. Please take one of our wine wagons if your horse can pull the cart. I am asking you to rest here for a few days, and so should your mount," Grandmother said softly but sternly.

"I also need you to further discuss Prussia's future and what you think Napoleon's next tactic is," Papa said.

At that point, Lieutenant Ferré began to sob. I quickly rose to my feet and sat beside him, embracing him with my arm over his shoulders while he cried uncontrollably, his head in his hands.

"I should have saved him! He had no fear and I saw it coming! The time was not right to plan the battle. We didn't have all the facts."

I burst into tears and Papa got up and cradled me in his arms. I just couldn't believe that my Hans was gone.

"Do not blame yourself," Papa said to the lieutenant. "We insist you stay here until you are stronger. It will take time to properly pack your supplies."

Gretchen entered the room and announced she had prepared a meal. I didn't feel hungry, but Grandmother insisted that I eat to keep my strength up. I felt numb, as if I were living in a fog. I knew the lieutenant needed to eat as well; he had to have been famished.

After the blessing was given, Papa said a prayer for Hans. "Oh, Holy Father, hold Hans into your loving care in heaven. We all loved him and honor him for his valor. Give us strength in the days to come. Help us to be grateful that he served our nation and give us courage to contest Napoleon in the days to come. Amen. The British will conquer Napoleon, and he will not make it through the winter if he plans to invade Russia. Amen."

Papa wiped the tears from his eyes. "You both are young and have your lives ahead of you," he said to me and Lieutenant Ferré. Then Papa turned to me. "All is not lost, Annaelise. You have Hans's ring, you have his horse, you have his memory, and you have the future. You must see how the Americans fought the British and won their revolution, and so will we. You must be strong."

Lieutenant Ferré stood up and wearily made a toast. "To the freedom of Prussia, Germany, Alsace, and for all mankind;

in the coming years, freedom, equality, liberty, and justice. To Hans Roster, a devoted friend and companion."

The wine tasted bitter. While they talked of hope for the future, my grief took over. Hans, the love of my life, had been taken from me. My heart was breaking. Hans would never know his child.

CHAPTER 27

IN MOURNING

A loud knock at my door woke me up from a dead sleep. I forgot where I was for a moment. Then it all came crashing down on me. Hans was dead. I would never see him again. Hans died on October 14, 1806, at the Battle of Jena, a day that would forever live in infamy. The nightmare was here while I was awake. What would I do? It wasn't long ago that I woke up next to him and saw his face and his smile.

Gretchen entered my room with a very welcomed cup of peppermint tea. When I got out of bed, I felt dizzy.

"Are you nauseated, Fräulein? If you are, you could be with child." She looked me in the eyes.

I sat down and burst into tears. "Yes, I am! I don't know what to do!" As distressed as I was, I was grateful I had someone with whom I could share my secret with.

Gretchen patted my back. "You know you will be fine. Your father wants to see you downstairs after you dress."

"Oh," I replied. My stomach turned while sipping my tea.

"I'm so sorry about the captain," Gretchen said. Her eyes were teary.

"I am sad," I whimpered. "I don't know how I am going to face everyone regarding the child." I rose wearily out of bed.

"Well, maybe something will evolve into a good outcome. You never know. Keep the faith." She embraced me in a tight hug.

There had been too much hurt and pain, and I wasn't sure I could take any more news unless it was good news. Wearily, I drank my tea and chose a woolen dress to combat the cold of the early November morning. Brushing my hair off my face, I viewed my puffy eyes in the small wooden-framed mirror on the wall. They were still swollen and red from crying.

Hans's ring sat on the nightstand. I'd put it on last night, but it was too big for my finger, and I was afraid I would lose it. I picked it up and kissed it two times, one for me and one for our baby. Then I placed our wedding rings into a wooden box and slid it under my bed. It was just too painful of a reminder.

I met Papa at the dining table, which had been set with fresh bread, eggs, and cheese. Normally I would have eaten with enthusiasm, but today I chose only to drink the tea.

"Annaelise," Papa said. "I'm sorry to say, but we must return to Friedensthal. Your mother is ill."

"Maman is ill?" I spoke. My face paled at the thought of hearing more fatal news.

Papa reached for my hand. "She has been ill for some time. I only just received a letter from Gustave—it was dated a month ago. The mail has taken longer due to the war." He paused and then said, "There is more. The Duke of Enghien had been arrested for no apparent reason. He was taken to Vincennes outside of Paris and was executed."

I gasped. "Oh dear Lord."

Papa took the letter out of his pocket and showed it to me.

25 September, 1806

Dear Count Karl Theiss and Countess Louisa Theiss,

It is my regret to inform you that we have been requested to send this notification to all members of Count Karl Thiess's family:

The Duc d'Enghien was tried and sentenced to death in Paris on the date of September 12, 1806. The duke was accused of treason against Napoleon on the accusation that the duke was giving information to the British who rallied against France. He was the last royal from the Bourbon rule of the French nobility. This puts an end to the former dynasty. Please be informed that no more action is required at this time.

Signed,

> *Joachim Murat, Admiral of France,*
> *Grand Duke of Berg*

"Napoleon has gone mad," Papa spoke in a rage. "The Reign of Terror is over, and we have a new regime, yet Napoleon is hunting down the former members of the Bourbon aristocratic class from the Revolution. This is an outrage! He obtained his brother-in-law, Joachim Murat, to do his dirty work. He is using fear tactics to further gain control of his empire. I cannot believe this has happened!"

"Are we in danger?" I asked. "Is Maman in danger since we are distant cousins of the Bourbons?"

Papa sighed. "That is why we must return. Your mother is worried sick."

My stomach turned and growled, and I got up quickly and ran from the table. I dashed through the kitchen and opened the back door as the contents of my stomach erupted onto the ground. Gretchen was right there and put her shawl around my shoulders.

"I cannot take it anymore! I don't want to go on!" I spoke in distress.

"There, there, Annaelise." Gretchen led me over to a bench. My legs felt weak, so I was grateful for the respite.

Papa and Grandmother were standing there staring at me as I sat on the bench shivering. I was emotional, grieving, and confused after Hans's death, but this news about my mother was overwhelming.

Grandmother tenderly embraced me, speaking softly, "Come, child, your mother needs you. It will be all right. Winter is coming and I have Gretchen, and Albert is here now. You and your father will be safer in Alsace. You must return home."

My stomach gurgled again, but I was able to keep my sickness inside this time.

"Let's bring you inside where it's warm." Grandmother led me back into the house to sit by the fire.

Papa sat in the chair next to me. "You are of German blood, my dear, and do not fear," he added.

"But Maman and Uncle Gustave?" I asked in distress.

"We will provide safety for them. Remember, the duke was a direct descendant of the Bourbons, but your mother is married to me; therefore, she is under German protection. Their situations are very different," Papa explained.

"And Uncle Gustave?" I pressed.

"He is breeding horses for the French cause, and Napoleon is only thinking about what is good for himself and the republic and all the handsome soldiers who will be coming to purchase horses," Papa said.

I sat up straighter. I had to be with my mother. I had to see her face. "Then we shall leave as soon as possible," I said.

The preparation for returning home involved packing our clothes, supplies, and making sure our wagon and horses were in good condition for the journey. I tended to Excelsior's leg, and he regained strength and weight from the nourishment and rest we provided for him. Petite Held was restless knowing something was changing.

Lieutenant Ferré slept for two days. Gretchen washed what few clothes he had. Papa found an old trunk in the attic that held his own father's clothes; they appeared to be a suitable size for the lieutenant.

I brought the lieutenant some meals during those two days. I was able to prop up his ankle on a pillow and keep it cold from time to time. At noon on the second day, as I entered his room to serve him some rabbit stew, he managed to smile.

"You are an angel, and I am blessed to have you by my side," he said.

I placed a cold rag onto his brow and ankle. His hazel eyes were swollen and red.

"*Danke schön*, thank you. It is no wonder Hans loved you so," he said tenderly.

"If only he were here," I said.

"He is here in spirit, and I believe our loved ones can look down on us from heaven above. Fear not. We will be taken care of," the lieutenant replied. "Oh, and please call me Wilhelm."

"Hans was blessed to have a friend such as you, Wilhelm," I said.

"I am leaving tomorrow morning," he said with some regret, still not touching his stew. "I must check on my horse after eating, and I can meet you in the barn."

"Your mount is doing well and enjoying his rest and feed. What is his name?"

"Faithful Friend," Wilhelm said. "A simple name but so appropriate."

"Like you have been to Hans and me," I acknowledged.

"I loved his family and I love yours. Your kindness has been so appreciated," he replied in earnest.

"I would like to meet his family, Millicent and Mary, in Karlsruhe one day. It is a shame Hans could not be buried there."

"Yes, I know. We will go there one day with your father too," Wilhelm said.

This exchange of mutual appreciation finally brought back Wilhelm's appetite and he ate, complimenting the delicious taste of the stew.

"Gretchen has packed your clothes, and I believe you will not be wearing your Prussian blue uniform?" I asked.

Wilhelm looked away. "No need, as the battle was lost and all Prussian soldiers can return home. I am sure Napoleon is now focused on his next conquest."

"Papa found some clothes that were my grandfather's. I believe they will fit you," I told him.

"Thank you. It is much appreciated," Wilhelm said.

"We shall see each other again soon." I left the room and headed toward the kitchen. My thoughts were focused on seeing the Wolf Woman again before we left. She was correct in revealing that I was pregnant, and therefore she held accountability in my eyes, but she also said that my mother would die. I had to know if she was to be believed.

Upon passing the window, I saw snow falling. We would be leaving in two days' time. Perhaps tomorrow I could ride to see the Wolf Woman and take the bottle of wine she requested. I could do nothing but pray that the Wolf Woman was wrong.

Gretchen met me in the kitchen with some hot cocoa. I drank it quickly.

"Are you feeling better, Fräulein Annaelise?"

"Yes, but it is sad to see Lieutenant Ferré leave," I said.

"He is better, is he not? He has been a good friend to you

and your family, yes?" Gretchen said. "Maybe he will come to see you at Friedensthal?"

"How can I even think of such a thing at this time?" I replied in an abrupt tone.

Gretchen's eyes grew wide. "I-I didn't mean anything by it . . . I just meant that the lieutenant is close with your Papa and—"

"That's okay," I said in a soft voice. "I'm sorry to react in such a way. I'm not feeling very well."

I tried to eat the rabbit stew while watching the snow from the kitchen window, but my stomach felt strange. I didn't know why I had reacted in such a way when Gretchen said that about Wilhelm visiting me at Friedensthal.

Just then, Wilhelm trudged across the courtyard toward the barn amidst the newly fallen snow. How strange it was to refer to him by his first name after knowing him as Lieutenant Ferré all these months. I realized something in that moment as I watched him: Wilhelm was the only living reminder of Hans. I had Hans's ring and the memory of his face, but Wilhelm and Hans had gone to military school together. They had memories that I knew nothing about. My heart ached for all of the memories I would not have with Hans.

I realized I must check on my horses. I looked for the fur coat that Maman had given me before we left Friedensthal. She intended for me to look beautiful in it, and now it was essential to keep me warm. Perhaps she was more sensible than I gave her credit for.

As I made my way to the barn, I walked in Wilhelm's foot tracks in the snow. We were walking the same path in Hans's memory. We were both going back home to our loved ones in the approaching winter and cold, and we must face everything that we lost. It was true what Papa had said: we had our future ahead of us. Perhaps we could continue a friendship in letters. But I had no time to think of that now. I had to go home to Maman.

CHAPTER 28

FAREWELL TO BLUMENTHAL

The entire staff joined us for dinner, including Albert and Gretchen, as well as Claude and Simon from the winery. Wilhelm said grace and gave thanks, saying a prayer for all of the soldiers who fought so bravely and died for the cause. Tears came to my eyes as I said a secret prayer for my unborn child. Grandmother raised a toast for the welfare of Germany, Prussia, Alsace-Lorraine, and for our safe return to Alsace.

We had a delicious meal of pheasant, potatoes, turnips, fresh bread, and cheese that complemented the special single-vineyard Riesling wine that Papa had selected. Talk varied around the table. Grandmother spoke of her concern about our safety from beggars on our journey home, including those who would come to Blumenthal in search of food. Wilhelm spoke of his family and his concern for his aging father, as well as for his sister and younger brother. His brother had an interest in their father's apothecary shop in Heidelberg, and his sister planted and oversaw the growing of the herbs. Although Wilhelm was trained in the trade, his preference was to be outdoors, which was why the winery business was of interest to him. Even in wartime and hard economic times, the masses looked to wine to ease their mental and physical stress and pain. We all rose and toasted everyone responsible for providing these essential needs. For the first time in weeks, I found a sense of relief and optimism for the future despite the bleak times we might yet face.

Later, Wilhelm and I went into the salon and sat next to the roaring fire. Even though it hurt my heart, I wanted to hear more about Hans. Wilhelm relayed how he and Hans had met when they attended a military academy in Karlsruhe. The academy was a division of the Krieg Schule Academy in Berlin.

Our conversation changed to discussions about America and the development of their government. We spoke of a future with democracy, and to my surprise, Wilhelm was quite informed about the politics and government that had developed in America. The more we spoke of the ideals of Hegel, the passion of Goethe, and the idealism set in romanticism, I was impressed with his intellect. I told him about Madame de Staël and how she'd influenced my views on more rights for women.

"I think I would love to visit America one day when this war is over. Papa and I have studied the Founding Fathers and principles that founded the New World. It is so inspiring," I said.

"I am glad to hear you are so aware of what is going on in this world," Wilhelm said with a smile.

The fire was still burning brightly. I stared into the flames, feeling grateful for its warmth. "Tell me about your life," I said.

"Well, there is not much to tell. As you know, I was born and raised outside of Heidelberg, where we have our apothecary shop. My father ran the business, and my siblings and I ran the shop when we were older. On Sundays and Mondays, the shop was closed and we would go to the family farm outside of Heidelberg. My grandfather developed the land and became a cabbage farmer. I enjoyed going there, and I started an herb garden, growing herbs for medicinal purposes. I preferred the country living and farming. I would love to develop a winery or brewery there one day."

"That sounds lovely. It takes at least three years to establish a winery with enough vines to create enough grapes for production. Perhaps start first with a brewery. My father can help you with that, I am sure," I said.

"Your father is a fine man. You are blessed to have such a doting father. I am sorry to hear of your mother's health," he said.

I swallowed the lump in my throat. "What about your mother?"

Wilhelm's eyes grew sad. "My mother passed away four years ago, and we all miss her. My father, Frederick, is an old man, and we are now helping him run the farm and the store. My sister, Gerda, is about your age or maybe a little younger. She now runs the household and cooks for us. My brother, François, is the manager of the apothecary, and I run the farm and grow the herbs. I am looking to do something new, and I have often thought about going to America when the war is over, or maybe before. I have been told that the country is now free of Britain's rule and the colonists are thriving. I could start out with an apothecary shop and then perhaps buy my own land to farm. I understand that one can purchase land for a very reasonable price there." He perked up a bit.

"That's what I heard as well. But you would leave your family behind? That could be hard, yes?" I asked.

"Well, it depends on this war and how hard we are all suffering." Wilhelm looked me in the eyes.

I looked away. "Who knows what this war will bring for all of us."

The weather had broken and the sun was shining, casting silver diamonds on the snow. I walked to the barn in the early morning to bring Wilhelm smoked trout, bread, and cheese for his journey back home to Heidelberg. When I approached the stalls, Petite Held and Excelsior greeted me with whinnies. Wilhelm was attending to Faithful Friend before his departure. He was bent over to inspect the horse's hoof.

"How is he?" I asked.

"We will make the trip, as it's only a two-day ride," he responded. He straightened up and turned to face me. There was a gleam in his eyes. "Ah, Fräulein, your coat is magnificent and will surely keep you warm on your journey home."

"This was my mother's coat. She gave it to me knowing it would be cold in the Pfalz and when we returned to Alsace." I pulled the coat tighter around me.

"Your mother sounds like a wise woman and she must love you very much."

At that moment I began to cry, and Wilhelm took a step toward me. Then he embraced me in a hug. My body stiffened, so he pulled away. He handed me a handkerchief. I used the soft fabric to dab my eyes with.

"Keep the faith," Wilhelm said. "Maybe she will recover with having you home."

"I hope so." I paused. "Thank you for all you have done . . . for being there for Hans, and for being a good friend and gentleman."

He placed a warm hand on my shoulder. "You will take care of Excelsior?"

I raised my eyebrows. "Why, yes . . . but you should take him."

"No, you will do a better job. It was Hans's horse, and you

should have him. Your uncle can use him for breeding," he said with a sincere smile.

I nodded. I handed him the food, and he packed it in the leather bag on his horse's saddle. "Faithful Friend is lucky to have you," I said, handing the kind horse an apple.

Wilhelm chuckled. "I never knew Faithful Friend liked apples."

Excelsior whinnied, sensing his war buddy's departure, and then Petite Held whinnied too.

"Oh, they sense their friend is leaving," Wilhelm said with a laugh.

"No, they just want an apple." I managed to smile.

We hugged briefly with a kiss on each cheek. Wilhelm said his goodbyes. I was grateful I had a faithful friend in Wilhelm. It was no wonder Hans loved him.

"Remember, you can visit us in Heidelberg anytime," Wilhelm said while mounting his horse.

"Of course, and the invitation is always welcome to you," I responded.

Somehow, I had a feeling that we would see each other soon.

After Wilhelm left, Papa and Albert prepared for our departure. This time, on the journey home, we would travel through Mannheim rather than Karlsruhe. Papa and I arranged to stay the night at a tavern near Mannheim since the danger of war in our area was over. Papa was instructed to deliver a very important letter and the new map of the Confederation of the Rhine to the envoy for Baron vom Stein of the Prussian government and the Minister of Trade. Although I was proud of Papa being an aide for the cause, I worried about his possible arrest by the French.

Grandmother and Gretchen were in the kitchen cooking

for us so we would have rations for the journey home. Papa and Albert loaded all of the necessary supplies and equipment that we would need for the journey, including items for Friedensthal.

While everyone was busy with preparations, I made my way out to the barn to saddle up Petite Held. I wanted to visit the Wolf Woman one more time before I left. Since Petite Held hadn't been ridden in several weeks, I knew she would be frisky, but she also would not want to leave Excelsior. I also realized it would cause concern if she were found missing. It was in my mind that the danger of falling off her could cause injury to my unborn child. Changing my mind about riding, I chose to walk to the cottage instead.

Grabbing a bottle of wine, bread, and cheese, I decided to take Grandmother's dog, Jacques, knowing he could alert me to any approaching danger. I also packed my pistol in my bag. It was a nice morning for a walk, and it would take me about an hour. I surmised a walk would do me good, especially since I would be sitting in the wagon for two days.

On my journey, I passed a Prussian regiment with wounded soldiers. My mourning grew deeper as I thought of Hans. I was sorrowful for the veterans who showed so much courage. In that moment, I saw men on the battlefield screaming as the vision flashed before my eyes, and I saw Hans's face among them. I wondered how long Hans's death would haunt me.

I stopped to give some soldiers a loaf of bread. They quickly devoured it while Jacques stood near and barked as they got closer.

"Leisel is just ahead. You will find lodging in the village," I said, worried about them stopping at Blumenthal.

Jacques and I continued on the snowy path. A hawk rose in the sky and circled the small cottage as we approached.

The Wolf Woman opened the door as I drew near. "The hawk spoke of your arrival. Come in by the fire," she beckoned.

I followed her inside. I opened my bag and handed her the wine and cheese. I felt much calmer around her even though my anticipation grew.

"Many thanks, Fräulein." She laughed, tilting her head back. Jacques growled.

"It is all right, Jacques. She's a friend," I said, pulling on his collar.

"Please sit down while I pour you some tea. So, you are with child then?" she asked as she raised her eyebrows.

"Yes, I am," I confirmed while I looked down at the floor.

"The tea helps, does it?"

"Yes, but I do not have much time today," I replied wearily.

She responded by picking up the tarot deck, shuffling it without further ado. While she laid the cards down once more, my heart was in my throat.

Pulling the Knight of Cups, she asked, "You have a new lover?"

"Wh-what? No . . . just a new friend," I replied.

She turned over the Death card. "Your mother died?" she asked.

"She is very ill and we are returning to Alsace."

"She may not live much longer," the Wolf Woman replied.

"No . . . my fiancé was killed at Jena," I explained, feeling the sadness coming over me in full force once again.

She nodded and didn't say anything. The next card was the Eight of Wands. "You will have a safe journey home," she stated confidently. Then she flipped over the Nine of Swords. "This represents a final ending or death of some sort," she explained. "It also indicates danger for you. Be very careful with others and who you tell your secret to."

I didn't realize my leg was shaking until the table began to rattle. Why had I come here? It all seemed to be bad news—death and danger.

"My child, please do not fret," she said. "The Death card doesn't only mean the freeing of one's soul. It can be the death or end of other things not living and breathing."

"What do you mean?" I asked. Tears brimmed my eyes.

"With life comes death, you see. It heralds a new beginning." She raised a bony finger. The last card was the Sun. "You will have hope for the future, perhaps with the birth of your child?" she asked.

"I hope so." I tried to smile.

"Well, this is all good. I tell you something good is coming your way." The Wolf Woman grinned.

"Yes, maybe so, but I cannot face telling my family I am with child."

"You may be surprised. They may be excited for you. A new life is good when there is so much death. However, the times are very dangerous and poverty will be everywhere. Stay close to home at Friedensthal, my dear." She reached for my hand.

"Will Napoleon be defeated?" I asked.

"Yes, and Prussia will rise again, but it will take years," she answered. "That is also shown in the card of the Sun. Trust no one and keep your eyes open." Rising from the chair, she embraced me. "Thank you, and you can tell your grandmother Liselotte that we spoke. I may need to rely on her in the thick of the winter."

"How well do you know her?" I asked.

"I know her well, my dear. How do you think she met your grandpapa?"

Smiling, I left the Wolf Woman's cabin and stepped outside where the hawk was still in sight.

CHAPTER 29

A NEW OPPORTUNITY

The next morning came too soon, and to combat the cold I wore Maman's fur coat. I held back tears as I said goodbye to my grandmother. "Thank you so much for everything. Take care of yourself and have Gretchen help you as much as possible. I will be back." A feeling came over me that this would be the last time I would see her.

She took my hands in hers. "My child, you are stronger than you know."

I said my goodbyes to Gretchen and knew I would have a strong ally if I lived here someday. "Please keep in touch and send me letters."

Gretchen hugged me and whispered in my ear, "Please take care of yourself and the baby." I was glad she was my good friend.

Papa gave Albert his final instructions and was pleased that everything was now under control with the vineyard. Jacques was barking and I bent down to kiss him goodbye. *I will miss this place. Until next time.*

Dominique and Dàrtangan pulled the wagon, and we tethered Petite Held and Excelsior to the back of it. I had my pistol close to my side. The snow had melted and the road had become muddy. Fortunately, we were not laden down with artillery and barrels of wine.

Papa and I headed on our journey. Despite the mud, we

were fortunate not to have any problems on the road for a long while. It was quiet and peaceful. But as the sun rose higher in the sky, we started to see soldiers injured and battered from the war, walking home to their loved ones. How I wished Hans were among them.

"Just look forward. Don't look back," Papa advised.

Excelsior was excitable, sensing fear and devastation from the war and the energy of the downtrodden soldiers, letting out frustrated steam through his nostrils and trotting sideways.

Upon arriving at the inn in Mannheim, Papa made his connection with General Blücher's envoy. We took a break and went inside for a cup of hot tea. It was planned some months ago that Papa would deliver maps that indicated the new provinces of the Confederation of the Rhine so the Prussians could plan for future retaliation. Discovering the barn had no vacancy, Papa decided to continue on to Heidelberg in hopes that we could stay with Wilhelm's family or at another inn. I then told Papa that Wilhelm had invited us to visit at any time. It was out of the way, but it seemed like the simplest option to take.

We were fortunate to have daylight in our favor, so we continued our journey toward our destination. Arriving at the apothecary in Heidelberg before dusk, I entered the quaint shop with wooden beams and plaster walls while Papa tended to the horses. A bright warm fire was burning in the old stone fireplace. Herbs hung from the rafters, and the shelves were stacked with small corked bottles of tincture. A young Fräulein greeted me. Her blonde hair was tied in braids and wrapped around her head. She wore a long black skirt and a white ruffled blouse which was tucked neatly into her skirt with a colorful apron to cover her clean clothes. Her eyes were bright blue, and she had a beautiful smile. I asked if the Ferré family owned this business.

"Yes, this is owned by the Ferré family. I am Gerda Ferré."

I smiled. "I am Annaelise Theiss, a friend of your brother."

"Yes, yes! Wilhelm has spoken so highly of you." Then she quieted. "I am sorry for your loss of Captain Hans."

Before I could say anything, she embraced me. I was surprised and happy to meet her.

"Wilhelm is out at our farm making much-needed repairs," Gerda explained.

"Ah, we were going to stay in Mannheim, but there was no room for the horses, so we were hoping we could stay here for the night."

"Well, of course you can stay at our farm." Gerda clapped her hands in delight.

"Thank you, Gerda," I responded with a smile.

"We will close the shop in an hour. I will tell my brother François," Gerda said. "Please sit by the fire and I will make you some tea."

"Oh, that would be wonderful. Perhaps it will help my aching head," I accepted gratefully.

"We can apply some chamomile poultices to your eyes," Gerda said. "François is delivering some herbs and will return soon."

Papa entered and was elated to meet Gerda and to explore the lovely shop. "I am so happy to meet you, Herr Theiss . . . um, I mean Count Karl," she corrected herself, blushing and curtsying respectfully.

"And you as well," he said and warmly embraced her, which was out of character for him.

François Ferré returned sooner than expected, and we were

delighted to meet him. He had brilliant red hair like his older brother. At closing, they locked up the shop. Gerda rode in the wagon with me while François led the way to the farm. The snow was falling once more, but I hardly noticed. Gerda and I continued our warm conversation.

Approaching the farm on that dark and bitter cold evening, the sight of a lit forge in the stone barn was a welcome relief. The barn was lovely, and the glow of the forge outlined the silhouette of two men working. Gerda jumped down from our wagon and ran to the barn to tell the news of our overnight stay to Wilhelm. He came running out to greet us.

"Welcome, welcome! What a wonderful surprise! Please, François, attend to the horses. But first I must greet Annaelise."

"We decided to take you up on your kind offer." I smiled through the snowflakes dusting my face.

"We are so glad you did," Wilhelm said with a large grin.

"What a beautiful barn," I remarked.

"Yes, and maybe enough space to house some wine barrels," he answered. "Please come inside the house and meet my father and brother. We will find beds for you."

The house was clean, cozy, and comfortable. The beams showed some cobwebs, and the stone fireplace was warm and inviting. Old paintings hung on the wall that showed their years of age and darkness.

Wilhelm's father, Frederick, seemed happy to meet us. He had a twinkle in his eye, gray hair with a bushy beard, and he was slightly hunched over. He bowed and reached for my hand with his twisted fingers, well-worn from years of hard labor. Then he and Papa shook hands.

"Thank you so much for taking care of my son. We are so grateful," Frederick Ferré said.

"We are so sorry to come unannounced," Papa said.

"Of course," Frederick responded. "Wilhelm has spoken highly of your family."

Gerda heated some venison stew, and Papa opened a bottle of pinot noir Cuvée Exceptionelle wine from Leisel. I broke some bread. Gerda led the blessing, and we all said prayers for our country and for those who gave their lives. We raised a toast to the Prussian cause and I felt at peace. Perhaps it was the wine or the good company from Wilhelm's family.

I was to sleep in Gerda's room and Papa would sleep by the fire. Before retiring, Wilhelm and I went to the barn to stoke the fire and check on the horses. They were all resting comfortably.

"Please sit down on the bench next to the fire. I want to speak to you about a matter of great importance. We are friends, right?" Wilhelm said.

"Of course, and why should that be doubted?" I asked, curious.

He cleared his throat, then took my hand and said in a timid manner, "Would you consider being my wife? I know it's too soon and we have not known each other for very long, but—"

I pulled my hand away. "I . . . I am overwhelmed and don't know what to say."

Wilhelm's cheeks looked red. "I was going to come to Friedensthal over Christmas and propose formally in front of your parents, you see, but first I want to even know if you would consider this."

I opened my mouth to speak, but Wilhelm cut me off. "Open your hand," he said.

I did as he asked. He placed a gold ring that held a brilliant ruby oval stone into my palm.

"This was my mother's ring. She would have wanted you to have it," Wilhelm spoke lovingly.

"It's so beautiful," I managed to say. "But I don't think I can say yes at this time."

"Please, Annaelise. I know your heart belongs to Hans and always will. But we can learn to grow together and care for one another—"

"I am with child . . . Hans's child," I blurted.

Wilhelm looked like the air had been knocked out of him. His shoulders slumped and he let out a long breath.

"Hans didn't know. I only just found out, and then I received word that he . . ."

Wilhelm took my hands in his. "It's okay . . . it will all be okay." He smiled warmly. "This is all the more reason to marry. I know your father would be pleased. I can come and meet your mother and uncle as well, and I know they will be pleased. We could live at Blumenthal. I am interested in becoming a winemaker. I never was interested in the apothecary. We could have a new life—"

"Wait! This all too much," I said in a raised tone. "Please understand, I am still grieving over Hans, and my mother is dying. Don't you see that I have to consider my baby?"

"Of course, my apologies." Wilhelm nodded. "I was getting ahead of myself. I just want you to consider it for now. It is such a blessing that you have come to our home now."

I felt slightly dizzy from all of this talk. "I just—"

"There is no need to say any more. But I will say this: I would be an honorable husband to you and your child."

Suddenly, the side door of the barn shut, and I jumped at the noise. *Someone must have been listening to our conversation!*

"We must go inside," Wilhelm said. "They are looking for us to have some desserts."

I stood up. "Thank you, Wilhelm. I will consider your offer."

He slid the ring onto my finger and it fit perfectly. I slowly took off the ring and placed it in his hand. "It is as beautiful as your heart," I said.

The snow was coming down harder as we made our way back to the brightly lit house. We all enjoyed the apple strudel that Gerda had prepared with some warm brandy by the fire. I was surprised that Papa was so engaged in conversation. Thankfully, there was no mention of the proposal. We all retired for the evening. I slept in Gerda's room, and we talked until my eyes were heavy and I felt at peace. Before I drifted off, my thoughts returned to the possibility of marrying Wilhelm and living on his family's estate.

If we lived here, my life here would be modest. I certainly could provide the teaching for the child that Uncle Gustave and Papa had provided for me. I could raise horses, and perhaps in time we could afford servants. Only in the back of my mind did I briefly compare it to the promise of the kind of life Hans would have given me. But I really wanted to live at Blumenthal—my home—and take care of my grandmother. I wanted Hans's and my child to grow up with the memories that I had as a young girl, and I knew Hans would want the same. Then Wilhelm could work for the winery and be the distributer and sale of the wine. Could I leave Friedensthal and Alsace? Would I miss it? Once again, everything felt confusing, and I let my eyelids close in the hopes that Hans would meet me in my dreams.

I arose early and went downstairs where Papa met me with some tea before the others were up.

"Annaelise, I must speak to you in the barn," he spoke firmly.

I shivered. "The snows are deep and it is cold."

"Come put on your shoes and coat and we will walk out there," he insisted.

We took the tea out with us and trudged through the snow. The horses whinnied and it was time for their breakfast.

"Sit down. We must talk." He stoked the fire while putting a log on the dying embers. "I overheard your conversation with Wilhelm last evening, and I know you are with child." He turned to me. "How could you? You are going to disgrace our family," he said in a harsh tone. "I suppose it is all my fault . . . setting you up with the captain . . ."

I felt angry at my father's accusations. "Papa, I'm sorry, but I am a woman now, and I can do as I please. I truly loved Hans, and the child will make me think of him always."

Papa was quiet for a moment. Then he said, "Well, you cannot disgrace our families, so you must marry Wilhelm. He will take good care of you both. You both loved Hans, and it is the right thing to do. You can live at Blumenthal with your grandmother, and she can help you with the child while Wilhelm will work for the winery. It is perfect. Can't you see?"

"But I do not love him!" I shouted. "He is a kind man, but I do not love him."

"You will learn to love him! He is honorable and will be perfect in our family. Let's face it: the days of balls and elegant living is over for a while. We are at war! It is survival time, Annaelise! You must think of the future of this family and the future of your child."

I had never been so angry with Papa. Maybe it was because I knew he was speaking the truth. Marrying Wilhelm was a considerable option. In a few months' time, my belly would be swollen, and I needed to think about my child's needs before my own.

Suddenly, there was a knock on the door and Wilhelm walked into the barn.

"Oh . . . um . . . I am wrong to intrude at a time like this; however, the horses must be fed and I do not think it is advisable to be on the roads today." Wilhelm barely looked at me. I knew he had overheard our conversation.

"Yes, of course. The horses need tending to. My daughter and I were just chatting about our journey," Papa said.

"I am ashamed to admit that I overheard your conversation," Wilhelm said, and he looked at me this time. "I will not force Annaelise in her decision; however, I do love her with all my heart. I will wait for her in earnest."

Papa hesitated and then walked over and embraced him. "You have my blessing, and I could not think of a finer man than you." They shook hands and then looked at me.

I stood up quickly and said, "I will let you know my decision by Christmas." Then I ran from the barn. The icy-cold air burned my cheeks. I just wanted to get away from it all.

When I got back to the house, I was greeted by Gerda, who had breakfast waiting. I was flustered and told her that I must go upstairs and change into something suitable. I didn't wait for her answer as I went up the stairs.

I entered the bedroom and closed the door. I stuffed my handkerchief into my mouth to stifle the cry that was rising in my throat. It wasn't that I didn't care for Wilhelm. He was a good man. But I missed Hans so much, and I was angry that he had been taken from this Earth. We would never grow old together. Our child would never know how his voice sounded. These thoughts were enough to send me into a tailspin, but I had to pull myself together. I dried my eyes and braided my wet hair that was dampened from the falling snow.

I can do this. I must be strong.

When I went back downstairs for breakfast, the scent of coffee filled my nostrils. Oh, how wonderful! It was a long time since we'd had coffee. Papa and Wilhelm entered, and we all sat down to a glorious breakfast. I was famished. Ham, egg soufflé, bratwurst, and trout with apple strudel—the food was delicious. The plan was to stay snowed in another night. The men would work in the barn repairing tools and equipment and the women would be sewing inside by the fire.

The day passed quickly. I was certainly relieved I was not on the road or in a dark, dreary tavern. As we sat by the fire, we talked of many things, and I was comforted by our conversations. The snow stopped and the sun came out later that afternoon. I was glad because I so wanted to see Maman and get home to Friedensthal.

Gerda and I started the oven fire early and roasted a pork loin and cabbage to make sauerbraten by adding potatoes, carrots, and parsnips. Papa brought another bottle of wine from the wagon. It was a joyous time, and I found myself laughing for a change. It was still awkward to make eye contact with Wilhelm.

After supper, Wilhelm took me outside while the sun was setting over the back of the house. "My love is true, Annaelise. And I will wait for your answer before Christmas. I will come and honor your family with my proposal again."

I took Wilhelm's hand and gently embraced him. "Thank you. This is what Hans would have wanted." I knew those words to be true.

CHAPTER 30

RETURN TO FRIEDENSTHAL

The next morning, after Papa and I said our goodbyes, we made our way home. It was heart-wrenching to see so many German soldiers on the road. Papa noticed the anger spring up in me. It was devastating to see the destruction that Napoleon had caused. I decided to ride Excelsior while Petite Held was tethered to the wagon. Excelsior was feeling the sadness, so I remained calm and talked to him to ease his nerves. What a magnificent horse.

"Remain calm, my dear, and be strong for your mother," Papa cautioned.

Fortunately, our journey was uneventful. We made our way south through the town of Bruchsal and other small villages that looked peaceful and lovely with no evidence of being war torn and ravaged.

While we proceeded down our road to Friedensthal, Hansel and Gretel came running from the manor house to greet us. When I bent down, they licked my face, pawing mud on Maman's fur coat. I ran to the house where Giselle met me at the door.

"Welcome home, Mademoiselle Annaelise. Your mother is in her room. Please be prepared to meet her. She has been very ill," Giselle warned.

Quickly removing my fur coat and handing it to Giselle, I ran up the stairs. Before entering Maman's room, I straightened my hair and dress and took a deep breath. It had been two months since I had last seen her. Would she be able to tell that I was a changed woman? That I was with child? That my heart was broken?

Maman was asleep. I walked slowly to her bed, reaching for her hand. It was shocking to see the color gone from her lips and cheeks and her hair grayer than before. Papa came into the room and moved to the opposite side of the bed to hold her other hand. Maman slowly opened her eyes and smiled.

"My family . . . my family is here. God bless you. I missed you so," she said in a shallow voice.

Giselle offered hot tea. After setting the tea down, Papa gently lifted Maman to a seated position. It was devastating to see her in this condition, and it was all I could do to hold back the tears.

"How was the Pfalz?" she asked wearily.

"All is well there," answered Papa, squeezing her hand tenderly. "We are here for you now, *mein schatz*, my love. Albert will help with the winery there, and we are grateful to have him at Blumenthal. I will relay that good news to Richard."

Maman then looked at me. "Why, Annaelise, you have a glow about you! You must be in love, *n'est-ce pas?*" She smiled weakly.

I didn't say anything. I couldn't find any words.

Maman fell into a cough fit.

"Please have some tea," I urged.

Giselle came over and held the teacup to Maman's lips. She took a small sip, which seemed to ease her cough.

"We are here and will not leave your side, Maman," I promised.

"I want to hear all about your time away." She squeezed my hand.

"You will, Maman, at dinnertime," I replied.

As she drifted back to sleep, Uncle Gustave entered and motioned for us to follow him down the stairs. Papa continued on ahead. My uncle stopped and sharply turned to me. His eyes looked tired.

"Please tell me what happened," he said.

"The Battle of Jena was a terrible loss for the Prussian Army. Hans was killed in battle," I managed to choke out. I then remembered that Papa instructed me to not talk about my relationship with Hans. Not a word that would indicate our alliance was with the Prussian forces against Napoleon. I controlled my tears enough to ask what the doctors said about Maman.

"Your mother is dying, Annaelise, and thank God you came when you did. You should have been here sooner," he admonished me.

I gritted my teeth. "We arrived as soon as we could. The war and the rule of an unsure dictatorship have made the postal service unreliable. What has happened to our cousin, the Duke of Enghien? Wasn't he considered to be the Prince of Condé?"

"He was accused of making secret visits to Strasbourg, and the House of Conde was a branch of the House of Bourbon. Napoleon decided the duke was plotting against him and the new French regime and ordered a small detachment to arrest him." He leaned in closer. I could smell the alcohol on his breath. "Apparently, the duke's secret visits were to his mistress and not for plotting against the regime. The police chief of Strasbourg, Chief Joseph Fouché, did not even know the duke was under investigation. It was Napoleon's brother-in-law, Joachim Murat, who had him arrested. The duke was then taken to Paris. He was arrested still in his hunting clothes with his dog at his side. Both the duke and the dog were shot.

This was all a pretense to assure the public that Napoleon's anti-aristocratic sentiments still held true. I am horrified and outraged, and so is your mother. This is what caused her to be ill! How can we go about our lives like this?"

"This is inconceivable!" I said angrily. "We received a letter from Murat stating that Napoleon accused him of plotting with the British to overthrow him. All lies, I tell you!"

Just then, Papa shouted, "Annaelise, come to the kitchen at once!"

I quickly left my uncle, grateful for the interruption. Upon entering the kitchen, Papa ordered me to sit down as he closed the doors and asked the cooks to leave. With his hand on the mantle, he glared down at me.

"You must bear in mind we are spies for the Prussian and German cause, as well as Alsace, yes?" Papa whispered.

I nodded.

"Then you must control your anger. Your uncle, despite his outrage over the injustice regarding your cousin, wants only to be a part of Napoleon's cause and the new regime. His main interest is to sell the horses to the handsome French officers. Do you understand?"

"Yes, Papa," I demurred.

"Then you will stay with your mother at this time. Remember your condition and the future. You must not outwardly show emotion for Hans, and do not tell anyone you are carrying his child, not even Giselle or Marie. In fact, you are forbidden to see Marie. We are fighting for the new cause, and Napoleon will be overthrown or beaten in battle. You will have a bright future in Heidelberg, Blumenthal, and Friedensthal after Napoleon's defeat. You will have all of these estates to pass on to your children. So be disciplined and be brave. Understood?" Papa spoke sharply.

I felt weak. "Oh my God, of course, of course!" I said.

What was I thinking? I had been gone too long and had forgotten my place. Papa was right: I did have a future, and our wineries had a future in the Pfalz. I knew we would overcome Napoleon's cruel dictatorship and one day we would be free.

CHAPTER 31

THE LAST CHRISTMAS

Maman grew weaker by the day. I sat in her room listening to her speak of her happy childhood memories in Obernai at Adlershof when she left Paris with my uncle. She asked about Hans while Papa was in the room with us. Papa told her of his tragic death, holding her hand gently. She could only respond, "He died for the French cause. He was so handsome and brave. I am so sorry for you, Annaelise. Have courage, my love."

Sadness overwhelmed me. My mother was dying, and I was grieving the loss of my true love. I didn't know how to deal with my emotions. My thoughts ran wild about Wilhelm's proposal. I was unwed with a baby growing in my belly. I couldn't bring shame to my family. My decision was then made. I would marry Wilhelm.

A weight had been lifted. I could love Wilhelm. He was a kind, honest man, and he would be the perfect father for my child. We could live in Heidelberg for a while and then move in the spring to Blumenthal and he could expand the winery. I could educate my child with all of Papa's teachings. We could be self-sufficient there, and with any luck, Excelsior could sire foals from Petite Held. It all started to make sense. *This is what Hans would have wanted.* I wrote to Wilhelm to request fabric from Heidelberg. More importantly, however, I informed him that I accepted his proposal. I knew it was the right thing to do.

Papa had suggested we tell Maman the news with an official engagement celebration at Christmas. We thought this would give Maman more peace of mind and something to look forward to. This proved to be a wise decision, and she became hopeful. Her optimism and excitement for planning a wedding made it possible for her to sit up in the bed for longer periods of time and to walk more. Her enthusiasm actually gave me hope for a future as well.

It was only two weeks to Christmas, and I became occupied with the requisite preparations. Papa was busy slaughtering a hog as well as one of our turkeys. Uncle Gustave and Richard selected the wines and planned the Christmas dinner. Giselle was busy baking bread and cakes. We were able to keep our food fresh by utilizing the cool condition in the springhouse. I was at peace while riding on Petite Held through the forest in search of greenery for the house, including a Christmas tree. I received a letter from Wilhelm announcing his arrival on Christmas Eve with his sister Gerda. The preparations gave us hope and joy. Even in the face of death, new life springs eternal, as represented by the birth of our Lord.

My appetite had returned and my condition became harder to conceal. I wore coats and long shawls to hide my growing belly. I needed to sew some new dresses. Fortunately, the classical empire waistline style, still in fashion, allowed me some more time before my condition became obvious. I managed to find some old woolen blankets that I fashioned into long shawls. I also took the liberty to look in Maman's closet, requisitioning the dresses that were too large for her shrinking body.

As if overnight, food tasted much better and, despite my worries, I was grateful I could share this special time with Maman for her last Christmas.

On the day before Christmas Eve, we were surprised by the

early arrival of Wilhelm and Gerda late in the evening. I was truly excited. Papa accompanied me outside to greet them just as large snowflakes began to fall and land softly on the ground.

"What a nice surprise!" exclaimed Papa.

I rushed from the door without my coat. Wilhelm and Gerda stepped off the cart and we exchanged embraces of warmth and elation. We were happy, and the cloud of death and despair was momentarily lifted.

Christmas Eve was joyous with all of the activities and preparations. Papa and Richard brought the tree into the salon. Popcorn was cooked, eaten, and also made into a garland to adorn the tree. Gerda and I made ornaments from goose feathers, red silk, and velvet ribbons that added the finishing touches. I had sewn a dress for Gerda and a shawl for Maman. I had knitted a woolen scarf for Wilhelm, Papa, and Uncle Gustave. All the presents were neatly nestled under the tree.

Maman managed to sit at the table, although with great difficulty, but her spirit and will were strong. I sat next to her, assisting her with eating. She made apologies for her appearance, but then she cried as the toast and official announcement of our engagement were made. Wilhelm made a show of presenting me with the ring with the ruby stone, and another round of congratulations and toasts was exchanged.

We enjoyed the roast of wild boar, venison, potatoes, turnips, and carrots for our dinner. We drank a Tokay Vendange Tardive wine, which enhanced the food wonderfully. After we ate, we exchanged gifts and included the staff for dessert in the salon. Giselle had made a delicious chocolate cake, which we enjoyed with a Crémant d'Alsace sparkling wine. We reveled in the joy of life and the reality of its fleeting preciousness that was apparent to us all even in these hard times.

Early the next day, Giselle awakened me. She had cooked

another elaborate breakfast. Wilhelm and Gerda were preparing to leave. While splashing water over my face, I suddenly felt the baby kick. I quickly sat down and looked at my belly. There was another kick. I gasped and then burst into tears. How amazing to have this life growing inside of me. A piece of Hans. I was filled with an unquestionable joy over the life I would bring into the world.

After breakfast, I went to the stable with Wilhelm. When we approached the barn, Excelsior whinnied, somehow sensing his battle companion, Faithful Friend, was leaving. Entering the stall, Wilhelm reached forward and, for the first time, drew me close to kiss my lips. His bold approach spoke to me of his joy and true intention of loyalty. But there was no passion in the kiss. As I looked up at his smiling face, I softened. He was a kind man, and I loved him for his companionship, and I knew I could grow to love him the way that he loved me. I was grateful that he would be the father of my child. I had to really believe that we could be happy together. I had to trust that Hans would want this for me and his child.

"I cannot wait until we wed, my love," he said as he looked deeply into my eyes. "I was speaking with your father, and we both agreed that the wedding should take place in the spring before the baby is born."

"Yes, I agree," I said. A woman giving birth out of wedlock would bring shame upon the family. "Let's get married in May. It's my favorite month."

"As you wish, my love."

"I felt the baby kick this morning," I said.

Wilhelm's eyes widened. "I know Hans would be proud." Then he pulled away and sat on a bale of hay. He ran his fingers through his red hair.

"Is everything all right?" I asked.

"Oh yes, everything is fine. It's just . . ." He paused a moment, then said, "I love you, Annaelise. And I love Hans. He was like a brother to me. But it's moments like this when I'm reminded that you and he were in love, and that you were supposed to get married and start your life with him and your child."

I sighed. Everything he said was true. I looked off into the distance, my eyes glazing over. A feeling of guilt washed over me. Wilhelm was a good, caring man, and he would make a great husband, but I wished Hans were here sitting next to me having this conversation.

"You're right," I said. "Hans and I were supposed to have a family and spend our lives together." I turned to him. "But that didn't happen. Hans was taken from this world unjustly. But I am sitting here now next to you, living and breathing with Hans's child growing in my womb. And that is what God wanted."

Wilhelm took my hand in his. "I promise to be everything I can for you and Hans's child."

I managed a smile. "This is our child now. I will join you and your family."

"Thank you for the privilege of becoming a father to Hans's child, my dear friend."

"Thank you for a future," I said, "but you must promise me this." I took a deep breath. "Please do not go into battle. You are the head of two households now. You will have a wife, a sister, and a child, as well as a family business. Your father needs you too."

Wilhelm nodded. His hazel eyes beamed joy and reflected the promise for passion and happiness. "Yes, and please don't worry. My brother is of an age where he will be the soldier in the family."

As we embraced once more, I heard footsteps and a door slam, and I jumped back.

Someone was eavesdropping. I had déjà vu of when Wilhelm had overheard me and Papa talking. My heart raced. Who could it have been? Then it felt like my world was caving in. *Uncle Gustave.* He was always so nosy. My throat felt tight. Did he hear me talking about Hans's child?

"I have to head inside now," I said, and raced out of the barn into the cold morning.

CHAPTER 32

AN EAGLE'S CRY

Uncle Gustave met me at the door. His eyes were blazing, but I couldn't tell if it was from anger, accusation, or something else.

"Come quickly now. Your mother is asking for you. Richard has gone to find the doctor."

I dashed up the stairs and entered the room. Papa was sitting next to Maman with tears in his eyes. I approached her and she held out her hand to me, trembling. Taking her frail hand in mine, I sobbed uncontrollably. "Please, Maman, don't leave me," I whispered.

While waiting for Dr. Frank to arrive, I spoke to her about all the happy memories she had in her lifetime. "Remember the happy times you had at Versailles when you were a child?"

She would smile and then drift back into her dream world.

I continued to tell her stories about the happy times we had when I was a young girl. I talked about the beautiful autumn days when we were harvesting the grapes. The fun of going to Adlershof and our walks together. Then I remembered the ball in Strasbourg, and I cried not only from losing her, but Hans as well. I would treasure that memory for the rest of my life.

Maman would fade in and out and occasionally smile, and somehow I knew she heard me.

Dr. Frank came from Kehl and we backed away from her bed. He felt her forehead for fever and checked her heartbeat.

Then he took a step back and looked at us. He had a sad look on his face.

"Her heart is going. It's time to just let her go in peace," he said.

Papa came close and held her hand. She looked up at him and whispered in French, "*Mon amour, mon amie, je t'aime.* My love, my friend, I love you."

"As I have loved you," Papa said, wiping his tears.

Uncle Gustave came forward, bent over, and kissed Maman's cheek and hand. "I just don't know what I will do without you, sister. We have been so close." He cried into his handkerchief.

Giselle was not able to speak as she was crying so much. Isabelle approached Maman's bedside and said, "We have had so many good years together. I love you, Louisa."

I was having trouble speaking. It was as if something had clamped my tongue down. I knew these were Maman's last moments on Earth, and I needed to say something more. Tears blurred my vision and mucus dribbled down my nose into my mouth. "Please . . ." I managed to say. "I love you, Maman."

Suddenly, Maman opened her eyes and looked at me. "My beautiful Annaelise. Always so sensitive and strong. You are the future for freedom, faith, and fortitude, beautiful one. Shine your light."

Then Maman exhaled, and her grasp went limp.

I closed my eyes and prayed for her. I didn't know what else to do. When I opened my eyes, I looked over at Papa. His face was crumpled in anguish. He gently closed Maman's eyes. She looked so peaceful. I touched her cheek. It was still warm.

Perhaps feeling he had lost his very last ally of his previous life in Paris and Versailles, Uncle Gustave didn't handle his sister's passing graciously. Over the next several days, he was despondent, drunk, and angry. Papa and I took the time to quickly plan the funeral. The Wolf Woman had again been correct in her predictions. I went to our small chapel and prayed for strength and courage.

We held the funeral in our family cemetery on December thirty-first. Richard and Henri, joined with surrounding neighbors, had dug the grave before the cold, bitter weather set in for the anticipation of Maman's imminent death. Fortunately, the cold weather was in our favor for Maman's preservation.

Isabelle managed to dress Maman in her finest clothes. I could not look at Maman except for the night of the wake. She looked small and fragile, but surprisingly sweet, as if she were finally resting in her silk dress, finished with the weariness of the world. Several of our staff residents and neighbors came to pay Maman their last respects. Uncle Gustave had continued to drink but managed to hold off on drinking for the wake, showing up with dark circles under his puffy eyes and a stiff manner as if holding himself together by will alone. Being the matriarch of the family now, I made great efforts to greet everyone with calmness and contained sorrow.

We had a visitor I did not immediately recognize. She was the wife of the Duke of Enghien, Charlotte Louise. I expressed my sympathy over the tragedy of her losing her husband. His horrific death had taken its toll on her; she looked significantly older than when I last saw her at the ball when she was so youthful and vivacious.

The darkness of winter, the war, and death were overwhelming. Our priest came, and I had never seen him look so distraught. Candles were lit throughout the house. Papa was strong, and I knew I had to be as well. A stranger came and was introduced to me simply as "Papa's old friend." He was dressed in black and had sunken eyes and a long gray beard. They left the salon and walked into the kitchen. Discreetly following them, I stopped outside the slightly open door and heard the quick conversation as the man handed Papa a letter. Then the man went out the back door. Papa put the letter into his pocket upon my passing the kitchen. I knew, of course, this had to do with espionage and the war effort. Papa looked even more distressed. I just wanted to have more wine. *If only Grandmother, Wilhelm, and Gerda were with me during this horrific time.*

The next day the snow began to fall as we made our way to the family cemetery. Excelsior drove the open wagon with the casket, his black coat stark against the snow. He somehow sensed death again, so I chose to walk close to him to calm him down, lending my strength to his restless being. Apart from breathing a heavy white mist through his nostrils, he stayed brave and strong. I was warm in Maman's thick fur coat. Somehow, I sensed her looking down on me with a smile. The wind began to blow as the icy hand of death gripped our hearts and shook our souls. I cried while Isabelle and I hugged each other.

The cemetery was on a knoll overlooking the Rhine. When the casket was lowered into the ground, a magnificent eagle cried over us as if to say, "Be strong, have courage. She is at peace."

CHAPTER 33

DARKNESS DESCENDS

The few weeks of winter were quiet and cold. Papa informed us that he was going away to Karlsruhe to attend a wine merchants' gathering, but I knew his true intentions had to do with the letter he received from the bearded man. I had confronted Papa and asked if he was going away for war business, which he confirmed. "Annaelise, that's all you need to know."

Exhaustion from the last several months of intense drama took its toll on my weary soul, and I needed to rest for the baby's sake. Fortunately, January in the new year of 1807 was off to a quiet start.

Daily, I found myself looking for Wilhelm's letters, but none came. I was somewhat encouraged because no other household letters arrived either, which was common during this time. How I wished I could see Grandmother or even visit the Wolf Woman, but I told myself it was a good time for me to heal my wounds and prepare myself for my new life. The baby was kicking more, and my pregnancy was becoming more obvious. It was lonely without Maman, and I wished to have her at my side in planning my wedding. My heart ached. I missed my mother and Hans. Sometimes I wondered if I would ever be the same.

Papa took his time returning from his trip to Karlsruhe. It was lonely in the house, and the harsh January cold had set in.

Uncle Gustave continued to drink, and his behavior became all the more hostile. I avoided him as much as possible. Finally, toward the end of January, a letter came from Papa stating his return trip was detained another week. I mostly slept and had dreams of war with battles and cannon fire. Hans came to me in a dream and said, "Take care of yourself and our child. Wilhelm will come for you."

One early cold and dark morning, I woke up from a dream, sweating and panting. Unable to return to sleep and also with an intense hunger that seemed to be a part of me these days, I went down to the kitchen for some hot tea and bread. Uncle Gustave was sitting in front of the kitchen fire. He was very drunk, swaying slightly as he took another slug from a wine bottle. I decided to return to my room, but he turned to face me before I could do so.

"Ah, Annaelise, my dear niece. What brings you here so early? Having trouble sleeping?" he said. His eyes were bloodshot, and his speech was slurred.

"Yes, Uncle, I'm a bit parched. I shall be retiring after I have some water to drink." I quickly scurried over to the basin, realizing I would not have time to make myself some tea. I needed to get away from him as quickly as I could. I grabbed some bread and water and moved to return to my room.

"I see the winter has been treating you kindly." His eyes raked over my body, and I suddenly felt self-conscious of my growing belly under my nightshirt. "While the peasants starve in the streets, you are getting plump. Are you the next Marie Antoinette, eating all the cake? Be careful, my dear, or those starving peasant traitors will have your head."

I glared at him. My cheeks burned. *He knows.* I tried my best to cover my stomach. "You're tired, Uncle. I shall go."

As I turned to leave, Uncle Gustave leapt out of the chair

and lunged toward me. A pot fell off the table and hit the floor, making a loud clattering sound. He gripped my arm tightly and spun me around to face him.

"Are you looking for your lover?" he asked. He had an evil grin on his face. "I know the secret you share with Captain Roster and Lieutenant Ferré. You are spying against the French cause. Maman would have been so disappointed in you. I know your secret that you share with Papa and Wilhelm. You are having Hans's baby. I know everything that goes on in this house!"

I ripped my arm out of his grasp. "How dare you!" I shouted.

He stumbled forward, staggering. I dashed out of the kitchen and hurried away. Once in my room, I locked the door and sought to find my pistol. While searching, I heard Uncle Gustave approach the door.

Bang, bang, bang he pounded on the door.

"Let me in, Annaelise! I won't hurt you," Uncle Gustave said.

My heart was in my throat. In a dizzy stupor, I rummaged through my things. I wasn't thinking straight. Where had I put the pistol Papa had given me?

"Annaelise my niece . . . Annaelise my niece . . ." my uncle chanted in a singsong voice as he pounded on the door. It sent a chill down my spine.

I rummaged through my chest of drawers opposite to my bed and located the pistol in the top drawer underneath some clothes.

Suddenly, the banging stopped. Everything went quiet. I was frozen in place, not sure what to do. Had he gone? I took a step toward the door. Then I heard clattering and the door flung open. Uncle Gustave was standing there with a maniacal look on his face.

"Tsk-tsk, my dear," he said as he held up a key. "We don't lock doors in this house. But if we do, there's always a key."

"Leave me alone or I will shoot you!" I shouted. I held up the pistol and aimed it at him.

Uncle Gustave's face contorted. "Let me tell you a little secret, Annaelise. I have been following you. I have heard your conversation with Wilhelm in the barn. I've seen the letters from your dead lover. You're a German whore. I know you laid with Captain Roster, who was a spy. You miserable traitor. I will punish you and your child!"

He raced toward me, grabbed my shoulders, and threw me down onto the mattress. The pistol fell from my hand and landed on the floor just under the bed. He grabbed my wrists with one hand while dropping his breeches with the other hand. He then raised my dress, but the movements unbalanced him in his drunken state, and I managed to kick him to the floor. I leapt off the bed and reached for the gun. In his inebriated stupor, Uncle Gustave took no notice of the gun and lowered his head to tackle me by the waist, and I fell to the hard floor. The wind was knocked out of me for a moment, and I gasped for air.

But this time I kept hold of the weapon, and as he rose above me, I yelled, "Get off me, you devil!"

I fired the pistol into his left shoulder.

Uncle Gustave screamed in pain and went flying backward, hitting the floor hard and slamming the back of his head on the dresser. He groaned in pain.

I got up. The room was spinning for a moment, and I held the bedpost for support. Gustave was lying on the floor, writhing in agony. Blood pooled around him.

"You bitch!" he shouted.

I ran past him, but he grabbed my ankle. I kicked and freed myself, then left my uncle lying bleeding on the floor. I raced as fast as I could down the hall and descended the stairs to Richard's room.

"Richard, please help," I yelled, beating my fist on his door.

Richard quickly opened the door. "What has happened, Annaelise?" he asked hoarsely.

"My uncle . . . he attacked me, and I grabbed my gun—"

Richard's eyes grew wide, and he abruptly cut me off. "Stay here," he said in a low voice. I was trembling in fear as I watched him run up the stairs.

Isabelle and Giselle had been awakened by all the noise and met me by Richard's door. "Mademoiselle, are you ill?" asked Isabelle in surprise.

"It is too horrible to speak about," I said.

"Let's go to the kitchen and make some tea," Giselle offered.

A few moments later, Richard yelled down the stairs to the servants' floor, "Get Henri and the others from the winery. We need Henri to ride quickly and find Dr. Frank."

Giselle went out into the bitter cold to retrieve Henri from the winery. Isabelle led me to the kitchen, holding me as I sobbed uncontrollably. I sat in one of the chairs. I couldn't stop my body from shaking.

Suddenly, Richard and Giselle entered the room with Uncle Gustave. They were helping him walk. Gustave was pale and sweat dotted his brow. He didn't seem to have any life in him. Richard managed to hoist him onto the kitchen table. My uncle passed out. Horrified, I became aware of the injury I had inflicted upon him. Would he die? *Oh my God, I was only trying to protect my child.* Distraught by my thinking, Isabelle led me away and I began to tell her everything. She assured me it was an accident.

"I never meant to fire . . . the gun just went off in the struggle . . ."

Dr. Frank came as the sun was coming up. He removed the bullet and said it had penetrated the top of the scapula and broken Uncle Gustave's collarbone. Fortunately, it wasn't close to an artery. He was to rest and have no alcohol. He would have to be watched for the next few weeks. *If only Papa were here.* The snows had set in deep. I was stuck here with no way out. How much longer could I endure this agony?

CHAPTER 34

AN UNWANTED JOURNEY
TO COLMAR

A week after the shooting incident, Uncle Gustave's condition began to improve. He continued to take his meals in his room. His bedchamber was on the opposite side of the house, and it was a great relief that I didn't have to see him.

I became larger and my pregnancy became noticeable. I took long walks in the snow and my appetite increased. I also found solace in the barn with Petite Held and Excelsior. Being so lonely, I spoke softly as I encouraged them of the return of spring as well as our new life in Heidelberg with Wilhelm's family and our reunion with Faithful Friend. I longed to ride and to see Marie. We kept in touch by letters, yet she knew nothing of Hans and the baby—only the wedding in May.

A letter arrived from Papa saying he would return home by February twentieth. He knew nothing about Uncle Gustave and the attack he'd made toward me and my child. Richard and I decided it was best to tell him of this horrific encounter in person. I was relieved that Wilhelm's letters arrived, and they assured me of his intention to wed me and be a father to my child.

One morning while walking along the road, I heard in the distance what sounded like a cavalry wagon. I turned and saw four French soldiers flanking the wagon, two on foot and two mounted, and they were all armed. I moved off to the side of the road for them to pass. Instead, they stopped and surrounded me.

"Annaelise Theiss, you are wanted for treason against Napoleon while assisting a spy in the Prussian government, as well as attempted murder of the French citizen Gustave Guerlain."

I felt faint, but I had to maintain my composure. *Stay calm, Annaelise. Choose your words carefully.* I smiled sweetly. "Oh, believe me, good sirs, but this is a misunderstanding. Monsieur Guerlain is my uncle, and he attacked me and tried to take advantage of me—"

"Mademoiselle, we have it under great authority that you are to be arrested for treason." The soldier stared at me with his piercing dark eyes. I squirmed under his gaze. Then two soldiers stepped toward me, and frightened, I backed away.

I started to panic. "Please, good sir, this is a misunderstanding! I am with child!"

The soldiers grabbed my arms.

"You cannot take me!" I screamed. "Gustave Guerlain lied about me being a spy! I am faithful to Napoleon! Ask the emperor yourself!"

But my cries fell on deaf ears. I was seized and lifted into the wagon with a gag in my mouth and my hands tied behind my back. I cried uncontrollably. The ride in the wagon was hours long. There was only a small window in the back of the wagon where I was seated to take in the views. I needed to see where we were going. The scenery was familiar, and I could soon tell we were approaching Strasbourg. While approaching the bridge into France, I heard one of the mounted guards announce, "We have a prisoner. We are taking her to the prison in Colmar."

I had been to Colmar with Papa when he had business with

other wine merchants in the old city. I remembered the canals and that it was a center for tanning leather. Drawing closer to the city, the familiar smells of tanning yards brought back memories. Papa had a good reputation as a brewer and wine merchant; perhaps this would be favorable in granting my release. Feeling hopeful, I realized Gustave's background in a court hearing could be tarnished as a former Bourbon. Many people thought the Duke of Enghien, a Bourbon, was wrongly executed, but in the eyes of Napoleon's government, the duke was rightly executed. Perhaps Uncle Gustave's character would be in question too.

As we continued on, I recognized the streets from my visits with Papa when I was a child. Storks nested in the chimneys, and I remembered fairy tales about how these birds represented fertility and birth. How strange it was to be returning here when I was with child. The familiarity brought me some comfort in the hopes that the birth would be happy with a fairy-tale ending.

Tears formed in my eyes. Would I see my family again? How could this be happening? I thought about Wilhelm's ruby ring on my finger and wondered if I would ever see him again. Once my hands were untied, the first thing I would do would be to take the ring off and hide it in the secret pocket Maman had sewn into the coat.

We reached the prison. Its imposing height backed up against the canal. I always thought it looked forbidden, and now I knew why. The roofline was steep and went straight down to a balcony surrounded with steel pickets and patrolling guards. When exiting the wagon, I felt sore, exhausted, and hungry. The guards removed the ropes that had irritated my wrists. They'd used brutish force and hurt my hands and arms. Then they pushed me forward and forced me into a small room.

The warden was a thin man with leathery skin and thin lips

that he pressed together in dislike. He leaned over his desk and wasted no time in giving me my verdict.

"Annaelise Theiss, you are accused of being a traitor to the French government and for assisting a spy from Prussia. You made contact with a former French citizen, Captain Hans Roster, who posed as a French officer. He, however, was serving the Prussian army as a spy. You are also accused of attempted murder of a French citizen, your uncle, Monsieur Gustave Guerlain."

"This is a misunderstanding! My child—"

"You are with child?" he asked. Without waiting for an answer, he nodded to the guard.

One guard locked me in his arms while another guard lifted my dress to expose my belly. The warden nodded again, and the guard let go of my dress. I felt ashamed and humiliated.

"You will remain here until your child is born," the warden said. "Then you will be executed for these crimes."

"No, no," I cried. "I was innocent in the knowledge of Captain Hans Roster's identity, and I was attacked by my uncle who tried to defile me. I used the gun in defense. The gun exploded into his shoulder when he tackled me. I never intended to shoot him in advance. Please, I must have a fair trial. My father is an upstanding citizen, and my family has a good reputation in Alsace. We have hosted Napoleon at our home, had a reception for Empress Joséphine, and we have attended balls in Strasbourg. This accusation of treason is not true! How can this happen after the Duke of Enghien's unjust trial?" I screamed in anguish.

"Quiet, woman!" the warden responded sternly as he rose from his desk in anger. The color of his face quickly turned redder. "You have no husband, and your character is in jeopardy as well. Enough! You will be taken to your cell!"

I was led down a dark stone corridor. Torches lit the dingy narrow hallways that smelled of mold and mildew. The guard opened the iron door and shoved me inside. The cell was cold and damp. There was a south-facing window with a shutter over the bars that looked out over the canal. A dirty cot sat under the window. My knees felt weak, so I sat down. I buried my face in my hands and sobbed.

"Mademoiselle," someone said. "It will be all right. Have faith."

I looked up. There was an older woman in the cell across from mine. She had gray hair and missing teeth and was dressed in rags. I wondered what she had done to be here.

"Ah, you are lucky you are with child," she said. "You will get more food. It gets warmer at night. They light fires at night from below."

"How did you know?" I asked. But when I looked down, I realized that I was cradling my belly. "I am too tired. Please, I must lie down."

I still had my fur coat on, so I curled up on the cot. It was cold, and I heard people screaming in agony. I shivered with fear. To my horror, rats ran across the floor. Despite the horrible conditions, I was exhausted. I fell into a deep sleep and saw Hans in his Prussian uniform. He reached out his hand for me and we were walking in the moonlight. He touched my belly and said, "Oh, my love, how I miss you. I am here, watching and waiting. The child is a girl and she will be fine. Have no fear. Wilhelm will come for you. Your father will come. Be brave, my love."

Suddenly, I was awakened by a loud noise as a bowl of cold soup and bread were shoved through a small opening in the door. The old woman in the adjoining cell continued to babble, wanting my food. Rising slowly from the wonderful dream, I was exhausted, yet I was comforted from my reconnection with Hans. After eating voraciously, although not feeling full, I felt greatly revived. Hans's presence reassured me he was with me and all would be well.

CHAPTER 35

A RAY OF HOPE

Around midday I was ushered out into a courtyard to sit on an old wooden bench in the warmth of the sunshine. The heat radiating from the large fortress walls brought a certain relief. I was considered a priority inmate because of my unborn child, and there were other inmates who were considered special and selective.

Relaxing, lifting my head toward the sun, I prayed for protection for my child. Mother Mary seemed to whisper, "All is well. You will be free."

Halfway opening my eyes, a tall shadow loomed in front of me.

"Bonjour, good day." An older man dressed in rags approached me. At first I was startled, but I could tell he had refined manners and had apparently recognized me as being of a nobler class.

"My name is Jean Michele Taquet," the man said as he bowed and kissed my hand. His once handsome face was framed by a long, thin beard. Despite his outer appearance, there was something about his piercing blue eyes that had a sparkle of intelligence and intrigue. "May I sit down?" he asked with a beautiful Parisian accent.

"Yes, monsieur," I said.

Jean Michele sat on a bench opposite to me. "Whatever were

you accused of, my dear?" His bony hands clutched the end of an old cane.

"I fell in love with a Prussian spy who portrayed himself as a French officer, and he captured my heart," I replied. It pained me to speak of Hans in such a way, but I had to do what I could to survive this place. "I was accused of treason for aiding a spy. I am also carrying his child. The drunken man who is accusing me of this crime also tried to rape me, and I wounded him in self-defense. To make matters worse, he is my uncle."

"Do not despair! Perhaps you will go to the Dominican Nunnery of Unterlinden where they will attend to you and give you proper care," he said. "All women who are brought here with child are taken there to have birth because they receive better care. You see, no Catholic wants to be charged with murder of a child! Also, I have not seen women return here after having their child. I think you will be fine," Jean Michele spoke with encouragement.

I sighed. "Oh, if only. I was told I would be executed after the child is born."

"Oh yes, of course. We are here only to provide the French government what they want. They want my knowledge of science and mathematics. I was a student of Antoine Nicolas, the Marquis de Condorcet. Do you know of him?"

My eyes widened. "Yes, I know of him. My father and I studied his manuscript . . . the title is escaping me."

"He wrote *Sketch for a Historical Picture of the Progress of the Human Spirit*," Jean Michele said.

"Yes, that's it!" I managed to smile. "You studied with the marquis and assisted him in the writing?" I asked, surprised. "Oh, please, I would like to know more." I felt a sense of lightness come over me.

Jean Michele explained that the Marquis de Condorcet was

arrested during the Revolution and was imprisoned for his writings of The Enlightenment. The marquis promoted equality for women and for all races. He believed in a liberal economy and a constitutional government, just like in America. It was a very confusing time with the Reign of Terror when everyone was suspected of treason. The marquis's views were avant-garde, so he was arrested and stayed in prison for a number of years before he died in prison.

"I was going to America when I was intercepted in Marseilles before I boarded the ship. The book was in print when Napoleon seized control, at the perfect time when everyone and everything was questioned in the decay of France. The book was banned and burned. After his death, I was hunted because I posed the threat of spreading views of The Enlightenment thinking and philosophy. I never made it to America, and one day I hope I will."

"If I get out of here, I will do everything in my power to petition your release," I said.

"My heart would be grateful, mademoiselle." Looking over his broken glasses, a ray of hope burned in his faded blue eyes.

"Madame de Staël was banned from Paris because she was an enlightened thinker. She was fortunate to return to Switzerland where her family is from. I met her when my family visited the Duke of Enghien. I was greatly impressed with her," I whispered.

"Do you know what happened to the duke?" Jean Michele asked with a raised brow.

"Just horrible," I said, and I stood up and stretched, motioning him to walk with me in the sunlight away from the guards.

"You see, the marquis also believed the progress of mankind is based upon scientific knowledge and mathematics. Science and mathematics, my dear, is the way to the future. We also must believe in freedom for mankind and the human spirit. Have you heard of Thomas Jefferson and Benjamin Franklin?" His eyebrows lifted, his hands resting on his cane.

"Why, yes. My father—"

We were interrupted by the guards and ordered to head back to our cells. I smiled at Jean Michele. A ray of hope shined upon me. If only I could speak to him again. We could share our philosophies and knowledge. It would help to keep me going, I was sure, until I was sent to the Dominican Nunnery of Unterlinden. Then a sinking feeling overwhelmed me. Could I trust Jean Michele? As I looked at the other prisoners who were lining up to go back inside, I wondered if I could trust any of them. The Wolf Woman told me not to trust anyone. I silently chastised myself for being so forward and expressing my view to a stranger. What if he was a spy gaining information from the prisoners only to report back to the guards? I could hear Papa saying that I must be cautious and trust no one. A feeling of dread overwhelmed me at the thought that I had potentially doomed the life of my child.

It rained for the next several days. The cold and dampness set in, and I developed a cough. I worried that I was getting sick. But then the sun returned and my cough faded. I went back to the courtyard and saw Jean Michele again.

We sat across from each other just like we had a few days ago. I promised myself that I would approach our discussion with more caution this time around.

"Have you been keeping track of the days? You must do so in order to maintain your sanity," he said.

"How do I do that, Jean Michele?" I inquired.

"Take a stone or a chip from the wall and scratch the month and then just mark in the days."

"How long have you been here?" I asked.

"Ten years. The year is 1807, correct?"

"Yes," I said. I couldn't even fathom living in this godforsaken place for years. "Why have you been here that long? Why haven't they executed you?"

"They think I hold the knowledge of science and mathematics. So, one day they will seek my counsel, I was told." He shook his head.

There was a familiarity in his eyes that reminded me of Papa, which gave me comfort. "Jean Michele, I must ask you something," I said.

"Go on," he responded.

"You must understand my hesitation toward confiding in you. I am, after all, an unwed soon-to-be mother who has been caught up in something bigger than myself. I want to trust—"

"Say no more," Jean Michele said. His eyes softened. "I understand your mistrust. I saw you from across the way and could tell that you were someone I could talk to about literature and philosophy. I will leave you be." He stood up, then said, "'Under the finest constitution, ignorant people are still slaves.'"

I recognized those words. Papa had said them, or I had read them somewhere. "No, please!" I said in desperation. "I recognize those words. Who said them?"

"The marquis," he responded with a smile.

I tapped the bench with my hand. "I need your companionship. Please sit."

We continued our discussion about politics and literature. Jean Michele told me stories about meeting Benjamin Franklin and Thomas Jefferson.

"Jefferson embodies all the hopes, all the ideals, all the vital and universal intellectual curiosity of his time," Jean Michele said enthusiastically. "He has been influenced by the English and German philosophies, the French Enlightenment, and is one of the Founding Fathers of America. The Declaration of Independence is a statement declaring freedom from British rule, but also for mankind." He continued, "Now Humboldt, as a Prussian scientist and botanist, explored the New World, including South America. He is an acquaintance of Jefferson. Have you not heard of him from your father's studies?" He raised a bushy eyebrow.

"I am familiar with Humboldt. I was fortunate to read his documentaries from when he traveled to America." Just speaking about these things made me miss Papa.

"I have a copy of the marquis's book in my cell. It is hidden under a stone in the floor. If you go to the convent, I want you to take it with you. Annaelise, the world is changing, and you must keep the faith for your child. Do you have a name for your child yet?"

"Louisa Liberté," I replied proudly. "My fiancé and I have discussed the distant possibility of going to the New World when the child is older."

"If only I could go to America. Your possession of the marquis's book gives me great hope that his philosophy will be spread to the New World," he said in a low voice but with intensity.

I told him to be prepared to deliver the document when we met in the courtyard next.

Two weeks went by before receiving notice I would be going to the Nunnery at Unterlinden. It was my understanding that all pregnant women would go to the nunnery to have their child, as Jean Michele stated. Happy and however relieved, I became most anxious to see Jean Michele once more to say goodbye. The day before I left, we were instructed to go to the courtyard. I was saddened that this would be our last visit.

As I made my way to the courtyard, I saw Jean Michele looking frailer than ever. The lack of nourishment had taken its toll on him. Over his rags, he wore a coat his cellmate had given to him. We talked of music and how he reveled in hearing Mozart at Versailles and Beethoven in Bonn. I talked of Madame de Staël and how her writings on women's equality had influenced me. The memories brought me comfort and entertained Jean Michele, whose weathered face briefly came alive.

When I discreetly stuffed his document into the secret pocket in my coat, I began to cry, knowing I would never see him again.

"Go to the New World and spread his teaching!" he responded. "It is my final wish."

We embraced, and I sobbed as the guards jerked me from his arms.

CHAPTER 36

SANCTUARY AND SOLACE

I was released on March third. It was a cold and windy day, and our drive took us through the dreary streets of Colmar. The convent and the Cathedral of the Dominican Nuns of Unterlinden was built in the thirteenth century. It provided a haven for the nuns who escaped the Revolution. It was currently in the process of renovation and would eventually serve as a museum for fine art. The cathedral had a certain charm and beauty, and it was a welcome relief after the dreary prison at Colmar.

Mother Superior Michelle Devereaux met me at the main entrance along with two other nuns. Mother Superior said in a commanding voice, "Welcome to Unterlinden, my child. You will be cared for by Sister Madeline and Sister Frances, who will be able to assist you with any of your personal needs."

The two sisters politely bowed their heads toward me. They all led me to my bedchamber. When Sister Frances opened the door, I was welcomed by a roaring fire and a bright room with a south-facing shuttered window. Bursting into tears of relief, I spontaneously hugged Mother Michelle. She smiled briefly but tried to speak solemnly. "You will be expected to attend meals and Mass, and you will be wearing the traditional habit and veil."

The sisters left, but Mother Michelle quickly turned and

handed me a letter from Papa. I closed the door and eagerly
tore the letter open.

Dear Annaelise,

*It is with great news that I have for you! I went to Strasbourg
and made the appeal to General Joseph Fouché, the Minister of
Police, for Gustave's arrest. I explained that you were acting
in self-defense after he attacked you. Also, Madame Germaine
de Staël has spoken to General Fouché on your behalf. We feel
certain that the court will look favorably on your case! The
hearing has been scheduled at the end of May.*

*As you may remember, Fouché was horrified by the quick
execution of your mother's cousin, the Duke of Enghien. He
ordered the execution, as per Napoleon's command, without
knowing the duke's true identity. It was Napoleon's brother-in-
law, Joachim Murat, who had the duke arrested and executed.*

*We are all looking forward to your wedding day. You and
Wilhelm Ferré are to be married at Unterlinden on May
sixteenth. Father Juergens will perform the ceremony. I will be
traveling in your direction soon, my sweet daughter.*

Your loving Papa

I took a deep breath and sat down. I was profoundly grateful
and relieved to hear of this news. It was reassuring to know I
had Madame de Staël's support. Uncle Gustave would be held
in prison until the trial. The hearing was to take place at the end
of May, so my wedding had to happen before then. Appearing
as a married woman in court would strengthen my case. The
odds were developing in my favor.

After bathing and changing into my habit and veil, I was

most grateful to have a nourishing meal. I felt as if I hadn't slept for days. Dr. Benedict came to visit me, and after I was examined, he reported that everything with the pregnancy appeared fine.

As the days passed, I got into a routine. I attended Mass regularly and sought great comfort kneeling at the altar with the painting of the Virgin Mary of the Rose Bush. Feeling protected by the Virgin gave me a great sense of peace. I felt the baby kick, and I sang to her while walking and talking with her down the long corridors of the cathedral, and to the dining hall out into the bright sunshine in the atrium. I would often sit there and feel the bright sunshine caress my body. The snow was melting and the birds were singing. It was healing and peaceful.

My focus shifted to the wedding. Writing to Wilhelm, I relayed my dream and my chosen name for the child, Louisa Liberté Ferré. After Hans had visited me in a dream when I was in prison, I felt sure the child would be a girl.

Father Juergens came to see me after breakfast one morning, and to my surprise he hand-delivered a letter from Wilhelm. Suddenly life seemed hopeful; I was so happy to receive my first letter from Wilhelm in what seemed like an eternity.

My Dearest Annaelise,

I cannot imagine the pain, anguish, and fear you have suffered over the last several months. The horrific attempt that Gustave made toward you was inconceivable! Your father has gone to great lengths to obtain a fair trial. The war is still going on around us, and we are keeping alive with provisions from our root cellar and venison. The apothecary shop is active, treating many illnesses over the winter. Have faith, my love. I think about you daily, and I am relieved you are in a safe place.

Gerda sends her love and kisses. We will see you in May for the wedding.

All my love,
Wilhelm

For the first time in weeks, I slept soundly, knowing my life could be at peace. I kept praying, however, for a favorable trial and a healthy child. I yearned to gaze upon my daughter's face and hoped to see some of Hans in her eyes.

CHAPTER 37

SISTER SOFIA

T he baby's kicking awakened me from a restless sleep on the night of the March full moon. I suddenly felt intense hunger. After struggling to get out of bed, I took my candle to light the way down the corridor toward the kitchen. Paintings of the crucifixion lined the long halls, and under the dim lighting, the suffering of Christ seemed even more haunting and torturous. Walking closer to the kitchen, I passed scaffolding and ladders as renovators were repairing and painting walls. I noticed an unfamiliar light at the end of the hall. To my surprise, a door was open to a quaint library with a balcony surrounding the back wall. How wonderful that reading could become my salvation while residing here.

I was suddenly startled when I saw a woman sitting at a sturdy oak desk. "Oh, so sorry, but I was going to the kitchen."

"Mademoiselle Annaelise, do not be alarmed. I am Sister Sofia, the head chef from the kitchen," she said in a strong Parisian accent.

"I am so hungry I cannot sleep," I responded. Then I saw freshly baked bread and cheese on the table where she was working.

"Please, have this food. I am researching books about the planting of herbs for our kitchen garden, which I hope to begin soon since it is early spring," she said with enthusiasm and pride. "I couldn't sleep either," she added, knowingly pointing a finger up to the sky indicating the full moon. After I devoured some bread and cheese, Sofia encouraged me to browse among the books.

I was drawn to the balcony. Making my way up the narrow spiral staircase, I managed to squeeze up the narrow passage to that cozy loft lined with bookcases. Lucky for me that my habit was comfortable and accommodating to my large shape. I could not believe what I saw—Madame de Staël's books! I selected these books and carefully made my way back down the steps.

"Look what I found," I said to Sister Sofia. "Madame de Staël is an acquaintance of my family."

Sister Sofia smiled. "Yes, and she is in the balcony books because she is Protestant, tucked away from the other sisters here," she confided. "I think she is a great voice for women and has come far in making her views known against Napoleon. I heard her speak in Paris before the Revolution. She has been very inspiring for me. I was a cook at Versailles, and I would take old bread to the streets for the hungry until I was let go. I came to the nunnery after my aunt died in Paris and have remained here peacefully as the head cook. Since I had no children or husband of my own, I sought refuge here. It was time to leave before the Reign of Terror."

"Oh, could it be you knew Gustave Guerlain?" I asked, pulling a chair in front of her.

"Oh oui, I knew *about* Monsieur Guerlain." She nodded while raising her eyebrows. "Mademoiselle, how on earth do you know this man?"

"He is my uncle and also the man who assaulted me. I am on trial for shooting him in my own defense. He had only a slight injury but reported me as being a traitor. Please tell me what you know about him," I said.

"He would often drink heavily late at night after the galas were completed. We were concerned for his sister, who was cared for by nannies at his home."

"That was my mother," I said in dismay.

"Oh, I see," Sister Sofia said. "Often one of the assistant cooks would offer to have him stay the night since he was unable to go home in his drunken state. He also loved men, as you might know. He loved to dance and continue the party long into the night until dawn. He loved to dress up in elaborate clothes no doubt stolen or borrowed from one of the courtesans in the palace. His late-night shenanigans were rumored throughout the court. It was no wonder he was ousted from Versailles!"

"Oh yes, I have heard all about my uncle's despicable ways," I said. "But what about my mother, Louisa Guerlain?" I sat back in my seat to help ease the tingling in my feet.

"Well, I only remember meeting her once when the children took a tour of the palace. She was a young girl at the time. The staff baked cookies and cakes for them as it was near Christmas." She paused. "Oh yes, I remember it well. She had dark curls piled on top of her head, and I gave her a candy-cane lollipop. She only wanted that and no other sweets."

I smiled. "Do you remember Isabelle Fontaine? She was my mother's nanny and mine as well."

"Why yes, she was a delight and young at the time, maybe only sixteen, with red hair and a beautiful smile," Sister Sofia said.

"She is residing with our family in Friedensthal. She is still employed by us and is like a member of our family. I miss her so."

We continued on into the wee hours of the morning.

"The other sisters and I will pray for your release from these accusations and for the safety of your child. God will be merciful," Sister Sofia said kindly.

When I went back to retrieve my books, I noticed the sunrise coming through the stained-glass window from beneath the balcony. The morning light revealed a scene of Jesus blessing the little children. I prayed he would bless mine.

CHAPTER 38

A SURPRISE VISITOR

The month of April was quiet and rejuvenating. I prayed every day for the health of my child and that I would soon be free. The sisters were more than accommodating, and they became my companions.

I found myself buried in books. Studying the values of The Enlightenment, the principles of parliamentary government in England, and the Constitutional government in America made me wonder about Wilhelm and his interest in the possibility of moving to the New World. He had said he wanted to move to America after his father died, and I hadn't really thought about what that meant. It would mean leaving our families behind along with the farms and businesses that were developed by our relatives. It would mean leaving the only home I knew, with memories of Maman and Hans. I didn't know how I felt about that. Fortunately, I was able to occupy my mind with my reading and plans for the wedding. I enjoyed my solitude. I often sat in the courtyard while enjoying the spring sunshine and the reemergence of birds singing. My body was changing. My feet would swell and sitting was a comfort.

One afternoon, Sister Sofia and an elegantly dressed woman approached me. The bright light blocked my view, and I stood up shielding my eyes with my hand.

"Annaelise, you have a visitor," Sister Sofia announced happily.

The elegant woman said, "I have come to visit you and help you plan your wedding!"

I gasped. I recognized that voice. "Oh, is it you, Madame de Staël? I am so happy to see you!" I exclaimed. I gave her a hug and a kiss for each cheek.

"After the unjust execution of your cousin, the Duke of Enghien, I kept in touch with his wife, Charlotte Louise, and she informed me of your unfortunate experience with Monsieur Guerlain. I was absolutely horrified and shocked to hear of this misfortune," she said. "I appealed to the General Fouché and informed your father regarding my approach and discovered he has made an appeal for you as well. I truly believe the Lord will be on your side and you will be exonerated."

"Thank you so much, Madame de Staël. Papa said this in his letter, and I am so appreciative and honored by your actions."

"I am thrilled you are here. I am one of the benefactors of this nunnery, both for the women and for the art preservation. You know this will become a museum one day. I petitioned families in the area to temporarily reopen this cathedral until they can get complete funding," she said.

"How wonderful, Madame! You are a saint," I said happily.

"Not according to Napoleon!" We both laughed and hugged one another.

"I am gravely sorry to hear of your Maman's passing. No woman should be without their mother on her wedding day. I hope you will oblige me to help you."

"Yes, I would be honored," I said. I hugged her again.

"Now, my dear, we have a wedding to plan! Becoming a new bride, you will need my assistance. There are the things your mother would have given to you. First, I have found a large dress that we will alter to fit your current condition. The wedding is in a month's time. We cannot have you marry in a nun's habit." She placed her hands on her hips. "Come, let us go to your quarters. Sister Frances will bring the dress."

I followed Madame de Staël to my room. As I unboxed the dress, I remembered finding Maman's dress in the attic at Friedensthal, the one we had altered for the ball in Strasbourg. Tears came to my eyes, somehow knowing she was here with me. It seemed as if that occasion was a lifetime ago.

"Now, no time for tears, my dear," said Madame de Staël as she lifted the gown over my head. It had an empire waist, and the silk flowed down my maternal body and cascaded to the floor. Being nearly six months along in the pregnancy, the empire waistline was a blessing. I suddenly did not feel so large when I saw my reflection in the mirror.

"Excellent! You are such a beautiful bride, and I know your Maman is smiling down on us." Madame de Staël beamed with a large smile. Aside from Maman, she was, without a doubt, the most wonderful woman I had ever known.

CHAPTER 39

THE WEDDING

T he spring wind withdrew its angry breath, and the days became longer and brighter. We were all hoping for a beautiful day, and our prayers were answered with the early morning sun. Today was my wedding day.

It had been Christmas when I last saw Wilhelm and Papa, and I was both excited and nervous. Papa would come early since he would be escorting me down the aisle. I wondered if I would still have love for Wilhelm when I saw him. Would he be attracted to me in my maternal state?

I sank onto the bed, cradling my belly. The baby was kicking a lot. *I'll see you soon, my girl.*

I'll see her too, Hans said.

I turned around but no one was there.

"Hans?" I whispered. "Are you here? Can you hear me?" I closed my eyes and imagined him sitting on the bed next to me.

This will be a beautiful day and you will be happy, Hans said, his voice an echo in my mind. Chills crawled down my spine and up my arms. I wished Maman were here. I tried not to get overwhelmed at the thought.

"Annaelise, do you want me to fetch your breakfast?" Josie asked, pulling me from my daydreaming. She was a sweet child of ten, an orphan the nuns had taken in.

I smiled. "Thank you, Josie, I would like that very much."

"Sister Sofia is busy in the kitchen with the day's preparations. I will make sure you get some food," Josie said and disappeared.

Not too long after, Sister Madeline brought toast, tea, and oatmeal to my room so I could be more rested. She conveyed that Sister Sofia was preparing a lunch with the best aged cheese and finest wine from deep in the cellar. Sister Sofia was also cooking a turkey, venison, potatoes, carrots, turnip greens, cabbage, and sauerbraten. Sister Madeline announced this with a broad smile, showing some of her missing teeth.

I felt a tightness in my womb and convinced myself it was just nerves. Sister Frances came to my room with my newly altered dress. Delighted with the contour, I was happy to see my image in the mirror despite my condition. There was a knock on my door, and Madame de Staël entered carrying a beautiful bouquet of spring flowers, including lilacs and roses, tied with a silk ribbon embroidered with pink flowers.

Wanting to style my hair, Madame de Staël asked Sister Frances to leave. She arranged some of my curls to cascade down my back, with the greater amount swept up on my head and tied on the top with another silk ribbon. For the finishing touch, she placed a pearl pin that shone brightly in my dark hair. It complemented my mother's pearl necklace that I wore when I took the vows with Hans.

"This is my gift to you, these pearl earrings," Madame de Staël said as she gave me a hug. "I am so happy you can wear them." She placed the exquisite earrings on my earlobes.

"Maman is smiling from heaven at us, and I know she is somehow so grateful to you. And I so hope you can return soon. Paris is not the same without you," I said with a laugh.

"I have another gift for you. This is my latest book, *Corinne*, about a young Italian poet who falls in love with a conflicted

Scotsman who was committed to marry a prim and proper English woman."

"Oh, this is so wonderful!" I opened the book. Madame de Staël had written an inscription on the first page in her beautiful handwriting:

> *Love is the emblem of eternity: it confounds all notion of time: effaces all memory of a beginning; all fear of an end.*

Tears formed in my eyes. She handed me a handkerchief. "You have been through so many heartbreaks. Let love carry you through this. You have a new life, a new family, and a bright future ahead of you! Come now, your father will be here soon. I will see you at the altar as your matron of honor." She had a tender look in her eyes.

"I'm truly honored you are here and will be by my side," I replied while she kissed my cheeks.

Soon after Madame de Staël left, I heard a knock on my door and then Papa's voice. I knew we would be shocked by one another's appearance. When I opened the door, I was surprised. His look was one of harsh distress, with dark clouds of despair around his eyes. Surprised by my large circumference, he was unsure how to embrace me. Nevertheless, he pulled up a chair and grasped my hands while we both sat down.

"Papa, it is so wonderful to see you. I've missed you."

"My dear Annaelise, it is wonderful to see your beautiful face. You look just like Maman on her wedding day." Tears brimmed his eyes. "She would have been very proud of you."

I squeezed his hand. "I think of her every day." I didn't want to cry, so I quickly changed the subject. "What is the news of the war?" I asked.

Papa sighed and shook his head. "The Battle of Jena took Hans from you, and Napoleon has crushed Prussia. My contacts tell me they expect a harsh treaty from France with both loss of land and expense-tribute payments to be made to France. How can Prussia continue? Baron Stein, who is now Minister of State, is working with commerce and taxes to try to save the nearly bankrupt Prussia. He is apparently working on an Edict to Emancipation of the old feudal system so that large estates could be sold and free trade would be encouraged between all casts of citizens. It should be approved by the end of this year. Apparently, the emperor is in favor of this. This will turn the citizens of Prussia into grateful and productive men who will all want to build and defend Prussia for the future."

The Battle at Jena had taken Hans, but if Prussia would change for the better, at least his sacrifice would not be in vain.

Papa must have sensed my sadness. "I apologize, my Annaelise. I should not have discussed politics at a time like this. Your Maman would have scolded me for doing that. This is your special day. We can discuss more after the wedding. Wilhelm and I will be here a few days after the wedding. No time for remorse. I have the wedding rings and must be sure that yours will fit your left hand."

When he took out the ring and placed it onto my finger, I was delighted it fit under Wilhelm's engagement ring. More importantly, I was so happy to discover it was Maman's wedding ring.

"I am happy you managed to keep Wilhelm's ring while in prison," Papa said, raising his bushy eyebrows.

"I hid it in the secret pocket of Maman's fur coat."

"Funny, she hid her jewels in the same coat when she left Paris," Papa revealed with a smile.

Mother Michelle then knocked on the door, and Papa took the wedding rings to give to Wilhelm before the ceremony. "I will see you in the vestibule soon," he said, then he kissed my cheeks. "You really are a beautiful bride, baby and all. Maman would be proud." He winked at me before closing the door on his way out.

Mother Michelle held the train of my gown when I carefully walked down the steps. When I reached the doors to the cathedral, Papa extended his arm while Sister Madeline and Sister Frances opened the large, wood-carved double doors. The bouquet was placed in my hand. I exhaled and then smiled, seeing Wilhelm smiling back at me. He was standing at the stone altar and was elegantly dressed in civilian clothes, wearing a navy-blue waistcoat and tails with brass buttons and a high collar starched in a white shirt with a stock tie. His breeches were white, and I was quite taken aback by his appearance. He was quite fit and trim, and he appeared taller than I remembered. His shiny red hair was neatly tied in a satin black tie. He wore a stylish top hat. Feeling elated by the realization that for the first time I did feel a spark of true love and exhilaration, my eyes filled with tears.

The nuns were singing "Ava Maria." As I walked down the long aisle, it was amazing to see all the unfamiliar guests who had come. Papa quietly said in my ear, "See, my Annaelise? You are loved by so many who support our cause. These are Madame de Staël's friends too."

Papa was talking but I was focused on Wilhelm. When we reached the altar, he held out his trembling hand, bowing gracefully to kiss mine. Looking into my eyes, he said, "You are so beautiful and beyond my greatest joy."

At that moment, we turned to Father Juergens while I handed my bouquet to Madame de Staël. Father Juergens smiled and started the ceremony by binding our hands in a sacred sash.

The ceremony far exceeded my expectations, and I was

overjoyed by our union. There were so many wonderful people who attended, and they were non-judgmental toward me. I felt a sense of reconciliation and renewal, almost as if I had been reborn. Father Juergens was joyful. I saw such emotion in his wrinkled, soulful face.

We left the cathedral and proceeded to the dining hall in the lower level under the nave of the church. Sister Sofia had set a magnificent buffet with all the food Madame de Staël had suggested. Another table was full of desserts including cakes, pies, and apple strudel.

After speaking with a few dignitaries, Wilhelm led me to our dining table just before Father Juergens delivered an elegant blessing for our lives together. The sisters of the choir sang another a cappella blessing in perfect harmony. Toasts were given all around with the wine flowing freely at the nunnery. Even I had two glasses while Wilhelm told me briefly about his family.

"I'm sorry they could not be here, but Father is not well, and I can tell you later about his condition. We will have a beautiful reception when you return home to Heidelberg. If we decide to have a ceremony at the chapel, Excelsior and Faithful Friend will pull our carriage," he said enthusiastically, gently embracing my arm.

"Oh, how I have missed them." I squeezed his hand.

"My family has missed you too," Wilhelm said with a big smile.

I laughed. "I meant the horses . . . and of course I miss your family!"

Wilhelm also burst forth in laughter, something we were unaccustomed to doing. It felt good to feel so free with our emotions. We were enjoying a meal without the shadow of war or death over our heads. People were laughing and smiling. The food was glorious and the wine was perfect. I felt true joy, and I knew Hans was feeling it too.

Madame de Staël was responsible for inviting the many dignitaries she knew in Colmar. We were able to have more private discussions at the tables, and Papa in particular enjoyed the conversations.

Before Madame de Staël departed, I took her aside. "I have a document, the writings by the Marquis de Condorcet, which had been given to me by his apprentice, Jean Michele Taquet, whom I had met in prison at Colmar. He wanted this to be published in America, and I promised him I would see to it somehow."

"Oh yes. I remember learning about the marquis in the early days of the Parisian salons. I am outraged that Napoleon would arrest such a brilliant man. Yes, I will make sure that it is published in Switzerland and sent to America," she said reverently.

"Jean Michele was my only ray of hope while in prison. The marquis was for women's rights and a constitutional government."

"Yes, how well I know it feels." She rolled her eyes.

"When do you think Napoleon will be defeated?" I asked.

"It is difficult to say, but his armies are dwindling, and if he makes a campaign to Russia, it would take the wind out of his sails. Russia is a long journey and harsh in the winter. I predict the English will be the cause of his defeat, maybe in two to three years."

I expressed my deep gratitude for all of her intervention and interaction in Colmar and making my wedding a beautiful experience. The intense feeling of sheer exhaustion came over me. "Please tell the others goodbye. I will speak to my family tomorrow. I am so exhausted now and must sleep."

"You are like a daughter to me, and we will always be close," she said as I hugged her.

It was the first time I had ever seen tears in her eyes. As she departed, I somehow had the strange feeling I would never see her again.

CHAPTER 40

THE END AND THE BEGINNING

I had no memory of one of the nuns removing my bridal gown. I remembered Wilhelm, my husband, coming into the room to kiss me goodnight and to wish me a peaceful sleep.

Drifting into a deep sleep, I saw Hans sitting by a riverbank. He was shirtless and looked strong and powerful. I walked over to him, and when he looked up at me, he smiled and patted the ground.

"Annaelise, my love, please sit."

I wrapped my arms around him from behind and inhaled the scent of his hair. I rocked him back and forth. There was no child in my belly, so I was able to press my body against his strong back. "This is where I need to be," I said. Then I let go and sat down next to him.

"What shall we do today?" he asked. He dipped his feet into the clear water.

"I don't need to do anything." I quickly removed my shoes and dipped my feet into the water. At first it was cold, and then it was warm, and the warmth crawled up my legs and soothed my belly.

Hans laughed. "We must do something," he said.

As I stared at the beautiful river—it flowed strong and fast and proud—I realized that I didn't want to do anything. I didn't want to leave this space where I sat next to the man I loved.

Hans looked so peaceful, with a glimmer in his eye and a smile on his face.

"Hans?" I spoke softly.

He turned his head to me. "Yes, my Annaelise?"

"Hans?" I said again.

But this time he was speaking, and I couldn't hear what he was saying. His mouth was moving but no words came out. They were drowned out by the sounds of cannon fire, and men screaming, and horses' hooves, and the smell of gunpowder.

"Hans!" I shouted and stood up quickly. The warmth of the river disappeared and I felt cold. The landscaped morphed into mounds of dirt. Bodies of soldiers were piled high, their faces bloodied and frozen in horror.

I searched among their faces for Hans, but I couldn't find him. Smoke filled the air, a sickly sweet scent of blood. Soldiers were battling each other with bayonets and gunfire. Cavalry was coming from everywhere, horses rearing and charging forward in fearless assaults.

It was the Battle at Jena.

Hans was a few feet away on Excelsior, yelling with rage as he fought a French captain on horseback. Swords were clashing.

"No, Hans!" I screamed, but no one could hear me.

Suddenly, another French cavalryman came from behind and thrusted his saber into the back of Hans's left shoulder. Excelsior reared, dislodging Hans to the ground.

"No!" I screamed. I ran toward him, but my feet were stuck in the mud. I tripped over a soldier who was missing an arm and fell down. My white wedding dress was stained with dirt and blood, but I didn't care. I had to get to Hans. I crawled on my hands and knees while soldiers engaged in battle all around me.

Wilhelm rode past on his horse, then jumped down and rushed over to Hans. He frantically placed his hand over the wound, but it was gushing blood, so he gently laid Hans down on the ground. Then he scurried over to a fallen soldier and ripped off the man's pants leg to secure a bandage.

"Stay with me," Wilhelm said in a panic as he tried to dress Hans's wound. He sat Hans up and wrapped the cloth around his chest to try to stop the bleeding.

"Lieutenant, we have to retreat!" a soldier said as he raced up to Hans. "They're closing in!" Then the young boy ran off.

Dozens of men on horses raced by. Others were running. Pieces of their uniforms were ripped and bloodied. Horns sounded in the distance. The air was heavy with the scent of gunpowder and death.

"You must go," Hans said. "But please, you must tell Annaelise . . . I need you to take care of her. I have known you loved her as well. You are the only one who can provide for her. You will have a good life with her. She must know this to give her courage."

"I promise," Wilhelm said. "You've always been like a brother to me. I will live the rest of my days in your honor." He rose, then leapt up onto Faithful Friend. Excelsior followed them as they retreated in absolute terror.

Hans lay there staring at the sky, trying to make out the sun hidden behind the clouds. His breath was ragged. His lips were moving but no sound came out, an inaudible prayer of some kind. Then his body healed. His skin was clean of blood and dirt and injuries. His uniform was clean with no rips. His hair was perfectly combed. He was without pain. He looked up toward the sky and a light shined down on him. Then his healed body ascended toward a light, higher and higher and higher . . .

I awoke screaming. I looked down and screamed again. Blood stained my nightshirt and the sheets, and I felt the gush of warm water. "She's coming," I said.

Clumsily arising from my bed, I shouted for help outside my door. Sister Madeline and Sister Frances came running down the hall and into the room. Sister Madeline informed me that Mother Michelle had sent for the doctor. I touched between my legs and my hands were covered in blood. I felt faint. The pain became worse in my abdomen.

"We must get you back into bed," Sister Madeline said.

Sister Frances was dabbing at the bloodstain on the sheet with a cloth.

"We don't have time," Sister Madeline snapped. "Help me get her into bed."

They grabbed under my arms and hoisted me onto the bed and scooted my body up toward the front. The sheets were still moist from my blood. The pain became worse and worse, as if I were being stabbed with a sword.

"I am trained in midwifery," Sister Madeline said. "Do not worry." She held my hand while wiping my forehead with a cold rag with her other hand.

Dr. Benedict finally came at noon. I continued to breathe while trying to lie still. As soon as he entered the room, he looked at me and his face paled. He placed his bag onto the nearby table and rushed over to my side.

"Now, Annaelise, I am going to examine you. Keep breathing. Both sisters will be at your side," he assured.

I held onto the sides of the bed, my hands clutched and hurting, but I finally relaxed, trusting he was competent. My breaths were longer and deeper now, yet the pain was increasing by the minute. The sisters stood on each side of my bed, one of them pressing a cool cloth on my forehead.

Dr. Benedict pressed his cold hands on my belly and pushed down. Pain shot up my spine and I screamed out in agony. An ache settled deeper in my pelvis.

"I think the baby is coming within the hour," the doctor said. "I will tell Mother Michelle to have your father and husband come as soon as they can."

My heart quickened at this news. *This can't be. I can't do this alone.*

Dr. Benedict stepped outside the room to speak to Mother Michelle. They were whispering, but I could hear their heavy words.

Something is wrong! It felt like my world was spinning out of control.

"I am afraid I have some bad news," the doctor said. "The baby is coming sooner than expected. This will be a caesarian birth. I will have to make an incision if she cannot birth the baby."

No, no, no, this cannot be happening!

"Oh, dear God!" Mother Michelle murmured. "I must inform the sisters to pray immediately."

"Have your friar go to the hotel in Colmar and ask her family to come as soon as possible," Dr. Benedict said. "Do not tell anyone about the seriousness of this."

"We will do our best," Mother Michelle responded with sadness.

The doctor stepped back into the room and took the sisters aside. He whispered in a low voice, "We will have to perform a cesarean birth. I will need your strength and courage." The sisters had a look of dismay while crossing themselves.

No, please, no! Hans, I'm scared! Becoming weaker and weaker, I said quickly, "What's wrong, doctor? Is the baby fine? Please save my baby!"

"The baby has turned the wrong way. Be brave and we will save the infant for you. The sisters will be giving you valerian root to ease the pain."

At that moment, the pain was so overwhelming it was almost blinding. Someone put a spoon in my mouth and I tasted something bitter. It numbed my tongue. My eyelids were getting heavy. I fought to keep them open. I was soon in a semiconscious state of mind, almost relaxed.

Stay awake, Annaelise!

My head felt cloudy and dizzy, and my entire body felt heavy and limp. The nuns hovered over me and held down my shoulders and feet. I wanted to fight back, but I was too tired to move. Then the doctor approached me with some sort of instrument: a knife.

"Please," I begged. "I am afraid."

"Hold her down," the doctor said.

A shadow passed over, darkening my vision.

I felt the pressure of someone holding me down. A sharp pain erupted in my abdomen and I opened my mouth to scream . . .

Suddenly, I felt my body rise above me, and I felt the baby being drawn from me. I witnessed a beautiful baby girl being placed in my arms.

Louisa Liberté.

I saw Hans's strong jaw and high cheekbones in her lovely little face. She had my mouth and eyes. She had dark hair inherited from both of us. I couldn't wait for Papa and Wilhelm to come.

"She is beautiful and healthy as you will be, my love," Hans said in my dreamlike state.

Fading into unconsciousness, I then saw a vision of Hans

riding Excelsior in a lush meadow with me at his side riding Petite Held. I saw my body and the bloodstained sheets. Then I saw my beautiful baby girl, Louisa Liberté. She was free and would have a wonderful life with Wilhelm in the New World.

At that moment, Papa and Wilhelm entered the room when Mother Michelle carefully pulled the sheet over my face. I felt myself rising above my body and looking down on myself. Was I dead? I felt no pain. Where was I?

No, please! I don't want to die. I need to be with my daughter.

Wilhelm held Louisa Liberté and looked down at her. His face was red from crying. He rubbed her cheek gently with his thumb.

Papa burst into tears. "Annaelise!" He broke down in sobs and held my hand.

My body felt lighter and lighter as I rose farther away from my family. Then I was drawn to a heavenly light from above, pulling me even higher when glorious angels appeared. I felt true peace, joy, and love I had never known before. Out of the golden light, Hans appeared with an outstretched hand.

I reached for his hand. "I want to be with you, my Hans. How I have missed you!"

"Not now, my love. You must be there for our daughter," he said.

Hans's face was pristine. His blue eyes sparkled, reflecting their warmth and love. His smile reached me and filled up my heart. I suddenly felt something pulling on me, our distance growing.

I then heard Louisa Liberté cry, and in the next moment I descended back into my body. My eyes snapped open. The pain was immense. Wilhelm, Papa, and Mother Michelle were staring at me as if they'd seen a ghost.

"My dear," Mother Michelle said. "You were . . . you were—"

"Dead, the life had drained out of your body, but you are back," Wilhelm said, caressing my brow.

Tears spilled from my eyes as I gazed upon my beautiful daughter. "I wasn't dead . . . I was alive. I saw—"

"Quiet now, dear, you need your rest," Mother Michelle said.

"Annaelise, you cannot give me a scare like that again," Papa said. He kissed my cheek. "Would you like to meet your daughter?"

Despite my intense pain, the miracle came to me. Wilhelm carefully placed my baby girl in my arms. She had a splash of dark hair. Tiny hands and fingers and toes. She puckered her little mouth.

"What is her name?" he asked.

"Louisa Liberté."

I smiled and a new life had begun. My sweet girl opened her eyes. I saw Hans looking back at me.

CHAPTER 41

GOING HOME

It took many weeks to recover from the loss of blood and my trauma and for me to regain my strength. I was lucky and blessed to have such good care from the nuns. Wilhelm stayed in Colmar, and he visited me almost every day. Louisa Liberté was brought to me for nursing, and the nuns brought my meals, which I was grateful for. Liberté had our dark hair and my eyebrows and nose, with Hans's mouth and cheekbones. She was simply beautiful.

Wilhelm was so supportive for both of us and would bring me Liberté after she woke up from her naps. I was so weak and had lost so much blood. My abdomen had been stitched; the dressings needed to be changed frequently. It hurt to move, so it was a long road to recovery. The hearing had been postponed because of my condition, and I was grateful for the delay.

Wilhelm was so encouraging and loving. I loved watching him cuddle our child. I was so relieved to see his tenderness toward her. He would be the father she needed. I now referred to Liberté as "our child."

"Everything will be just fine, my love. We will be settled in Heidelberg, and Gerda will help you with the baby. When you are stronger, we will move to Blumenthal, and you will have your grandmother to help you. However, I have a better plan that you may like the best," he said as he cradled Liberté in his arms.

"What is your idea?" I squeezed his hand. "Please tell me your thoughts."

"Last night I spoke to your father, and he gave me a great idea. Why don't we live at Friedensthal? Your father can teach me all about the winery business, and you will feel safe there. I also spoke with him about Gustave—no matter the outcome of the trial, he has ordered Gustave to leave Friedensthal and return to Adlershof. He will not allow Gustave on the property. How would you like to go home, feel safe and secure?" Wilhelm smiled.

I bit back tears. Nothing sounded better than the thought of going home. "I would love to go home," I said. "It would be wonderful to have Isabelle as our nanny. After all, she was my nanny and Maman's as well." I managed a weak smile.

Wilhelm nodded. "I knew you would like this idea."

"Thank you, and that is so considerate of you," I said. "I wanted to ask if you would like to call her Libby? Not always, but a pet name for her? How do you like that?"

"I think that sounds like a wonderful idea." Wilhelm smiled. "What do you think, Libby?" He gently rubbed her cheek. She grunted in response.

I laughed. "She is just the sweetest rose. I must sleep now before the nuns bring Libby in for her lunch. You have given me hope, my dear." I gently rubbed the top of Liberté's head.

"I will see you tomorrow then. Sweet dreams, my love."

There were no more nightmares, no more visions of Hans, just restful and peaceful sleep.

Over the next few weeks, I continued to heal. I was glad to rest and spend time with my new family. But despite my happy disposition, the trial hovered like a gray cloud. A new date had been set, and it was to take place in a month. I didn't even want to look at my uncle's face, let alone stand before the court and give my testimony. I had lost so much and come so far for it all to be pulled out from under my feet.

One day, Wilhelm brought me some lovely flowers and a letter from Papa.

"I have some fantastic news!" he exclaimed. "It does seem that God is watching over us."

I was sitting in the chair by the window holding Liberté. "What is it?"

Wilhelm practically hopped over toward us. I had never seen him so giddy. He got down on one knee and kissed the top of my hand. "Let me hold her while you read this letter."

I handed him the baby and he handed me the letter. My heart was in my throat as I read Papa's words.

Dear Annaelise and Wilhelm,

I hope by now, mother and child are much stronger and well. The trial date was set, but it appears that Gustave has changed his story. He now claims that the gun had gone off accidentally when he was giving his niece a lesson on how to use a pistol. He claims that in his emotional and wounded state, he had been confused about what had happened, thus giving the authorities the wrong testimony. In truth, Gustave must have learned how many people would be testifying on Annaelise's behalf—Madame de Staël, Richard, Isabelle, to name a few. Should he be found guilty of perjury in his testimony, a prison sentence would surely await him. The case has been dismissed.

Madame de Staël is a very visible and well-respected citizen in Germany and Switzerland. General Fouché would have also testified that Gustave was a cousin of the Duke of Enghien.

General Fouché is disgusted with all the wrongful killing, and he clearly admits that it was a case of missing identity and the duke was wrongly executed.

In my estimation, Gustave Guerlain may need to pay a penalty, and his reputation will further be ruined. But one thing I do know: Gustave Guerlain will leave Friedensthal with his horses and go back to Adlershof or wherever he chooses, and he will never be allowed at Friedensthal again. I look forward to being with my new family and granddaughter.

All my Love, Faith, and Fortitude,
Papa

My hands were shaking. I dropped the letter on the floor. "Does this mean that this nightmare is over?" I asked.

"It appears that way. Gustave has no evidence to claim that Hans was a spy, nor that you were an accomplice. How much of a fool would he look in his testimony making these bizarre claims about the Theiss family? When you have so many witnesses to speak to your character?"

I must have looked ill because Wilhelm placed Liberté on the bed, then knelt beside me and took my hand.

"This is all good, Annaelise. God is in our favor and justice has prevailed. We are now free to put this behind us." He picked up Liberté and then placed her in my arms.

I couldn't believe this had happened. Heavy sadness filled my being at what Maman would think of all this. But Wilhelm was right. We could finally move on . . . except for one thing.

"Can I ask you something?" I said cautiously.

"Sure, my love. You should always feel that you and I can speak openly."

I hesitated. I didn't want him to think me mad. "Now that

we are husband and wife, I want to share everything. When I was dying . . . I felt like I was floating above near the ceiling, and I was able to watch all of you. I saw Papa burst into tears and you were holding Liberté. I rose higher to a beautiful white light, almost as if I was in heaven. I felt incredible peace and joy. I saw Hans."

Wilhelm furrowed his brow. "You saw Hans?"

"Yes. He told me that I needed to go back and raise my child. Then I came back to Earth, and I was in my body. I saw everyone and especially this little bundle of joy." I held my little angel's hand as she cooed at me.

"Well, that does not seem crazy. Remember when you were crying about your mother? I gave you assurance that she would be looking down on you. I still think my mother is with me from time to time. I am glad that Hans, or the angels, or God brought you back to us."

"There is something more . . . I had a dream before I went into labor and I witnessed the Battle at Jena."

Wilhelm's face dropped. "Anna—"

"Please, let me speak. I can't really explain it, but I was there. It was horrible. I saw myself walking over dead bodies through the mud. I was looking for Hans. I saw you with Hans after he fell off Excelsior. You ripped off the pant leg from a dead soldier and tried to stop the bleeding by wrapping a tourniquet around his chest. Hans spoke to you, and he told you to leave. He asked you to keep a promise: Please take care of Annaelise." Tears spilled from my eyes.

Wilhelm's face was pale. His cheeks were blotchy red. "I . . . how could you know all of that? Dear God . . ."

"Please, Wilhelm, I cannot explain it. I only know what I saw."

He looked at me, and there was pain behind his eyes. "I

would do anything to forget being on the battlefield. To get the stench of death out of my nose. To erase the look on Hans's face as he died in my arms. It's true, Hans asked me to take care of you. I will make true on a promise to a friend who was like a brother to me, but I have loved you from the moment I laid eyes on you. I am a lucky man to have you as my wife and that I can be a father to our Libby."

I closed my eyes and took a deep breath. I imagined the charming homes in the Alsatians villages with the storks nesting above. I saw the vast green valleys and vineyards in Alsace. I saw Maman sitting outside on a blanket in the grass while Papa chopped wood near the stable. I felt the wind on my face as I rode my trusted steed Petite Held through wooded paths. Hans was riding ahead of me on Excelsior—he looked over his shoulder at me and smiled. I saw Liberté running along the Rhine in a white dress, pausing to pick up rocks and flinging them into the water while Wilhelm and I chased after her, laughing.

In that moment, a breeze swept into the room and I opened my eyes. I felt rejuvenated, happy, hopeful. I looked at Liberté in my arms—her rosy cheeks, her expressive face, her blue eyes. I grabbed Wilhelm's hand.

"Thank you, my love," I said in earnest. "Let's go home."

ABOUT THE AUTHOR

Martha (Marta) Anne Tice has been
a native of Virginia for the majority
of her life and is now a resident of
Nelson County, Virginia. She obtained a degree in interior design
from the American University in
Washington, DC, and became a li-
censed interior designer in 1997.
Marta is a member of the American
Society of Interior Designers (ASID)
and continues to be active in the

interior design industry. Marta also has a lodging business,
Leap of Faith Lodging, at Wintergreen in Nelson County,
Virginia.

Marta's love of horses and equestrian sports kept her active
in foxhunting for thirty-five years. She became a member of
Bull Run, Loudoun, and Farmington Hunt Clubs. She loves
riding her senior horse, Comanche, on the beautiful trails in
Nelson County. As a conservationist, Marta also enjoys fly fishing, kayaking, and snorkeling.

As a member of the Daughters of the American Revolution
(DAR), Marta's interests include fundraising for veterans, researching genealogy for writing, and pursuing her neverend-
ing thirst for knowledge about history and art.

Allegiance to Alsace is her debut novel.